ALWAYS ENCHANTING . . .
NEVER A LADY

"What are you you doing here, Virg?"

"This is *my* bed," Virg told Max. "Where else would I be?" Instead of waiting for him to answer, Virg asked a second question. "Tell me, my lord, what are you doing in my bed?"

A reasonable question, but not one he wanted to answer. "I, ah, became lost and blundered into the wrong room," Max improvised.

Her hypnotic scent of orange blossoms and the warm, inviting curve of her hip and thigh sparked his desire, and he surreptitiously edged closer to her.

"I can understand why you would hardly know this castle," she said wryly, "having only lived here for what—fifteen or twenty years?"

"I have occasional memory lapses," he lied. "Please accept my most sincere apologies."

"Why don't you get out of my bed, and I'll think about that."

"Must I?" he asked, loath to comply. He stroked her leg, slowly and rhythmically, moving a bit farther up her thigh with each sweep of his hand. "I promise you will enjoy my staying. . . ."

Other **AVON ROMANCES**

THE DEFIANT ONE *by Danelle Harmon*
THE MACKENZIES: JOSH *by Ana Leigh*
MUSTANG ANNIE *by Rachelle Morgan*
MY LADY'S GUARDIAN *by Gayle Callen*
NEVER KISS A DUKE *by Eileen Putman*
ON A LONG AGO NIGHT *by Susan Sizemore*
WOLF SHADOW'S PROMISE *by Karen Kay*

Coming Soon

ALWAYS AND FOREVER *by Beverly Jenkins*
MUCH ADO ABOUT LOVE *by Malia Martin*

And Don't Miss These
ROMANTIC TREASURES
from Avon Books

THE HUSBAND LIST *by Victoria Alexander*
LION HEART *by Tanya Anne Crosby*
THE MOST WANTED BACHELOR *by Susan Kay Law*

MARLENE SUSON

Never A Lady

AVON BOOKS
An Imprint of HarperCollinsPublishers

This is a work of fiction. Names, characters, places, and incidents are products of the author's imagination or are used fictitiously and are not to be construed as real. Any resemblance to actual events, locales, organizations, or persons, living or dead, is entirely coincidental.

AVON BOOKS
An Imprint of HarperCollins*Publishers*
10 East 53rd Street
New York, New York 10022-5299

Copyright © 2000 by Joan Sweeney
ISBN: 0-380-80567-7
www.avonromance.com

First Avon Books paperback printing: August 2000

Avon Trademark Reg. U.S. Pat. Off. and in Other Countries, Marca Registrada, Hecho en U.S.A.
HarperCollins® is a trademark of HarperCollins Publishers Inc.

Printed in the U.S.A.

WCD 10 9 8 7 6 5 4 3 2 1

*To Donna Sweeney
for more reasons than I can count*

Chapter 1

England, 1873

Two Americans, a Mrs. Blair and her daughter Virginia, have bribed Duke Esmond's mother to persuade him to marry the girl. His Grace is infatuated with Virginia and will undoubtedly do as his mother wishes.

"Over my dead body, he will!" muttered Lord Maximilian Chartwell, the duke's first cousin. Max crumpled the warning note from the steward of Esmond's estate and stuffed it into his pocket.

Anger as hot as wildfire raged within Max at the prospect of his young cousin, sweet-natured and naive, being manipulated into marrying a crass, conniving creature who was totally unsuitable to be his wife and duchess.

Everyone knew what crude, uncouth people Americans were, only a half-step—if that—above the savages who had previously occupied their godforsaken land.

In recent years, a horde of American mamas, even more ambitious than they were rich, had descended on England in search of eligible nobles for their nubile daughters to marry.

Max cursed Daphne, the duke's greedy, extravagant mother. As calculating as he knew her to be, he had not thought she would stoop so low as to sell her son in a disastrous marriage merely to benefit herself.

Clearly, he was wrong.

A man of action, Max ordered a horse saddled and immediately left his Essex estate for Castle Penrose, the duke's country seat in Suffolk, to prevent this shocking misalliance.

Why the hell could his cousin not have fallen in love with someone like beautiful, demure Lady Priscilla, the earl of Stonybrook's daughter, whom Max intended to marry?

He rode hard and changed horses often at posting inns along the road, determined to reach his cousin's estate as quickly as he could.

Finally Max saw his destination ahead of him, crowning the highest hill in the area. A ribbonlike wisp of cloud floated past the haphazard collection of gloomy gray towers, turrets, and parapets that was Castle Penrose, home to Chartwells for nearly eight centuries.

Max slowed his brown gelding to a trot and turned the horse off the highway onto a drive that meandered through the green of the estate's carefully landscaped park up to the castle. Colorful tulip trees, their leaves now a bright autumn gold, lined the road.

Hooves pounded across a meadow beyond the leafy yellow screen of the trees. Curious to see who was racing there, Max nudged his mount toward the sound.

A chestnut horse streaked past Max. He caught a blurred glimpse of a young woman riding sidesaddle. She had lost her hat, and her long dark hair, glinting with red highlights in the sun, streamed out behind her like an exotic flag in a stiff wind.

No woman would willingly ride a horse at that speed.

Bloody hell, the chestnut must be a runaway!

Max instantly spurred his mount after the woman to try to save her. It was a minor miracle she had not already fallen off.

Her silence astonished Max even more. All the ladies Max knew would be screaming hysterically for help. Apparently, however, she was too terrified even to do that.

As Max chased her, the trees and bushes edging the meadow rushed past him at breathtaking speed. Although the gap between him and the runaway chestnut shrank a little, he could not close it.

He shouted at her until she finally looked back at him.

"Stop!" he yelled. "Pull on the reins."

Instead of doing as he instructed, the panicked creature did the opposite. In her terror, she kicked her feet against the horse's sides, urging the confused beast on.

Fortunately, her chestnut was tiring. The space between the two horses narrowed.

Max maneuvered his gelding as close to her mount as he could. As he came abreast of her, he threw his arm around her waist and yanked her from the sidesaddle.

To his amazement, she tried to fight him, and he came within a hairsbreadth of dropping her.

Max could only manage—and then barely—to dump her over his horse in front of the saddle, with her head and feet hanging down on opposite sides of his gelding.

Her arms and legs flailed like windmills gone mad, unnerving Max's mount.

He halted the gelding so he could lower her to the ground.

She instantly turned into a wildcat, clawing at Max's face and arms, and he lost his grip on her. She dropped to the ground, somehow managing to land on her feet.

He jumped from his horse, but she did not look at him. She bent her head over her fingers, and her long auburn hair tumbled wildly about her face, shielding it from Max's inspection. For some inexplicable reason, she was hurriedly unbuttoning the jacket of her fashionable emerald green riding habit.

His patience snapped. "What the hell were you trying to do, fighting me like that? Kill us both?"

She glared at him as she pulled a small pistol from inside her jacket and pointed it at him. "No, only you!"

Max stared in disbelief at the weapon in her hand, its barrel aimed at his groin. "Be careful where you point that," he cautioned uneasily.

"I know where I'm pointing it. I always shoot where it'll do the most good."

He blinked. Surely she could not mean what it sounded like . . . of course not. "Is that a toy?"

"No, it's a loaded derringer."

Her calm coolness flabbergasted Max.

"Unless you want me to prove to you it's loaded, you'll hand me your horse's reins and walk away from me."

Bloody hell, the woman was stark raving mad.

Max's work as a secret agent for the crown had placed him in dangerous, explosive situations, but he felt more nervous now, facing this lunatic female armed with a pistol she probably had no idea how to use.

Incredulous, Max studied her delicate oval face, with its high cheekbones and determined chin. "You are not joking, are you?"

"No, I am . . . *deadly* . . . serious." Her voice puzzled him. It was firm, with a foreign accent, soft and pleasing, that he could not identify.

She held out her hand. "Now, give me the reins."

Despite the gun aimed at him, he made no move to comply. "Why the hell should I do that? This is my horse. Or have you forgotten?"

"But since you robbed me of mine, I am perfectly justified in taking yours." Again she spoke with a softness that belied the infuriating content of her words.

"Robbed you?" he sputtered. "Apparently you failed to notice that your damned horse ran away. Christ, is this the thanks I get for saving you from a runaway horse, you ungrateful woman!"

She looked as though he'd royally insulted her.

"Horses don't run away when I'm riding them. I don't allow it."

She sounded as regal as Queen Victoria herself.

Her eyes narrowed suspiciously. "Is that the defense you intend to use, you were only trying to save me, not rob me or—"

"Do I look like a robber?" Max interrupted, incensed. He gestured at his impeccably tailored clothing in the first stare of fashion. He'd never been so damned insulted in his life.

She studied him for a moment. "No," she admitted. "More likely you're a rapist."

His jaw dropped. He did not know which shocked him more: that she could think such a vile thing of him or that she would actually speak the word aloud—and to a man. No lady in this modern Victorian age would dream of letting it cross her lips.

Nor would she falsely accuse a lord of the realm of such a crime as this creature had just done.

"Furthermore," she continued, "if you do not start walking away from me immediately, no other woman will ever have to worry about what you might do to her."

The glint in her eyes told him she was as serious as she had warned.

"You belong in Bedlam!"

And Max wished to hell she was there.

Or anywhere else except in front of him, pointing that damned derringer at his family jewels.

Moreover, she had grievously insulted his honor. "I would never rape a woman. For your information, I am Lord Maximilian Chartwell, the—"

He'd expected her to be impressed. Instead disdain flashed in her eyes. "Being a lord and a rapist are not mutually exclusive."

Max started to protest, then remembered the predilections of one lord in particular. He said instead, "I swear my only intent was to save you from what I thought was a runaway horse."

"A likely story." She kept the gun pointed at his crotch.

His anger and exasperation got the better of him. "So you intend to repay me for trying to save your life by blowing off my balls."

The words were out before he realized what he was saying. No gentleman—and he was one—spoke so crudely to a lady. Max, who had not blushed in twenty years, felt his face redden.

He hoped to hell she did not understand what he was referring to, but nevertheless he said, "I beg your pardon."

To his astonishment, she laughed, a delightful, musical trill that reminded him of a rippling harp. Her expressive eyes twinkled like a pair of twin Venuses in the night sky. "Yes, they were my target, but I've decided to spare them for now."

Max felt his face growing still hotter. And, damn her, she was clearly enjoying his discomfort. "May I ask why?"

"I've concluded you're telling the truth. So, as you pointed out, it would be most ungrateful of me." She lowered the pistol to her side.

Max took a long, deep breath of relief, and his nostrils filled with her fresh, pleasing scent, reminiscent of orange blossoms. Now that she no longer threatened him, he turned his attention to studying her.

She was young. In her early twenties, Max guessed.

Petite, too. The top of her head barely reached his mouth.

And she was a beauty, although a critic might carp that her cute button of a nose lacked proper aristocratic length.

Her large eyes were a rare shade of aquamarine, shaded by thick curling lashes. Her lips were wide and full, particularly the lower one, and her smile dazzled Max.

A sudden, ridiculous desire to kiss that tempting mouth gripped him. He hastily suppressed the urge.

He had no wish to become a eunuch.

Max dropped his gaze to her body, displayed to perfection by her stylish riding habit. Her curves were equally alluring. An unwanted wave of lust surged through him.

Bloody hell, how could he want to bed a madwoman who'd been on the verge of unmanning him?

He was as crazy as she was!

"Who are you?" Max asked.

"My name's Virginia Blair."

This was the brazen, title-hunting American? She was not at all what Max had expected. Nor did her accent sound like any American's he'd ever heard. Nevertheless, his growing attraction to her shriveled instantly.

"I heard you and Mrs. Blair were visiting Castle Penrose. I am on my way there."

"Willingly?"

She sounded so astonished that he nearly laughed. "Of course willingly. Unless you intend to aim your pistol at me again and force me there at gunpoint."

"But why would you willingly go to that damp, dreary pile of gray flint?"

Clearly Miss Blair was not enamored of the castle—only of its owner's title.

"To visit my cousin, the duke of Penrose."

"You must be a very distant cousin. You look nothing like him."

"Perhaps not, but he is my first cousin. His father was my uncle."

She seemed puzzled. "Then how is it you're a lord? I thought boys born to younger sons of dukes were mere misters."

Miss Blair had obviously made a thorough study of the British peerage, no doubt so she could make certain a prospective husband was at least a lord.

But a duke would be best of all, Max thought cynically. The title-hunting vixen was just like cousin Esmond's mother, though considerably more interesting than Daphne was. "I was not born to my title. I earned it."

"How could a male aristocrat earn anything? Work is beneath you."

Much offended by her scornful tone, Max demanded, "Is it? Who do you think governs this country?"

"*Her* Majesty, Queen Victoria."

"You do not need a gun for protection," he grumbled. "You have your rapier tongue."

"Why, thank you." Her smile was brilliant, as though Max had just paid her a great compliment, rather than insulted her.

Looking around, he saw her chestnut placidly

munching grass in the shade of an English oak on the far side of the meadow.

"Your horse, which you falsely accused me of stealing, is over there, peacefully eating. I will retrieve it, and we *both* can ride to the castle." Max glanced down at her pistol. "Do you really know how to shoot that, Miss Blair?"

"I am an excellent shot."

Max could not hide his incredulity, and her eyes narrowed.

"See that cone?" She raised the pistol, pointing the small barrel at a white pine on the edge of the meadow, perhaps thirty feet away.

It took him a moment to locate the long, tapering cone hanging from one of the higher branches. "Yes, I see it."

He folded his arms across his chest, struggling to hide his amusement at her presumption. The tree was far enough away that he would be astonished if she managed to hit any part of the damned thing.

She aimed and fired.

The cone shattered into fragments.

Gulping, Max fought a strong, instinctive impulse to clasp his hands protectively over his groin.

Chapter 2

Virgie watched Lord Chartwell ride toward her, trailing her chestnut behind his brown gelding. She admired a skilled rider, and he rode as though he'd been born in a saddle.

Although she'd been careful not to betray it to Max, she was still embarrassed at how badly she'd misinterpreted his attempt to rescue her. No one had ever tried to save her before, and she found his concern touching.

Certainly her three rambunctious older brothers, whom she'd done her best to emulate as she grew up, would have scoffed at the idea of her needing help.

A lump rose in Virgie's throat at the thought of them. They had always been a close family, and she missed her father and her brothers dreadfully. She ached to go home to their ranch in California, but . . .

11

She squared her shoulders. That day was still months away.

His lordship reached Virgie with her chestnut in tow. "Here is your 'stolen' horse, Miss Blair."

"Thank you . . ." She broke off. She'd been about to say Lord Chartwell.

But perhaps she was supposed to call him Lord Maximilian.

Or Lord Maximilian Chartwell.

Unlike her odious stepmother, who studied *DeBrett's Peerage* as though it were the Bible itself, Virgie could never keep straight the variations in how a lord and lady were addressed. And English aristocrats were so stuffy about people getting their titles exactly right.

Chartwell swung down from his gelding. "Let me help you onto your horse."

He did so, and Virgie settled in the sidesaddle she loathed. In California, she wasn't subjected to such saddles, or to all the other foolish strictures that imprisoned ladies here in England even more rigidly than those ridiculous corsets that scarcely permitted them to breathe.

Chartwell remounted, and their horses moved forward. They quickly left the meadow behind and cantered along the road between the golden-leaved tulip trees.

Virgie surreptitiously studied her companion out of the corner of her eye. He was a big man, tall, with wide shoulders and a posture that proclaimed confidence and strength. He would have made a far more impressive duke than his cousin did.

The features beneath his hat were too sharp to be handsome. Yet his thick black brows, prominent

cheekbones, straight nose, and hard chin combined
to make a striking, distinctive face that Virgie much
preferred to one that was conventionally good looking.

"Why were you riding alone at such an insane
speed?" Chartwell had a vibrant voice, deep and
surprisingly pleasant, considering his hard face.

"I love to ride flat out." That was true but not the
reason Virgie had been doing so today. She'd quar-
reled more hotly than usual with her imperious, dic-
tatorial stepmother, and she'd been trying to ride off
her fury.

"That can be a dangerous habit," he observed.

"Not for a skilled rider."

"What if her horse stumbles and breaks a leg?"

His inquiry startled Virgie into turning her head
to look at him. "I would never knowingly endanger
a horse."

Chartwell's slate gray eyes had a piercing quality
to them that made her feel as though he could bore
through to the dark secrets of her soul.

Not that Virgie had any. She was too used to
speaking her mind freely and candidly to hide any
secrets, dark or otherwise. Her frank tongue often
landed her in trouble, especially with her stepmother, but Virgie prized honesty.

"Why, when I was trying to catch you, did you
think I meant you harm?" he asked.

"I apologize for misjudging you, but you have
the look of an outlaw about you," Virgie replied
with her customary candor.

He looked so insulted that she felt she must defend herself. "I can hardly be blamed for mistaking

you for a highwayman, especially after the warning
I received this morning."

"What warning was that?"

"A robber in the area is preying on women by
themselves. He sneaks up on an unsuspecting victim, grabs her reticule or cuts it from her grasp, and
flees before the victim realizes what has happened.
He's already robbed more than a dozen women in
Ipswich and smaller villages in the area."

His lordship frowned. "He must be a footpad, not
a highwayman."

"He is, but when I saw your face, I thought he
must have purchased a horse with the money he's
stolen and become a highwayman."

Chartwell had scared Virgie half to death, but she
would never admit that to him or any other living
soul. Her brothers, who had taught her to ride, rope,
and shoot, had also instilled in her that a Blair, no
matter how frightened, did not show fear. To do so
gave the adversary an advantage.

Now, though, what most astonished and discon-
certed her about the man riding beside her was the
strange, excited fluttering that he evoked in her.

And him a damned English lord too!

Her social-climbing stepmother, Rowena, would
have bartered her soul to be part of the English aristocracy, but Virgie had only contempt for its titles
and endless entertaining. She considered lords and
their ladies a parasitic blight on society.

"How long do you and your mother plan to stay
at the castle, Miss Blair?"

"Rowena's my stepmother. Please don't insult the
memory of my mother, who was a wonderful, generous, loving woman." And as different from her

father's second wife as sugar was from sulphur.

He raised one of his black brows. "I gather you consider your stepmother none of those things."

"We are not the best of friends." *The understatement of the century, maybe the millennium.*

"You did not tell me how long you will be staying at Penrose."

Virgie looked at the imposing castle towering against the sky ahead of them, and she shivered. Once a medieval fortress, it was perched on the highest hill in the area, like an enormous sentinel guarding the flat green countryside sprinkled with groves of trees and newly harvested fields.

"I would love to leave today," she said. "The castle is the most depressing place I've ever stayed."

"Then why do you remain?"

"My stepmother refuses to go. She glories in being the guest of a *duke* in his own castle." Virgie also was convinced that Rowena hoped to make a match between her stepdaughter and the duke.

Over Virgie's dead body!

"Then depart without her." Although Chartwell's voice was casual, he was watching her intently with those probing gray eyes.

If it were that easy, Virgie would have been gone weeks ago. She could hardly confide to this stranger, however, that what she wanted most in the world was at stake. Even if it were not, she would deeply disappoint her father, and she could not bear to do that. She loved him too much.

Virgie and Chartwell crossed over the castle's moat. The hooves of their mounts thudded dully on the worn, weathered planks of a creaky drawbridge she doubted had been raised in centuries.

They passed between the twin turrets of the gate-house, and then through both the outer and inner curtain walls that had been built as part of the castle's medieval fortifications.

When they stopped by the steps that led to the entrance of the castle's principal building, Chartwell dismounted and helped her down from her horse.

She shivered a little at his touch as he set her on the ground with a gentleness that contradicted his dangerous appearance.

What would it be like to have a strong, masterful man like Chartwell look at her as though he were besotted by her? Virgie was startled at how much she wanted to find out.

Not that she was likely to do so. Strong men perversely seemed to prefer dainty little flowers—coy, helpless females who looked at them adoringly.

Virgie did not do coy. Or helpless. Or adoring.

She looked up at her companion. "What am I to call you: Lord Chartwell or Lord Maximilian? I can never keep straight whom I should address as what in your silly aristocracy."

"Silly?" he echoed, looking mortally offended.

"Yes, silly. All that bowing and scraping to people who've done nothing to deserve it." She turned and briskly climbed the uneven stone stairs. Over the centuries, the feet of lords and knights, serfs and servants, had worn deep valleys into the center of each step.

"How did you determine they don't deserve it?" he called after her, an irritated edge to his voice.

She banged the knocker on the heavy oak entrance strapped with iron, turned, and looked down at him, saying with false sweetness, "Because, it grieves me to say, I have met too many of *you* lords."

Rapier, hell, Miss Blair had a hatchet for a tongue.

The door opened behind the American, and she disappeared into the castle.

She would be a match for Max's Great-aunt Elizabeth, who was famous for her witty, acerbic tongue.

Still, Miss Blair puzzled Max. She did not sound like a woman trying to trap Esmond into matrimony for his title. If she were, would she have been so candid about how little she cared for the aristocracy and for Castle Penrose?

Or had it all been an act for Max's benefit?

He had long ago come to appreciate the full deviousness and duplicity of the opposite sex. No doubt Miss Blair had been trying to mislead him about her real intentions.

Max handed the horses' reins to a groom, but he did not go into the castle. After hours in the saddle, he needed a brisk walk, and he might as well combine it with an inspection of the outer ward between the two curtain walls.

A quarter of the way around, he passed all that remained of Penrose's once splendid menagerie—two rusting cages, one empty and the other inhabited by an old lion. As the beast always did when he saw Max, he thrust his deadly jaws between the bars of his cage and snarled ferociously.

Max was tempted to snarl back. Actually, he was surprised to see the lion still alive. The last time Max had visited the castle, the beast had been skin and bones, his coat, dull and mangy. When Max had asked what was wrong, he'd been told the lion refused to eat.

Now, though, his coat was much improved, and he had gained weight. Clearly he was eating again.

After Max finished his walk around the outer ward, he went to the familiar stairs that he had climbed so often as a child. When he was six, his parents had been killed in a yachting accident, and his grandfather, the ninth duke of Penrose, had brought Max to the castle to raise him.

As he reached the top of the stairs, the ramrod-straight butler, Jenkins, who was at the castle when the newly orphaned Max came to live here twenty-nine years ago, opened the heavy, iron-strapped oak door and welcomed Max inside.

"A room is not ready for you, my lord," Jenkins fretted. "Neither the duke nor his mother mentioned you were coming."

"They did not know." Max walked into the castle's narrow entry hall, with its two-story-high walls that supported the soaring arches of a Gothic ceiling, giving the hall a top-heavy appearance.

As a six-year-old, Max had feared the vaulted ceiling might collapse on him. He had been terrified, too, of his grandfather, the gruff, authoritarian duke, but the boy had quickly come to love the old man.

Max said, "I decided to surprise Duke Esmond and his mother."

"And may I say what a pleasant surprise it is, my lord."

"Thank you, Jenkins, but the duke's mother would not agree with you."

"No, my lord." A small smile tugged at the corners of the butler's mouth, as though he enjoyed the thought of her displeasure. "Is there anything you wish?"

"Yes, to see Grigsby." He was the estate's steward who had written the note warning that the Blairs had bribed the duke's mother. Max wanted to learn what else Grigsby might have discovered. "Where is he?"

"He was called away yesterday to the bedside of his father, who is very ill. I do not expect him back before tomorrow at the earliest."

Damn the luck. Max wanted to see him as soon as possible. "In that case, where will I find His Grace?"

"I believe he is in the conservatory, my lord."

Virgie went to the castle's long gallery, its walls lined with musty tapestries, rather than to the guest apartment that she shared with her stepmother. She feared Rowena would be in their apartment, and Virgie hoped to avoid her for as long as possible.

Preferably forever.

She stopped before one of the tapestries, so faded and frayed that she could scarcely make out its cherubs frolicking in a forest. It had probably been hanging there since this castle was built seven hundred and eighty-three years ago. Too bad the Chartwells' medieval enemies had failed to destroy the drafty monstrosity.

"*Bonjour,* Mademoiselle Blair."

Recognizing the Comte de Beaucaire's voice behind her, Virgie suppressed a groan. She could not seem to go anywhere in the castle these days without bumping into him.

Not that he wasn't charming. That was the problem. He was too charming. Too practiced. Too slick.

He reminded Virgie of the cardsharps and fortune hunters she'd met in San Francisco.

Reluctantly, she turned to face the comte. Brown hair curled around a slender, sensitive face set with dark, sensual eyes that visually caressed any woman upon whom they gazed.

The scion of a noble French family that had fallen on hard times, he'd become an artist to support himself. The duke's mother, Lady Albert, had hired him to give her art lessons.

Virgie was convinced, however, that the principal duties he performed for her ladyship had nothing to do with paints and canvas.

He reached for Virgie's hand, and she hastily put it behind her to prevent him from kissing it. She was convinced her sole appeal to the comte was her father's fortune.

"Careful, Comte, Lady Albert will get jealous."

Something hard and cold glinted in his eyes for a fleeting instant. Then he was all charm and smiles again. "You flatter me, Mademoiselle. I am merely employed to give my lady art lessons. I must remind you, my lovely flower, I am nearer your age than hers."

"And I must warn you, Comte, you will find me more cactus than flower."

The conservatory was in the wing of the castle opposite from the entry, and Max decided to cut through the tapestry gallery to reach it.

At the gallery entrance, he stopped in surprise. Miss Blair, her back to Max, was talking to a stranger whose handsome face and bedroom eyes would capture any woman's attention.

Max heard him call Miss Blair his lovely flower in a French accent. The man's hot, seductive expression told Max he intended to make her one of his conquests—and he undoubtedly had scored many.

Who the devil was he and why was he at Castle Penrose?

Max could not make out Miss Blair's low reply, but whatever it was, the man's jaw dropped. Perhaps Max was not the only one on whom she used her rapier tongue.

She strode rapidly toward the doorway at the opposite end of the long gallery. The Frenchman recovered from his surprise and went after her. Max quietly followed him, intent on learning his identity.

By the time Max exited the other end of the gallery, however, both the Frenchman and Miss Blair had disappeared, and Max continued on to the conservatory.

Stopping in the doorway, Max did not see his cousin there, but the duke's mother, Daphne, was sitting beside a zebra plant, a dreamy look on her face.

Most likely she was considering all the ways she would spend the Blairs' bribe money, Max thought cynically.

Daphne still retained enough of the delicate, blond beauty of her youth for Max to understand how she had so captivated his uncle Albert, the marquess of Dolby. He had married her over the vehement objections of Max's grandfather and the rest of the Chartwell family.

Max stepped inside the conservatory. When he was a child, he had loved this large glass-enclosed room.

Now, however, Daphne had packed it with so many exotic plants and flowers—lilies of the Nile, flaming swords, a Canary date palm, several kinds of ferns, and dozens of others—that hardly any room was left to walk among them. Daphne did everything to excess.

The disparate smells in the moist room did not mingle well, and they tickled Max's nose.

He much preferred the scent of orange blossoms.

Max took a dozen steps into the conservatory before Daphne noticed him.

"Chartwell, what a surprise." Both her expression and her tone made clear how unpleasant the surprise was.

Since the day the will of Max's grandfather had been read, Daphne had hated Max more than any other human being.

When the dying man had realized that Esmond, rather than his favorite grandson, Max, would succeed him as duke, he had changed his will. He had stipulated that all of the entailed estate, including Castle Penrose, be placed in trust for the new duke, whom Grandfather had considered incapable of running the estate, and he had named Max its sole trustee.

In effect, the will had given Max control of the estate and made him Esmond's de facto guardian until the new duke reached the advanced age of thirty-five.

Esmond could do nothing without Max's permission.

Not even marry.

"Why are you here, Chartwell?" Hostility permeated Daphne's voice.

He shrugged carelessly. "I thought it time to inspect the estate. After all, I am responsible for it."

"It is my son's estate, not yours!"

"I did not say it was mine, only that I was responsible for it. I assure you that it is a burden I would happily have done without."

Which was true, although Daphne would never believe that, or that Max did not begrudge Esmond his title. The duke's affairs required far more of Max's attention than his own did. Managing Penrose was a particularly difficult and thankless task because Daphne was so unpleasant whenever he had to visit.

"But since my grandfather imposed the charge on me," Max continued, "I will not shirk my duty."

"Your pretty words about duty do not fool me in the least, Chartwell." Daphne stood abruptly, bumping the zebra plant, which tottered precariously. "You draw the greatest pleasure from denying me and my son what is rightfully ours."

He raised a brow. "Denying *you*? *You* have no claim whatsoever upon this estate. Grandfather made it my responsibility to protect Castle Penrose from your extravagance and ensure it remains in the Chartwell family for future generations." He gave her a grim look. "And I will."

Angry color rose in Daphne's face, and she opened her mouth. Max awaited a bitter tirade, but she caught herself and closed her mouth again.

Perhaps she remembered the stipulation in Grandfather's will that her son could not marry without

Max's consent? Although he doubted the provision was legally enforceable, he was not about to let her know that.

Especially not now. He would use whatever means necessary to save Esmond from his mother's selfish greed.

"This is where you are, Daphne, dear."

Now here was an accent that Max recognized instantly as American. It belonged to a large woman with gray hair, several chins, and an overbearing air. She sailed into the conservatory, reminding Max of a thirty-two-gun frigate that scattered all before her. She eyed him with a hard, assessing stare.

She must be Miss Blair's stepmother, the other half of the bribing duo.

Something akin to panic flashed across Daphne's face. She hastily moved toward the woman, trying to block her advance into the room. "I was just coming for you, Rowena."

The woman ignored Daphne, steaming rudely past her and up to Max, whom she surveyed with undisguised curiosity.

"I am Mrs. Leonard Blair." She sounded as though he should be vastly impressed by the name. "My daughter, Virginia, and I are staying at the castle. Who are you?"

Max was taken aback by the woman's audacity in failing to wait for her hostess to introduce them. "I am Lord Chartwell." His frigid reply was designed to quell the presumptuous American into silence.

It failed. At the mention of his title, her eyes glinted with interest. "What kind of lord?"

"I beg your pardon?"

Mrs. Blair did not seem to notice Max's icy tone.

"There are several kinds of English lords, from a marquess to a baron." Her nasal voice made clear the latter was beneath her notice. "Which are you?"

Max could scarcely believe he'd heard her correctly. The woman was a living, breathing caricature of the brassy, rude, determined American mamas who had invaded England, determined to buy noble titles for their daughters.

Well, damn her, Es would not be this obnoxious woman's trophy. With a deliberate incivility meant to match her own, Max said, "That hardly matters, since I have no wish to make your acquaintance."

Max turned on his heel and strode from the conservatory. As he passed through its door, he heard Mrs. Blair gasp in outrage. "Well, I never! Such rudeness!"

"Yes, he is a most unpleasant man," Daphne said.

Max intended to prove to Mrs. Blair that, as far as she was concerned, Daphne's description of him was correct.

He marched directly to the library. With its vaulted ceiling and stained glass windows, the library looked at first glance like the nave of a Gothic cathedral, and it offered solace as if it were. Only the many shelves filled with leather-bound books betrayed its real purpose. The old books' bindings scented the room.

Max stopped abruptly, puzzled by the painting that was displayed on an easel near the door, an honor that in the past had been reserved only for works by such masters in the Penrose art collection as Turner, Reynolds, and Rembrandt.

This painting, a landscape, definitely did not qualify.

It depicted Penmoor, the estate's village, but was so crude and lacking in perspective that the castle, instead of resting atop the hill in the background, looked as though it were sitting on the roofs of the cottages.

"Max, how good it is to see you!"

He turned at the duke of Penrose's warm greeting. Hard as Daphne had tried, she had not been able to convince her son he should share her hatred of Max.

Es had inherited his papa's less than handsome face and thin, diminutive body, but he also had been blessed with his father's genial, easygoing character.

Smiling broadly, Max gripped the duke's hands in his own. He was very fond of his young cousin and de facto ward. Although Es was not the brightest candle in the illustrious Chartwell chandelier, Max believed that Grandfather had seriously underestimated him.

"What brings you here?" Es asked.

Max could hardly tell him the truth. Instead, he joked, "I wanted to ride Black Lightning again."

That cantankerous stallion terrorized the castle's grooms. Several had quit rather than try to ride him. Max had the distinction of being the only person to remain on him for longer than a few seconds.

But it had not been easy. And, despite his quip, Max was not anxious for an encore ride.

"You are so brave, Max." Es's eyes shone with awe. "How happy I am that you are here. I have missed you."

"What, have you no visitors at the castle to entertain you?" Although Max knew the answer, he wanted to hear what Es would say about Miss Blair.

"We have three. Miss Virginia Blair and her mama, and Comte Jacques de Beaucaire."

That must be the Frenchman Max had seen trying to seduce Miss Blair. "Who is the comte and why is he here?"

"A very talented painter who is giving Mama art lessons. She says some of his paintings hang in the Louvre."

"I did not know your mother had artistic leanings."

Es gestured toward the painting Max had been examining. "That is her work. The comte says Mama has great hidden talent."

Very, very well hidden! "Hmm, I wondered who painted it," Max said with noncommittal politeness. "Who are the Blairs, Es?"

"Americans Mama invited."

"Tell me about Miss Blair?"

His cousin's face lit up. "Oh, Max, she is the most beautiful, witty, charming woman. You will love her."

Like hell I will. Although he would not mind in the least bedding her, a thought that startled him.

Unfortunately, Grigsby had been right. The duke was clearly infatuated with the American. Max glumly lengthened the probable amount of time he would have to spend at the castle freeing his cousin from the Blairs' clutches.

He hoped he succeeded before he had to go to London in three weeks to escort Lady Priscilla to a ball. If he did not, he would have to travel to London and then come back here.

"Even Mama likes her and thinks she would make me an excellent wife," Es confided.

"I am certain Mama does."

Max's ironic reply clearly puzzled the duke. "Why do you say that? She is very particular about whom I shall marry. Indeed, Miss Blair is the very first girl Mama has ever said that about."

"Do you want to marry her?"

"If she will have me."

Oh, she will have you, Your Grace. Never doubt that. "Where in America is she from?"

"California, where her father made his fortune from the gold rush."

Bloody hell, Max thought, disgusted at the idea of the duke of Penrose marrying the daughter of a common miner from beyond the frontiers of civilization, no matter how rich the man had become. Damn Daphne and her greed!

"I have never met another girl like her," Esmond said.

At least on that point Max agreed totally with his young cousin. Miss Blair was indeed unique.

But damn her, Max would not let her hurt his cousin. Es was too innocent and sweet natured for his own good.

And far, far too generous.

Max was as certain as his grandfather had been that had the young duke control of the Penrose fortune, Es would be unable to withstand the ceaseless, wheedling demands of his mother. He would indulge every one of her extravagant, expensive whims, just as his father had done before him.

Max attributed much of his grandfather's prejudice against Es to his being Daphne's son. After Dolby's death, Grandfather had let her take her son to Cornwall and keep him there with her. Max thought it had been his usually astute grandfather's most grievous mistake. He should have kept the boy at the castle and raised him as he had Max. If his grandfather had done that, Max was convinced his cousin would be a different man today.

Max would happily have taken Es under his wing and taught him what their grandfather should have, but Daphne's hatred of Max precluded that.

As though his thoughts had conjured her up, Daphne hurried into the library, clearly unhappy to discover Max alone with her son. "Esmond . . ."

"Mama, Max has come." Es's clear delight deepened her frown. "Now that you are here, Max, I hope you will make a long visit."

"Esmond dearest, Lord Chartwell is a very busy man and has many duties that call him elsewhere."

"Not at all, Daphne," Max replied with more spite than truth. "I am presently a man of leisure. Furthermore, nothing is as important to me as my responsibility to Castle Penrose and His Grace."

He turned to Es. "In answer to your question, I plan to stay at least several days, perhaps longer."

Daphne looked as though she'd just swallowed a mouthful of broken glass, but the duke clapped his hands in joy.

"Wonderful! Mama—I mean we—are having a shooting party in a fortnight or so. You must stay for it."

"Esmond," his mother interjected quickly, "come, we must dress for dinner." She was clearly determined not to leave her son alone with Max.

"Go ahead," Max told him. "I must do the same."

Normally Max loathed dining at the same table as Daphne, but tonight he looked forward to dinner.

And to matching wits with the scheming Miss Blair.

Chapter 3

⌒◯◯⌒

As Virgie dressed for dinner that night, the rain pounded and the wind howled against the windows of her bedchamber. A storm had roared in off the North Sea, sending the temperature plummeting. The castle's gray stone walls oozed damp and cold.

She had ignored the thin gown of pale pink tulle and silk, fussily covered with bows and ruffles, the steel-banded crinoline cage, and the corset that Rowena's maid had laid out for her to wear to dinner. She hated the gown, which her stepmother had ordered for her.

Virgie was too petite to wear all those frills. Her feminine curves disappeared beneath the ostentatious frippery, and she looked as though she were a grotesquely overdressed China doll come to life. Worse, the gown's square neck was cut so low that she'd blushed with embarrassment at her first fitting.

Virgie favored simple garments over the lavish, ornately trimmed gowns currently so fashionable. Nor did she wear pale, insipid pastels that were much in vogue among English ladies. She preferred vivid colors like the bright red of the simple wool gown she had chosen for tonight.

A fierce gust of wind rattled the glass. Virgie yearned to be back in California, enjoying a warm, pleasant autumn among the pines and cedars and redwoods, but she would not be allowed to see the United States again before January.

Virgie reminded herself firmly that what she most wanted in the world was at stake during this visit to England.

To instill character and tenacity in his children, her father had required each of them upon reaching adulthood to do what they most disliked for six months. If they succeeded in sticking with their assigned task, they were rewarded with what they most coveted.

Before her turn came, Virgie had thought of a dozen different challenges her father might give her. Never in a million years, though, would she have anticipated the one he'd picked.

She must forsake their California ranch and act like a genteel lady for six months in England, where her stepmother would introduce her to the aristocracy. Virgie suspected Rowena, who had wanted to visit England, of planting the idea in her father's head.

True, nothing was harder for Virgie than acting like a lady. It was such damned hard work, especially in oh-so-proper England.

But all her older brothers had successfully completed the task their father had given them, and she refused to be the first of his children to fail. Particularly when her reward would be the valley she loved so much. She would endure anything to obtain it.

She gritted her teeth, swearing to succeed.

Virgie had come to dread dinner at the castle, particularly during a storm. Tonight, however, despite the terrible weather, she was impatient to go down to the meal.

Or, more precisely, to see Lord Maximilian Chartwell again.

Why she should want to do so mystified her. So did the little flutter of excitement she felt when she thought of him. Even though he didn't look like a member of the British aristocracy she found stultifying and, for the most part, useless, he was.

He was *not*, however, dull. Nor, she suspected, useless either. She was still touched that he had tried to rescue her.

"Virginia, why are you wearing that dreadful dress?"

She started at the sound of her stepmother's grating, nasal voice behind her. "What a fright you gave me."

Virgie wished that just once Rowena would knock before she marched into her stepdaughter's bedroom. The woman acted as though Virgie were a child instead of a grown woman.

"Why aren't you wearing the lovely pink silk I had my maid lay out for you tonight? It is by far the most flattering gown you own."

Virgie, who thought it her most unflattering

gown, said as gently as she could, "I'm afraid I can't agree."

"You have no sense of what becomes you, missy."

Virgie bit her lips together to keep from retorting that her stepmother had no notion of style at all—only a slavish adherence to fashion's dictates, no matter how unsuitable or bizarre they looked on her.

"Put the pink gown on at once."

Rowena never requested, never said please or thank you to Virgie. She merely ordered her as though her stepdaughter were another one of her servants.

"It's too light a gown for tonight," Virgie explained, careful to keep her voice polite and non-argumentative. "With this storm, the refectory will be as cold as an icehouse. I chose this wool because I knew I would freeze in the pink gown." And she'd be damned if she'd catch pneumonia in this wretched old castle.

Anger flashed in Rowena's eyes. "A proper lady bears a little discomfort for the sake of fashion. I order you to wear the pink!"

If Virgie had a valid, sensible reason for doing something, her stepmother was certain to demand she do the opposite. "I'm very sorry, but I can't."

"How dare you defy me!" Mrs. Blair's voice rose to a screech. "Wait until your father hears of your unnatural behavior. You will be very sorry then."

In other words, Rowena would do all she could to convince her husband that his daughter had failed her test. Virgie would not allow her stepmother to see how worrisome she found this threat.

Virgie would not let her stepmother cost her the

valley she loved so much. Yet she could not shake the fear that Rowena would try to deny Virgie her dream even if she did everything her stepmother wanted.

A chill ran down Virgie's spine. Then she told herself firmly that surely, by now, her father was sufficiently disillusioned with Rowena that he would believe his daughter rather than his spiteful wife.

Virgie suspected that her father rued the day he had married Rowena even more than his daughter did. Poor man. He'd been so lonely after Virgie's mother had died. Ironically, now that he was married to Rowena, he was even lonelier.

"Furthermore, Virginia, your manners toward Duke Esmond are abominable. The duke is our host, and you all but ignore him. Tonight you will attend to him."

With each passing day, Virgie grew more convinced that Rowena was determined to make a match between the duke and her stepdaughter.

Virgie could think of no one she less wanted to marry than an English duke.

Any duke, but especially Esmond.

Not that she disliked him. He was too amiable and good-hearted for her not to be fond of him, but he would never interest her as a husband. Although he had reached the age of manhood, he was still a boy tied to his mother's apron strings with suffocating tightness.

He desperately needed to be freed from his mama's tentacles and to have a strong, patient, responsible male teach him to be a man, as her father had taught her brothers.

"You *will* treat His Grace with the respect a duke deserves, Virginia."

"But a title does not *deserve* my respect. The man who holds the title must earn it."

Rowena looked as though Virgie had just avowed she was a practicing Satanist. "You will do as I say."

Max expected to stay, as he always did during his visits to Penrose, in the apartment that had been his when he had lived at the castle. Instead Daphne had ordered that he be given a small, sparsely furnished guest bedchamber, uncomfortable and seldom used, in the oldest section of the castle.

When he asked why he was not assigned his usual apartment, he was told the Comte de Beaucaire now occupied it.

Max went to the high narrow slit in the four-foot-thick wall that served as the chamber's sole window. In medieval times, the slit had been used to dump burning torches and boiling pitch on enemy troops, but it proved to be considerably less useful as a window.

Had Daphne chosen this room for him because his view through the slit consisted of the cage housing that snarling, evil-tempered lion? It was exactly the sort of thing she would do.

Max listened to the heavy, wind-propelled rain beating almost horizontally against the castle. Damn, what wretched luck that the weather had changed. When the wind roared in from the north as it did now, the dining hall was aswirl in bone-chilling drafts.

Nor was his bedchamber much better. The fireplace poured out more smoke than heat into the room. Perhaps Daphne hoped either the smoke would suffocate him or he would freeze to death.

He left the room and strode toward the staircase. It was very early to go down to dinner, but Max wanted to be the first person in the withdrawing room, where the guests gathered before going into the refectory. He intended to observe how Miss Blair and the handsome comte behaved toward each other.

"Virginia, you are not wearing your corset. How shocking!"

Mrs. Blair's unmistakable voice drifted through a door that stood ajar twenty feet or so ahead of him.

Max grinned. The old frigate could not have sounded more outraged if her stepdaughter had proposed to go down to dinner naked.

An image flashed into his mind of Miss Blair's lovely body sans clothes. To his dismay, that elicited an instant response in his own anatomy. He had not expected the title-hungry American chit would raise that kind of interest in him.

But then he did not have to like a beautiful woman to lust for her body in his bed.

"Put on your corset, Virginia. I will not allow you to go down to dinner without it on, you wretched girl."

"I will remain here then." Miss Blair's dulcet voice contrasted sharply with her stepmother's shrill tones.

"Only to spite me, and I'll not allow that!"

Max, who was passing their door, almost laughed aloud. Clearly, the girl was not easily cowed by her harridan of a stepmother—or anyone else. He found himself liking Miss Blair despite himself.

"I hope that odious Lord Chartwell will not be at dinner." Mrs. Blair's voice drifted down the hall after him. "His manners are appalling! And why he should make Lady Albert so nervous is beyond me. The stupid creature is actually afraid of him."

"I suspect Lord Chartwell would be a formidable enemy," her stepdaughter observed.

Ah, Miss Blair was even more perceptive and intelligent than Max had realized.

"Fiddlesticks, I'm told he's nothing but a lowly baron. The duke is the head of the family. This Chartwell can do nothing."

Max's jaw tightened. Rowena Blair would find out soon enough what he could and would do—thwart her ambition to make the duke of Penrose her son-in-law. Max waited a moment, curious to hear Miss Blair's answer, but she said nothing, and he continued on his way.

Downstairs, he was the first to arrive in the long, narrow withdrawing room. Although the original castle had been built in Norman times, successive generations of Chartwells had vied to leave their own mark, resulting in a jumble of additions and "improvements" in whatever style was in vogue at the time.

The withdrawing room had once been a sliver of the castle's original great hall, but the seventh duke had made it into a separate room. Delicate plasterwork patterns, popular in the Georgian era, decorated the walls and false ceiling in an attempt to soften the stark cold stone of the castle.

When Max was a child, the room had been done entirely in Georgian furniture. Now, however, several heavy Victorian pieces had been added, cluttering the room and spoiling the classical effect. More of Daphne's tasteless meddling.

Max sat down on a graceful Georgian sofa, expecting ten minutes would pass before either the duke or the comte would come down, and at least twenty minutes before the first woman would make her appearance.

But Miss Blair proved Max wrong, joining him only a few minutes later.

He politely stood and less politely gave her a slow, appreciative appraisal. Her dark hair, the color of rich, strong coffee, no longer hung loosely about her shoulders but was piled high on her head in a way that enhanced the delicacy of her features.

She must have won the war of the corsets, for she could not have had time to don one. Actually she had no need of a corset. Her figure was lovely—and more pleasingly natural in shape—without it.

Max grinned, pleased to discover that the overbearing stepmother could not make Miss Blair do what she did not want.

But if that was the case, then Miss Blair must be an active participant in the scheme to marry Esmond. Otherwise, she would have flatly rejected the plan.

Max's grin and his reluctant liking for Miss Blair died instantly. Damn the presumptuous wench!

Her gown was striking for both its color, a vivid red wool, and its simplicity—long fitted sleeves and a narrow flared skirt instead of one of those huge pyramid affairs covered with flounces, puffs, and bows that were all the thing now. Her bodice eschewed the fashionably deep décolletage in favor of a high mandarin-style collar.

She should have appeared as the most demure and proper of ladies. On her, though, the red gown looked so sensual that Max again felt the stirring of unwanted desire.

He hid this behind a sardonic remark. "I must say you disappoint me, Miss Blair."

She eyed him suspiciously. "Why is that?"

"I thought all women are late because they are constitutionally incapable of appearing on time. But you are *early*, thus challenging my cherished belief."

She laughed, and again Max was reminded of a rippling harp. He loved her laugh. Beneath her long curling lashes, aquamarine eyes gleamed mischievously.

She was enchanting, damn her!

"Are you saying I should strive to be fashionably late, my lord, so I won't ruin my gender's reputation in your eyes?"

"Not at all. I enjoy having my deepest and most cherished beliefs challenged."

"You do?" she questioned with obvious skepticism.

"Yes, it so rarely happens. Besides, I am convinced you are the exception that proves the rule. Did hunger drive you down so early?"

"No, I wanted to escape my stepmother."

Although Max did not blame Miss Blair for that, her candor surprised him.

"But I'm thankful you're here, my lord."

"Why?" he asked, instantly suspicious.

Miss Blair took a step closer to him. Her scent

of orange blossoms tantalized his nose—and other parts of his anatomy.

"So I can ask you to take me into dinner tonight. Will you?"

He stared at her, uncertain whether he was flattered she sought his company or shocked by her forwardness.

More important, what was her reason for asking him?

Was she trying to make Es jealous? Max was not always so suspicious, but his responsibility to save Es from the pain and unhappiness his cousin's father had endured weighed heavily.

"Why do you ask me?" he inquired. "After this afternoon, I cannot believe I am a favorite of yours."

She grinned impishly, again drawing Max's attention to her tempting mouth, with its full lower lip that invited a man to taste it.

"Quite true, but the alternatives are even more unattractive."

For some reason, her reply stung. "How complimentary you are. I am glad to know that, unattractive as you find me, I am better than the alternatives. Which are?"

"The duke or Comte de Beaucaire."

Max seized this opening to try to discover her feelings for the Frenchman. "I am astonished you do not find the comte a most handsome and charming man."

"Oh, I do," Miss Blair assured him. "Exceedingly so."

"But you called him unattractive."

"Not his countenance—his company."

Max raised an eyebrow quizzically. "You do not like him?"

"I don't. Worse, I distrust him."

Her frankness was unprecedented among women Max knew, and he found that as refreshing as her scent. Once again he could not help liking her despite himself. "Why do you not trust him?"

She shrugged. "Intuition. And mine's almost always right."

"How modest you are," he teased.

Miss Blair's lips parted in a beguiling smile that intensified Max's desire to kiss them.

"You have not yet said, my lord, whether you will grant my request."

Although the prospect of having her beside him at the refectory's table inexplicably pleased him, he carefully kept his enthusiasm out of his voice. "Only if you tell me what you find wrong with the duke."

"Nothing really. He's a very sweet boy."

Max secretly agreed with her assessment, but he felt required to defend Es. "He is not a boy, but a man a year past his majority."

"Forgive me, but I differentiate between chronology and reality."

Did she think Max would not use her words against her? He quickly disabused her of that mistake. "My cousin will be devastated to hear your assessment of him."

Concern clouded her face. "Please don't tell him."

"Why should I not, if that is what you think of him?"

"I wouldn't hurt the duke's feelings for the world."

Of course she would not. Max's jaw clenched. The ambitious title hunter wanted too much to be a duchess. "Then why do you prefer to have me, rather than him, as your dinner companion?"

"It will infuriate my stepmother. She thinks you're dreadful."

Once again, her blunt honesty startled Max. He was used to Victorian ladies who spoke only in the most innocuous and polite euphemisms.

"Don't be offended, my lord."

She touched his arm placatingly, making him think of certain other parts of himself he would like her to touch.

"I can accord you no higher recommendation than that my stepmother dislikes you. She dislikes me even more. Will you escort me into the refectory?"

"Yes." Max told himself he wanted Miss Blair's company at dinner because he needed to learn as much as he could about her. *Know thine enemy.*

"Thank you, Lord . . . you never did tell me whether I am to call you Lord Chartwell or Lord Maximilian?"

"Max."

"Lord Max?"

"No, just Max. Why do you look so surprised?"

"You are the first English lord I have met who did not insist upon being addressed by his title." Miss Blair's eyes lit with amusement. "What did you do to make Rowena think you so odious? She has practically groveled before every other lord in England."

"Except for barons, who are beneath her notice. And I am only a baron, thank God."

Her rippling laughter sent a shiver of pleasure through Max. "You have a lovely laugh, Miss Blair."

"Thank you. If I am to call you Max, you may call me Virgie."

To do so would indicate a degree of friendliness that Max did not feel for her. Max also worried it would upset Es, which he did not want to do. "I fear that Virgie would be too familiar," he said diplomatically. "You will remain Miss Blair to me."

"You think Virgie is too familiar? You English are so damned stuffy."

Max had been accused of many things in his life, but never stuffiness.

A strong gust of wind billowed the curtains covering a window that had been left open an inch, aiming shafts of cold air at Max and his companion. Miss Blair shivered at the sudden draft and crossed to the offending window to shut it.

Comte de Beaucaire entered the room, his face lighting at the sight of her turning away from the window. He did not notice Max standing in the shadow of the door.

No answering warmth appeared in Miss Blair's expression. Was that because Max was in the room?

The comte advanced toward her, his hands out. "*Cherie*, I have you all to myself."

She hastily put her hands behind her back. "Not quite." She nodded toward Max.

The comte whirled around. "Pray, monsieur, who are you?" he demanded.

"Lord Maximilian Chartwell."

"*Mais oui*, the cousin of the duke." The comte's cold manner instantly melted, and he advanced with his hand extended. "I am most pleased to make the acquaintance of you, my lord. I am Comte Jacques de Beaucaire. I have heard much about you."

The comte's sudden warmth baffled Max. "From whom?"

"From your cousin, the duke. He has a case of—how do you say it—worship of the hero for you."

"And I am exceedingly fond of His Grace, too."

"If you were that, Chartwell," a querulous feminine voice behind Max said, "you would . . ."

"Mama, please," Esmond implored. He and his mother had entered the room together, her arm in his.

For once, Daphne heeded her son's plea, shutting her mouth in a tight, disapproving line.

Her gown of pink satin clashed with the vivid red of Miss Blair's. Indeed, the two gowns were stylistic opposites, with Daphne's cut so low across the bosom that it was only a fraction above indecent. Her huge skirt was a profusion of flounces and bows puffed out by several petticoats.

The comte hurried forward to kiss Daphne's hand. "Madame, how lovely you look tonight, like the first bright rose of spring."

When it came to women, the comte seemed to have a flower fixation.

Daphne's mouth dissolved into a flattered smile. "Oh, Comte, you are so *galant*."

"It is but the truth." His heated glance at Daphne was very like the one Max had seen him direct toward Miss Blair earlier in the day.

The comte was a very busy man.

The clock on the mantel chimed the dinner hour. Max looked expectantly at Daphne, but she made no move toward the refectory. He waited a few more minutes, then said to her, "Should we not go into dinner?"

She frowned at him. "One of our guests, Mrs. Blair, has not come down yet."

Max turned to Miss Blair. "I see your stepmother does not share your punctuality."

"Rowena's always late so she can make a grand entrance in front of everyone." Her stepdaughter's expression was embarrassed and pained. "That's one of the reasons I try always to be early."

Several more minutes went by before Rowena Blair swept into the room. "Oh dear, am I the last to arrive?"

Max fought to keep from laughing at Mrs. Blair's gown of purple silk and tulle. Its bodice was cut every bit as low as Daphne's, and its skirt boasted even more flounces, puffs, and large bows.

Given her more than ample size, she reminded Max of one of Egypt's great pyramids decked out in royal purple.

His amused gaze met Miss Blair's, and she rolled her eyes.

"We will go into dinner now." Daphne gave her arm to the comte. "The duke will take Miss Blair in and—"

"I have already promised Lord Chartwell that I would go in with him," Miss Blair interrupted, giving Max her arm.

Daphne glowered at Max. "But—"

He cut her off. "Precedence requires Esmond to

escort Mrs. Blair. She is by far the oldest woman here."

That won him a look of pure fury from Rowena, who clearly did not appreciate his pointing out the truth.

Max intended to do so frequently, in the hope of hastening her departure.

Chapter 4

The castle's refectory, a cavernous chamber with a soaring barrel-vaulted ceiling and narrow windows set high in its clammy walls, remained exactly as it had been when Max was a child. He doubted it had changed much since his Norman ancestors had lived here.

The hall was so large that it dwarfed the massive oak dining table that could easily seat forty. Tonight five places had been set at the head of this table and one at the foot with a vast amount of space between them.

Daphne said curtly, "Chartwell, you are at the foot of the table."

Esmond took his place at the head of the table. "Mama, why have you put Max so far away?"

Daphne ignored her son's question. "Miss Blair, come. I know you would much prefer to sit beside your mother."

Max glanced at the American, expecting her to seize this opportunity to escape his ostracism.

Instead she tightened her hold on his arm. "Not at all. I much prefer to remain with Lord Chartwell."

Her answer clearly displeased everyone at the table—except Max. Though he was gratified, he was also curious. Was Miss Blair trying to make Es jealous?

From the look on the young duke's face, she was succeeding.

Max led her to their mutual exile and pulled out a chair for her beside the place Daphne had assigned him. Miss Blair sat down, and a footman rushed up with china and silver for her.

As Max settled in the chair beside her, he asked, "Why do you want to share my banishment?"

She flashed him one of her brilliant smiles that raised dangerous desires in him.

"You'll understand soon enough."

Her lovely eyes sparkled so mischievously that, to Max's disgust, his desire intensified.

"You don't appear to mind being ostracized either," she said.

"Actually, Daphne unwittingly did me a favor. For some reason I have never been able to discern, this end of the table is warmer and less drafty than the other."

"Really? Wonderful!" she exclaimed fervently.

As they ate the soup, a creamy lobster bisque, Mrs. Blair recounted in excruciating detail other excellent soups she had enjoyed and the distinguished company in which she had eaten them.

Not one of these people, Max noted, was less than a lord or lady.

"Rowena loves to monopolize the conversation," Miss Blair whispered to Max.

"Even though she has nothing worth saying?"

She smiled. "Now you understand why I prefer this end of the table."

Max's soup spoon paused for a second on his way to his mouth. What the hell was her game? Was she trying to make him think she was not a willing participant in bribing Daphne?

When Miss Blair finished her soup, she said, "I believe you're right, Max. It is warmer at this end of the table. For that, I am most grateful."

"You clearly hate Castle Penrose."

"No, I simply can't imagine why anyone would want to live in such an ugly, inconvenient, freezing place."

Max studied her uncertainly. She sounded so sincere, yet he feared her frankness was feigned, designed to hide her real goal of marrying Esmond.

"Is the duke of Penrose so poor, my lord, that he can't afford to build a comfortable home?"

Although Max found the castle as uncomfortable as she did, his Chartwell family pride swelled in indignation. How dare this upstart from the American West, populated by savages, denigrate the castle that had been his illustrious family's home for eight centuries?

"Castle Penrose is considered a historical treasure and one of the few examples of Norman architecture still standing."

Miss Blair smiled sweetly. "Now I understand

why Norman architecture went out of style centuries ago—and will forever remain so."

Max could not help laughing. Damn, he did enjoy her.

Actually he had exaggerated about the castle. Only part of it dated from Norman times. Even though in his heart of hearts Max thought the hodgepodge of additions that had grown up over the centuries an abomination, he was not about to admit that to the critical American.

A footman removed their soup bowls and served them sole a la Normandie and crimped cod with oyster sauce.

Max picked up his wineglass. Before tasting its contents, he observed, "I gather you are not as fond of the English aristocracy as your stepmother."

"I have no fondness for any of you so-called lords."

He gave her a sardonic smile. "Only for dukes."

"Nor dukes either. I find the whole idea of aristocracy, particularly a male aristocracy, offensive."

"Why is that?"

She gave him a scathing look. "I see you are a typical sexist British lord who believes both the male sex and the aristocracy are innately superior."

"I do not *believe* that."

"You don't?" she exclaimed, clearly surprised.

"I *know* it for a fact."

Miss Blair gave a most unladylike snort.

Max's intended, Lady Priscilla, would never have uttered such an offensive sound.

"And as usual, you are dead wrong, my lord. We are all—male and female alike—created equal. Aristocracy, unless it is based on merit, is a . . . a crime against nature."

"This is the most ridiculous statement I have ever heard!"

"Is it? Why should you or the duke or any other man be considered better than another simply because you were born to a title?"

"I told you, I was not born to mine."

"How did you earn it?"

"For service to the crown."

"What kind of service?"

"That is between the crown and me." The clandestine work that earned him his title must remain secret.

By the time dinner progressed through the second course of grouse pie, roast goose, turkey, and saddle of mutton, Max observed that whenever Daphne looked elsewhere, the comte sent hot, seductive glances toward Miss Blair. She appeared to be oblivious to them.

Or was she merely pretending?

Max also noted in dismay how frequently Esmond's adoring gaze settled on Miss Blair. He mooned at her like a lovesick calfling.

She, however, scarcely glanced in the duke's direction.

Was the clever American minx indulging in the common female tactic of faking indifference toward the man she intended to marry to pique his interest?

In Max's youth, he'd had this wile used often enough on him, although it had never had its intended effect. Instead of fueling his jealousy, it inevitably raised his contempt.

And so it did now on his cousin's behalf.

Max had to prove to Es how unworthy of his regard the ruthless, sly creature was. Otherwise she would break his cousin's heart.

But what was the best way to show his cousin the American girl's true colors?

Perhaps Max should tell Es about the two Americans' bribe to his mother.

Max feared, however, Miss Blair had so dazzled his cousin that Es would not believe him. Max needed proof, not just Grigsby's word for it, especially since he did not yet know how the steward had learned of the bribery.

"How old are you, Miss Blair?" Max asked abruptly.

She was raising her wineglass to her lips, and she regarded him over its rim. "Twenty-three. Why do you ask?"

He answered with deliberate, insulting intent. "I am surprised that a woman as lovely as you is still unmarried at *such an advanced age*."

He expected her to react angrily. Instead she answered mockingly, "But, Max, you are still unmarried and far more advanced in age than I am."

The damned vixen sounded as though he had one foot in the grave! "But I am a man and still single by choice."

"So am I single by choice." She sipped her wine.

He raised an eyebrow. "You have found no man worthy of your hand?"

"I've found no man I love enough to marry."

Her answer so surprised Max that he exclaimed, "Love! What has that to do with marriage?"

She set her wineglass down sharply on the table, obviously outraged by his answer. "Everything. I would never marry a man I did not love."

Unless he is a duke. Was this her way of subtly alleging that she loved Esmond?

Max longed to tell her flatly that her feigned romanticism did not, for an instant, fool him about her real goal.

"Marriage among the aristocracy has nothing to do with love, Miss Blair, but with financial advantage, family alliances, and strategic connections."

In fact, Max was negotiating for just such a marriage with Lady Priscilla's father. He smiled at the thought of his bride to be, who was so much superior to this conniving American.

"What damned stupid reasons to marry!" Miss Blair protested.

Lady Priscilla would never curse. Nor, for that matter, would any other *lady* of Max's acquaintance.

"No one, neither duke nor the lowliest laborer, should marry except for love," Miss Blair continued.

Max firmly believed only a fool married for love. Love placed a man at great disadvantage in marriage, a prey to his wife's whims and demands.

Love had been his uncle Albert's downfall. Esmond's father had not been able to say no to any of his wife's extravagant demands.

"Surely, my lord, you would not marry a woman you did not love."

"I would not marry a woman I *did* love."

Miss Blair looked aghast. How very clever she was. If it was not for Grigsby's message, Max would not have tumbled to her real goal.

Prying his cousin from her clutches would not be easy, but Max swore he would succeed.

"We will adjourn to the drawing room," Lady Albert announced abruptly.

Virgie, who had not yet finished her dessert ices, looked up in surprise.

"You ladies go ahead," the duke said. "We men will stay here and enjoy our brandy."

"You know I cannot abide that ridiculous custom, Esmond." Lady Albert stood. "We will all go together. Come."

Her son protested no further but, to Virgie's disappointment, rose dutifully. If only Esmond would tell his mother he would do as he wished. After all, he was the duke and head of the Chartwell family, and he needed to act like it.

As Virgie stood, she looked speculatively at Max. He seemed fond of his young cousin. Perhaps she could persuade Max to train the duke for his role.

Max took Virgie's arm, and a tremor stole through her at his touch, warm and firm. She felt a pang of regret that dinner was over. She found him fascinating, although she was not at all certain that she liked him.

Or that he liked her.

Several times during dinner, he had looked at her as though he detested her, his eyes darkening, his frown making his hawklike features even sharper.

Not that his enmity should bother her, but somehow it did.

Max led her toward the castle's drawing room. "My belief love has no place in aristocratic marriages appears to have shocked you into silence."

"Your belief appalls me. Marrying for any reason other than love would be a fate worse than a medieval inquisition."

"Such hyperbole," Max scoffed.

"I understand now why lords and ladies of the English aristocracy so often go their own ways and rarely see their spouses," Virgie said in disgust. "If that's the type of marriage you want for yourself, I hope you get what you deserve."

His face hardened. "It will still be far happier than the misery the duke's father endured after he married Daphne for love."

"But did she love him?"

"The one and only thing about Uncle Albert that Daphne loved was the prospect of becoming the duchess of Penrose upon my grandfather's demise."

"But that didn't happen?"

"No, Uncle Albert died several years before Grandfather. Daphne is still bitter that she will never be the duchess of Penrose. My uncle, poor man, did live long enough to sire Esmond and to appreciate how right Grandfather had been in opposing the marriage to Daphne. I sometimes think my uncle, who was genial and easygoing, found the only escape from his wife he could—in a coffin."

"How awful!" Virgie exclaimed in genuine distress. "I suspected Daphne did not return your uncle's passion for her."

Max's gaze was suddenly piercing. "What makes you think that?"

"I doubt she has ever loved anyone but herself."

Max laughed, and for an instant, something like appreciation glinted in his eyes. "On that point, I heartily agree with you."

They entered the castle's so-called drawing room. Like the refectory, it was huge, with massive wooden trusses, beams supporting the barrel-vaulted ceiling, and four-foot-thick walls.

Unlike the dining hall, though, mullion windows, clearly installed long after the castle was built, were large and placed low enough that Virgie could actually look through them.

The hall was cold despite the flames dancing in a large but inadequate hearth at the opposite end of the hall. In tacit agreement, Virgie and Max moved toward the fire.

"So, Miss Blair, you are seeking a marriage in which you and your husband are both wildly in love."

The cynical note in Max's voice puzzled her, but she replied with her usual frankness. "More than that. What I want—indeed, what I insist upon—is a partnership in which I will have equal voice with the man I love."

If only she could find such a man.

If only he would love her as she would surely love him.

She thought wistfully of the way her brother Leo adored his wife. She wanted the kind of union they had, the kind her father and mother had had before she died.

"Good God!" Max looked at her as though she had just advocated voodoo. "No wonder you are still unmarried."

Virgie knew the marital partnership she sought would shock Max, convinced as he was that women were inferior creatures in both mind and body.

She knew better.

Unfortunately, though, the aristocratic British ladies she'd met did their best to live down to his expectations, with their mincing steps, hysterical vapors, and feigned helplessness.

At least Virgie hoped it was feigned. She'd hate to think her sex was that weak.

She had to concede, however, that apparently it was the best way to capture a desirable husband. Strong men seemed to fall over themselves trying to aid these ladies.

Nobody fell over her—at least no one who interested her.

Still, she was proud she neither wanted nor needed such help, although at times a small part of her wished that she was one of those women who fascinated men of strength and intelligence. Men like the one walking beside her.

From where had that renegade thought come?

Her brothers had warned her that she was too independent, too blunt, too threatening to the fragile male ego. She must be more demure and circumspect. But Virgie would not pretend to be something she wasn't. She prized honesty above all else.

Nor did she want a man with such a frail ego for her husband.

As Virgie and Max neared the hearth, Esmond fell into step with them.

Lady Albert immediately broke away from the comte and hurried to her son's side.

"Perhaps we can go shooting tomorrow, Max," the duke said.

"Esmond," his mother interjected quickly in a horrified tone, "you cannot go out when the weather is so ugly. You risk taking a chill."

"Well then, if the weather clears," he conceded.

"That is out of the question, Esmond," Lady Albert said. "You have guests to entertain. What will Miss Blair think if you desert her to hunt?"

Virgie would be damned if she'd be used as an excuse to keep Esmond in this dreadful castle. "I would be delighted that he is doing something he enjoys. Please do not stay home on my account, Your Grace."

Max studied her with an odd, inscrutable expression. Daphne looked as though she would happily boil Virgie in oil.

"Indeed, Your Grace," she continued, "I might be persuaded to accompany you."

Max's eyes narrowed disapprovingly.

Apparently proper British ladies did not hunt.

"Come with me, Esmond." His mother took his arm. "I have something to show you."

When they were out of earshot, Virgie said to Max, "Poor Esmond."

"Yes, Daphne has always coddled him, striving to protect him from even the smallest danger to his health. After all, he is her meal ticket. More so now than ever."

Virgie wanted to ask what Max meant by that, but she wanted even more to convince him to take Esmond in hand. "Lady Albert's wrapped her apron strings around him with the suffocating strength of a boa constrictor. He must cut them, but he needs the guidance of an older, wiser man. Would you be that man?"

"Of course, you would want that."

"What?" Virgie asked, bewildered by the scorn

that transfused Max's voice. "Why do you say that?"

"I am not a fool, Miss Blair. You know full well what I am talking about."

"Then I must be the fool, because I don't."

His incredulous expression baffled her. Instead of explaining, however, he tried to guide her toward the fireplace.

She obstinately planted her feet and refused to budge. "Be so kind as to enlighten me."

"Unfortunately, Miss Blair, I am not in a kindly mood tonight." His voice was colder than the storm raging outside.

She jerked her arm from his and would have walked away had she not seen the comte watching her. Max might infuriate her, but at least he did not bore her. Nor was he trying to seduce her for her father's fortune.

Yet why would Max refuse to help the duke, when he seemed fond of his cousin?

Deciding Max was the lesser of two evils, she let him lead her to the fireplace. "I am beginning to think my stepmother is right. You are odious."

"Why, thank you." Despite Max's words, his voice was as sharp as a dagger's edge.

"You are very welcome, my lord."

By now, they were within a dozen feet of the fireplace, and Virgie could at last feel a little heat.

"If this castle is this uncomfortable in autumn, it must be unbearably cold in the winter." The thought made her shiver despite her wool dress.

"You are right. You cannot imagine how cold it is."

The malicious undertone to Max's answer puzzled Virgie.

"Are you certain you want to remain here, Miss Blair, and find out how miserably cold it is?" The smile on Max's lips did not reach his hard gray eyes.

"I told you this afternoon I don't want to remain here at all."

"Where in England would you prefer your home to be? London?"

"Nowhere." Virgie moved closer to the hearth and held out her hands toward the fire to warm them. "I want to live in a very special valley in my own country."

"But where do you *intend* to live?"

"In that valley."

Max's obvious disbelief stung Virgie. "You seem to think I am playing some kind of word game with you, my lord, and I am not."

"Glad to hear that," he said blandly. "Tell me about this valley of yours. Where is it?"

"In the Sierra Nevada of California. The valley is truly nature's cathedral." Just thinking of it made her smile and her spirits rise. "Glaciers carved the valley from granite, leaving it surrounded by great gray cliffs. Even its trees are majestic, growing as tall and straight as cathedral spires."

"And how tall is that?"

"For Ponderosa pines, two hundred feet." Virgie loved to talk about the magnificent valley that would be hers if she could endure the rest of her English exile with Rowena. "The sugar pines are almost as tall. From a distance, the valley is all gray and green."

Max was studying her so oddly that she asked, "What is it?"

"Merely enjoying your description. What other wonders does your valley have?"

She ignored the sarcastic tinge to his question. "A spectacular waterfall plunges over one of the cliffs. My favorite time is late spring when the Pacific dogwood is a mass of white blossoms."

"You make it sound like paradise," Max said dryly.

"That's why it's named Eden Valley." The fire in the hearth had at last warmed Virgie, and she backed a little away.

Max did the same. "I am surprised you could bear to leave it at all."

"If I'd had a choice, I would not have."

His gray gaze became penetrating. "Why did you not have a choice?"

"It's a long story." She would not tell this arrogant English lord about the rite of passage that her father imposed on his children. "I won't bore you with it."

"Go ahead, I might enjoy being bored."

"No, it's a family matter."

But he did not give up easily. "To whom does the valley belong now?"

"My father," she replied with a curtness that warned him to push no further.

An awkward silence developed between them. Finally Max asked, "Have you seen our English mountains, the Pennines?"

"Yes, but they aren't mountains. Why, at home, the Pennines would barely qualify as hills. If you have a hankering to see real mountains, go to California and look at the Sierra Nevada."

He looked puzzled. "A hankering?"

"A longing, a desire."

"Thank you, but my only—er, hankering is for England. Indeed, I no longer have much interest in traveling beyond its borders. Certainly, I would live nowhere else."

Virgie felt an odd pang of regret. She would like to have shown him her special valley. "You might enjoy spending some time in another country."

"I have already spent too much time in other countries. I have lived in a half dozen. Tell me, is there anything about Castle Penrose that you like?"

"Very little," she admitted. "Even the menagerie is pathetic, with a doddering old lion its only inhabitant. Who was so unimaginative that he named the poor creature Lionel?"

Although amusement flickered in Max's eyes, he retorted coolly, "Chartwells prefer reason to imagination."

Virgie had been about to complain to him about Raffe, the lazy, incompetent servant in charge of the lion, but Max's chilly response dissuaded her. Most likely he would not care.

"Dear Miss Blair, come join us for whist," Daphne called. "Esmond wants you to be his partner. The comte and I will play against you."

Virgie turned from the fire to face Daphne. "The only card game I play is poker. If you wish me to teach you that—"

"Virginia!" Her stepmother's voice grated against Virgie's ear. "Stop pretending to favor such uncouth games."

"I pretend nothing."

Ignoring Virgie's answer, Rowena announced, "I will be the duke's partner."

Virgie glanced at Esmond. His expression reminded her of a man learning he'd been selected as a human sacrifice.

When she turned back toward the fire again, Max said in an undertone, "Perhaps you will teach me this uncouth game of poker, Miss Blair, while the others play whist."

"Certainly, but I must warn you I play only for money, the higher the stakes the better. Otherwise, why waste my time?"

"Your father must be a very generous man to finance your losses."

His automatic, condescending assumption that she must habitually lose infuriated Virgie. She was very good at the game—able to read and bluff her opponent without betraying her own position—but she would keep that to herself. To tell Max would only elicit more skepticism.

Virgie would let the arrogant man find out for himself—and it would cost him. She'd see that he paid a high price for his false presumptions about her skill.

Chapter 5

Max strode to the castle's stable so early the next morning that only a tiny sliver of sun poked above the eastern horizon.

Although the rain had stopped, the air was still heavy with moisture, and raw, blustery winds raked the land, bending saplings and bushes before it. A fierce gust hit Max, piercing his wool riding clothes with its bite, and he shivered.

Damn, but it was cold. Maybe he should reconsider his decision to ride.

Much disturbed by Esmond's infatuation for that American title hunter, Max had slept poorly and awakened far too early.

Well hell, who was he fooling?

It was his own attraction to Miss Blair, not his cousin's, that had had him tossing and turning.

The miserable night had begun with a dream in which Max had tried and failed to seduce her. He awakened in desperate need of a woman's body in the flesh and could not go back to sleep.

Lying there staring up at the ceiling, he considered Miss Blair and how she likened Daphne's apron strings to a boa constrictor's crushing embrace. He thought it a marvelous comparison.

He knew, however, that Miss Blair only wanted to free Esmond from his mother's tether so she could substitute her own leash. She had even had the effrontery to ask Max to help her.

But was that truly why Miss Blair had asked him?

By the time they had parted last night, Max thought she must be innocent of the bribery scheme. Never had he met such a candid woman. She did not seem to have a devious bone in her.

Seeing how she glowed and her eyes sparkled as she talked of Eden Valley, Max could not believe she had fabricated either the valley or her description of it. Nor could he doubt that she wanted to live there.

He did, however, doubt that the valley could be nearly so beautiful as she claimed it was. Beauty was in the eye of the beholder.

And why, if her father owned it, did she have to leave and come to England? He intended to extract that "boring" story from her somehow.

Still unable to sleep, Max had decided to get up and go riding, even though he considered any time before nine the middle of the night.

He was never in the best of humor in the morning, and his early rising had made him even more grouchy. Given his dark mood, maybe he ought to ride Black Lightning, the half wild stallion that terrorized Castle Penrose's grooms and stableboys.

As he approached the stable door, he discovered he was not the first person riding so early. A groom was exercising Black Lightning. And, to Max's amazement, doing an excellent job.

Max stopped and watched the rider guide the powerful gelding over the fences on the practice track.

Then Max's gaze focused on the rider's legs. They looked as though they had fur growing on them. Max was so tired that his eyes must be playing tricks on him.

He did not recognize the groom, who was so small that Max marveled the boy could control the big stallion so well.

Odd that Grigsby had not written Max about hiring a new groom, especially one who managed to control Black Lightning. The steward kept Max faithfully apprised of any action he took.

A stableboy Max recognized stepped outside and halted abruptly at the sight of him. The boy's weary expression instantly dissolved into panic.

What the hell was going on?

"Who is the new groom riding Black Lightning, Pauley?"

"Not a groom," Pauley mumbled, his gaze fixed on the toe of his boot.

"Who is it, then?"

"One o' the guests." The stableboy chipped at the hard ground with his toe, as though his life depended on his digging into it.

Max frowned. Surely, the rider could not be the comte. He was not that small a man. An unwelcome suspicion crossed Max's mind about the rider's identity, but he instantly dismissed it as ridiculous.

No female in her right mind—or, for that matter, many males, either—would mount Black Lightning. Still . . .

"Which guest?" Max demanded.

The stableboy kicked harder at the dirt with his toe. "One of the Americans." His voice came out in a hoarse croak.

Max's jaw clenched. "Miss Blair?"

Pauley nodded, his gaze still fixed on his toe.

Fear for her safety gripped Max. "Why the hell did you let her ride Black Lightning?"

"She wanted to."

"That's not an acceptable reason, and you damn well know it, Pauley."

The stableboy gulped visibly, still staring at his toe as though the intensity of his gaze was all that kept it attached to his foot.

"But . . . she's the only one . . . who can . . . 'cepting maybe yer lordship," he stammered.

Not for an instant did Max believe Miss Blair could stay on that mean sonofabitch for more than a few minutes.

As if to confirm Max's fear, the stallion veered away from the practice track and galloped hell bent in the direction of the meadow where Max had met Miss Blair the previous day.

"Saddle the fastest horse in the stable for me. *Now!*"

Pauley ran to obey.

As Max waited, he recalled the previous day's fiasco. If he cherished his manhood, he might be wiser to forgo any attempt to rescue Miss Blair from this morning's folly.

Yet it went against his grain as a gentleman not

to save a damsel in distress—even though it might go against his groin. Chivalry defeated caution. Max just hoped he would not pay a high price for his honorable intentions.

But then, after a hair-raising ride on Black Lightning, Miss Blair might well be overjoyed to see Max. That thought made him smile.

Pauley emerged from the stable leading a sorrel gelding. Max took the reins, mounted, and set out to save the foolish chit.

He kept a careful watch for any sign of her or the stallion.

Seeing none, Max grew increasingly uneasy.

Not until he reached the meadow did he sight Black Lightning, riderless and munching on grass. Damn! As he'd feared, the stallion had thrown her.

Much alarmed, he looked around the meadow for her. The golden-leaved tulip trees along the road edged one side. A wood, mostly oaks with a lush undergrowth of ferns, hazel, and holly bushes, ringed the remainder of the meadow's circumference.

Finally Max spotted the missing Miss Blair propped against the trunk of an English oak on the perimeter of the meadow.

Bloody hell, had the horse hurled her against the tree?

Max dismounted and ran toward her.

A strange kind of dark hair, thick and curly, covered her legs. What the devil was it? Had she pulled a peculiar kind of blanket over herself?

To his relief, she noticed him and rose. Apparently she was not badly hurt.

Then Max saw what she wore. He blinked in disbelief, so dumbfounded he could only stare. He'd never seen anything like it, not even on a man.

The curly black hair he'd thought was a blanket was not. It was . . .

Pants!

On a woman!

She turned, and Max saw they were not even real pants. They had no behind but ended at the top of her thighs, emphasizing her shapely derriere, which was covered by a second, skintight pair of pants.

It was shocking.

Shameless.

Obscene.

And it made him hard in an instant.

The lust that had driven him from his bed that morning hit him again with renewed force, like a landslide picking up momentum as it roared down the hill. That made him even angrier.

And this shocking American might become the next duchess of Penrose?

Over my dead body!

How dare she tantalize Max—and every other man within seeing distance—like this?

Lady Priscilla would never have dreamed of donning anything so vulgar.

"What the hell are you wearing?" he demanded.

"What?" She turned back toward him.

Max gestured at the black curly hair wrapped around her legs. "No *lady* would ever wear such an outrageous, revealing garment."

Looking puzzled, she glanced down. "You mean my woollies?"

"Woollies? Are you trying to tell me they came from a black sheep? I don't believe it." The only black sheep involved was the damned female wearing them.

"No, silly. They're made of buffalo skin and keep my legs warmer than anything else."

She had the nerve to declare Max silly.

Damn it, old women were *silly*!

Young children were *silly*.

Max was not.

"So you only wear these so-called woollies when it's cold?"

Miss Blair nodded.

Another gust of raw wind whipped through his riding pants, and he wouldn't have minded having a pair of woollies on himself. Woollies made sense—*for a man*.

"In summer, our chaps are made of leather."

What the blazes were "shaps"? Max looked at her in bewilderment. "Now what are you talking about?"

Miss Blair gestured at her woollies. "These are our winter chaps and in summer we wear leather."

"Why do you call them 'shaps'?"

"It's short for *chaparejos*."

She looked up at him, and his breath caught. Her eyes were a stunning melding of blue and green; her cheeks were pink from the cold, and her luscious lips were invitingly parted. It was all he could do to keep from kissing them, even though, damn her, she thought he was *silly*!

"Why are you staring at me like that?" she asked. "Is something wrong?"

"Nothing." Except his wayward desire. "Were you much hurt when Black Lightning threw you?"

"He didn't throw me! Why would you think such

a ridiculous thing? And what are you doing here?"

"I came to rescue you." His tone was disgruntled. "I should have known better than to think you needed it."

Amusement danced in her eyes. "Yes, you should have. Why on earth did you think that?"

His gaze dropped to the intriguing curves her woollies revealed, and the sudden urge to cup his hands over her enticing derriere was nearly irresistible.

What the hell was wrong with him? His body was responding to her as though he were a randy youth in a haystack with his first love. He balled his hands into fists and put them behind his back.

"Because I am a fool," he said testily. "And because Black Lightning is not a lady's horse."

"No, but as you told me only a minute ago, I'm no lady."

"True, you are not." He meant his answer as an insult that would infuriate her.

Instead she gave him a warm smile. "Nor do I want to be one."

Max studied her suspiciously. Was she subtly throwing down the gauntlet, telling him that she had no intention of being a mere lady and would settle for nothing less than being a duchess?

Well, he had a surprise for her and her ambition. "Why do you not want to be a lady?"

"It's so boring. All those nonsensical rules. An English lady isn't even allowed to read a newspaper. She might be contaminated by the contents, which report on real life, thus threatening the unnatural cocoon in which she is wrapped."

Max opened his mouth, but Virgie cut him off.

"Even more boring, she must change gowns several times a day and then submit to endless fittings for all those clothes. Such a waste of time! And she's lucky if she doesn't freeze in those ridiculous fashions she's expected to wear. Especially at Castle Penrose."

He raised a skeptical eyebrow. "But being a duchess would not be boring?"

"That'd be worse!"

Right. And the Sahara was a swamp.

A linnet, harshly calling "zee-chee-chee," flew past them and landed on the branch of an oak behind Miss Blair. She turned to look at the noisy bird.

As though drawn by a powerful magnet, Max's gaze slid downward again. Damn, but she did have the most alluring behind.

He thought of what it would be like to caress it as she rode *him* in bed. His body instantly responded. Embarrassed by the strength of his reaction, he forced himself to look up.

When she turned to face him again, he asked, "Whom would you consider the ideal husband for you, Miss Blair?"

"An American rancher who shares my philosophical views and my love of adventure," she answered promptly.

Her philosophical views! Max could scarcely believe his ears. Everyone knew a female's mind could not comprehend such a difficult subject. He could not resist saying sarcastically, "My, all that and passionate mutual love, too."

With another burst of "zee-chee-chee," the linnet

rose from the oak and flew westward, drawing Miss Blair's attention again.

No woman of Max's acquaintance willingly rose before noon. "You are up very early, Miss Blair. Could you not sleep?"

"I never have difficulty sleeping, but I love early morning. The air smells so fresh and clean, and I like to watch the sun rise. The sky is so beautiful at dawn."

The chit was stark, raving mad.

Or exceedingly devious.

"I think, Miss Blair, something more than your love for dawn brought you out this morning." Max's voice was considerably drier than the moisture-laden air around them.

"You're right."

Her frank admission caught Max by surprise.

"My stepmother hates to get up before noon, and everyone else but the servants are asleep too. It's the only time I don't have to ride on an abysmal sidesaddle."

"What is wrong with a sidesaddle?"

"Only a man would ask such a stupid question."

First, she called Max foolish and now stupid. She most definitely was not ingratiating herself with him.

"If you men were required to ride sidesaddle, the abominations would be outlawed within the month."

"Nonsense!" Max was still smarting from being branded stupid.

"Is it? Have you ever ridden sidesaddle?"

"Of course not. No man would."

"That's the crux of the problem. No man would think of doing so. I dare you to try it. Then you will not think my statement in the least ridiculous."

He chose to ignore her dare. "If you say so, Virg."

She gave him a quizzical look. "Why did you call me that?"

"If you dress and act like a man, Virg, you deserve to be called by a man's name." He meant the male name as an insult that would raise her ire, but she seemed delighted rather than angry. Her smile warmed everything in its vicinity—including Max.

"Promise you'll continue to call me Virg."

Incredulous, he stared at her. "You *want* me to call you that?"

"Yes, please."

Damn it, every time he insulted her she took it as a compliment. Max renewed his vow to prevent Esmond from marrying this farouche female who wanted to be called by a male name and wore those damned shameless "woollies" in the bargain.

How could Esmond look twice at this shocking American?

Max's own perverse gaze drifted downward.

Except when she wore woollies.

Chapter 6

❧~⦿~❧

Virgie's father and three brothers had called her Virg since she was a little girl, and she loved the nickname. Until today, however, no one outside of her family had done so.

Still smiling, she put her index and little fingers in her mouth and whistled loudly for Black Lightning.

Max stared at her as though she'd committed some scandalous sin.

Clearly, proper English ladies did not whistle, either.

The stallion came to her immediately.

"I cannot believe it!" Max exclaimed, sounding confounded. "That horse never does what anyone wants."

"He does what I want." And in proof of that, Black Lightning let Virgie mount him as docilely as if he were a gentle mare.

76

She was disappointed, however, that Max didn't help her as he had the previous day. Not that she needed it, but she had a strange hankering to have him touch her again.

Instead Max caught his sorrel's reins, which he'd left dangling on the ground. As he mounted, she couldn't help admiring both his graceful movements and the way the muscles of his strong, wide shoulders rippled beneath his riding coat. An odd warmth spread through her.

To quell this disconcerting feeling, Virgie challenged, "I'll race you to the stable."

Without waiting for Max's response, she urged Black Lightning forward. The stallion reached a gallop in seconds.

As horse and rider sped over the ground, the wind lifted her hair and blew it behind her. Virgie loved running at top speed in the damp, fresh morning air. She and her brothers had raced like this often at home.

She loved, too, the freedom—brief but blessed—from the constrictions of a "lady's" proper clothes and her stepmother's endless criticisms of her.

Virgie left the meadow behind, following a path through the oak wood. Most of the leaves had turned yellow, warning of winter's relentless approach.

When she pulled up at the stable, she looked over her shoulder. She was perhaps twenty yards ahead of Max. Before he could reach her, she dismounted.

"How slow you are today, my lord," she teased.

He gave her a dark, chagrined look.

She smothered a smile. Virgie trusted her instincts when it came to people. Despite Max's Neanderthal ideas about women and marriage, she detected beneath his arrogant, aristocratic veneer the kind of strength and integrity that she admired in her father and brothers.

She was touched that, even after she'd pulled a gun on him the previous day, he'd been worried enough about her safety this morning to ride after her and risk her ire a second time.

Pauley ran out of the stable, took the horses' reins, and led the animals away.

Max looked intently at something inside the stable.

"What is it?" she asked.

"I see someone with whom I have business. Go back to the castle without me, Virg."

Behind a smile, she hid her disappointment at losing his company. "Certainly."

As she walked away from him, she felt his eyes on her.

Max watched the provocative sway of Virg's hips in those damned "shaps" as she walked toward the castle. He cursed silently at the effect the sight had on him. Max tried to look away, but her derriere seemed to hold his gaze the way a magnet held iron shavings.

"You appear to be enjoying the view, my lord," said the familiar voice of Grigsby, the estate's steward.

"Tantalizing, is it not?" So much so that Max could not tear his gaze from it.

Finally, though, as Virg's figure receded in the distance, Max turned to Grigsby. "I thought I saw you inside the stable when I rode up. How is your father?"

"Better, thank you." The steward was a muscular man of medium height, with a square face, hazel eyes that missed little, and hair the color of sand. "I returned only minutes ago. What brings you to the castle, my lord?"

"You know very well what brings me. I came as soon as I received your note."

Grigsby nodded. "I see you have met Miss Blair. I was astonished to see her riding Black Lightning this morning and even more astonished at how well she managed him."

"So was I. He is the most difficult horse at Penrose."

"Unfortunately, that is no longer true. Our latest acquisition, Vesuvius, makes Black Lightning look gentle by comparison. Let me show you."

Grigsby led Max beyond the far side of the stable, past an ancient, tangled hedgerow, to a pasture enclosed by a circular wooden fence that was used to segregate and contain troublesome horses. Today only one horse, a roan stallion, occupied the corral.

When the roan saw the two men approaching, he reared and bucked. His hooves pounded against the wood fence like the beat of a crazed drummer.

The steward gestured at the stallion. "Meet Vesuvius, a gift to the duke."

Max frowned. "From whom? I did not think His Grace had any enemies."

"Lord Warwich, the earl of Kingsbury's eldest son."

Max raised his voice so that he could be heard over Vesuvius's racket. "Why would that damned bully Warwich give the duke a present?"

"He wants to marry Lord Asley's daughter Charlotte, who is horse mad. She hopes to marry the duke. Warwich knows His Grace is not a good rider and fears even gentle horses."

"So Warwich hopes to embarrass the duke in front of her by challenging him to ride Vesuvius," Max said.

"I fear you have the right of it."

"How does the duke feel about Miss Asley?"

"Scarcely notices her existence, but Warwich is jealous nonetheless."

"Walk to the castle with me. We will enjoy more privacy outside than in."

Grigsby obediently fell into step with Max. To give them more time alone, he led the steward on a roundabout path that wound through a grove of English oaks.

"How did you learn Lady Albert had been bribed?"

"I was taking a shortcut past the maze, and I overheard her and Mrs. Blair talking there."

The maze was rarely explored. Undoubtedly the two women had picked the labyrinth, thinking no one would hear them plotting there.

"They could not see me, and I could not see them, but Mrs. Blair's voice is—er, distinctive."

"What bribe persuaded Lady Albert to sell her son in marriage?"

"Mrs. Blair promised her husband would pay her ladyship a very large monthly allowance for the remainder of her life."

"How much is very large?"

When Grigsby disclosed the amount, Max's jaw

dropped in disbelief. "Why, that is a virtual king's ransom. I cannot believe he would pay her such a sum each and every month."

A former miner, even one who had struck it rich in the gold rush, would not have that much money to throw away on buying his daughter a ducal husband. Of course, that would never have occurred to the stupid, greedy Daphne.

Thank God she was not intelligent, or she would have been truly dangerous.

"The allowance, my lord, is only part of what Lady Albert supposedly will get. She insisted upon additional funds to refurbish the duke's London town house for her own use."

Max groaned. Daphne had long wanted to reopen Penrose House in London for herself and to staff it with a large retinue of servants so she might enjoy the season in the ostentatious luxury to which she thought herself entitled.

"Her ladyship also insisted on being guaranteed the use of the town house and the castle for the remainder of her life."

"No dower house for her." Knowing Daphne, she would hold on to control of both households and make Virg's life a living nightmare. And poor Es would be caught between his mother and his wife.

If Virg was so eager to be a duchess, she deserved the life she would lead.

But by now, Max seriously doubted she was that ambitious or even knew about her stepmother's scheming.

"Were only Lady Albert and Mrs. Blair in the maze?" he asked casually. "Or was Miss Blair with them?"

"I don't know. I did not hear her."

"Could it be Miss Blair is not a party to this brib-ery?" Max was startled at how much he hoped Grigsby would confirm she was not.

"She is very much a party to it."

The quiet certainty of Grigsby's answer hit Max like a blow to the gut. "How do you know that?" His voice was sharper than he intended.

"Later that day, I asked Miss Blair when her wed-ding with the duke would be. She replied as soon as her conditions were met."

So Virg had lied to Max. The candor he admired in her was false. Disillusionment ate at him like acid. He should have known better than to trust her. How much he had wanted her to be innocent, but she was not. He felt deeply hurt and betrayed.

How could he have been such a damn fool!

His anger intensified at himself, but it was noth-ing compared to his fury toward her. She'd even had the unmitigated gall to attach conditions. "What were her demands? Did you ask her?"

Grigsby nodded. "They were outrageous. The one I found most distressing was that the duke must agree to demolish Castle Penrose and build a mod-ern house in its place."

"What!" Destroy the centuries-old home of the Chartwells, would she? Damn her! Max would make the title-hunting vixen rue the day she set her sights on Es.

After Virgie returned from the stable, she hur-riedly bathed and changed into a simple morning gown before Rowena awoke and discovered her wearing pants and chaps.

Her stepmother was still sleeping when Virgie slipped silently out of their suite a few minutes before eight and went down to the kitchen.

Virgie believed the best way to learn about a foreign country—or one's own—lay in talking to people of all ages and walks of life. She genuinely enjoyed discovering all she could about them and their lives.

After she'd arrived at the castle, she'd made friends with the servants, including the cook and her helpers—something no visitor had done before.

Breakfast at the castle was served between nine and eleven, although Virgie considered the vast spread laid out each morning more banquet than breakfast. Since she generally rose very early, she hated waiting that long for food.

Nor did some of the dishes on the sideboard, like kippers, broiled sheep's kidneys, and dried haddock, do anything for her appetite.

Even less appealing was the company of the comte, Lady Albert, and Rowena. Virgie suspected that was why the duke always appeared for breakfast promptly at nine o'clock and was long gone before the other three, late risers all, appeared in the dining room, usually as the clock was about to strike eleven.

The cook had been shocked when Virgie had first asked to eat breakfast early in the kitchen, but she'd cajoled the woman into agreeing.

Virgie was very glad she had, for she'd learned far more below stairs about Castle Penrose and *all* of its residents than she ever would have above stairs.

And this morning, Virgie wanted to know more about Max.

She walked into the enormous kitchen with its great cast iron stoves, a hearth large enough for roasting a whole pig on a spit, a big wooden table, and narrow windows set high up in thick, sixteen-foot-tall walls. Doors sprinkled around the room led to various pantries and larders.

Cook, a tall, big-boned woman with gray hair, looked up from an enormous earthenware bowl in which she was beating batter with a large wooden paddle. "I saw the old lion this morning. Put on weight, he has, and his coat's improved, thanks to you."

"And to you," Virgie said. When she had arrived at the castle, the lion had been so thin beneath his dull, mangy coat that she had almost cried for him. Virgie, who could not bear cruelty to any animal, quickly ascertained he had lost his teeth and could no longer chew the joints of the tough raw meat that was all his keeper fed him.

When the man refused to listen to her, she'd convinced Cook to prepare a nourishing gruel that Lionel could eat. Each night and morning, Virgie slipped outside with a bucket of the concoction and gave it to Lionel, who eagerly lapped it up.

"Were it a good ride you had this morning, Miss Blair?" Cook asked.

"Yes. It was beautiful. Cool and crisp. Lord Chartwell joined me for part of the ride."

"But him ne'er gets up so early," Cook said in surprise.

"He stays here often?"

"Not as much since Lady Albert came to live

here, more's the pity. But he were raised here. E'eryone thought Lord Chartwell'd be the one to succeed his grandpa as duke. His uncle, the heir, had been married for years and had no children, but . . ."

"But what?" Virgie prodded, curious to learn everything she could about Max.

"But then his uncle's wife died, and he married Lady Albert, and the young duke were born." From her expression, Cook agreed with Virgie that Max would have made the better duke.

A place had already been set for Virgie at the big wooden table in the center of the kitchen. She sat down, and a maid served Virgie the simple breakfast—an orange, porridge, coffee, and brown bread still hot from the oven—that she preferred.

She slowly sipped her steaming coffee. "Once again, I must apologize to you for my stepmother delaying dinner last night."

Virgie made the same heartfelt apology each morning to poor Cook, who had to keep the many dishes of food she'd worked so hard to prepare warm and edible while everyone waited for Rowena.

Cook looked up from the mixing bowl. "She'd better be on time from now on. The duchess won't stand for her being late."

"The duchess? Who is she?"

"The dowager duchess of Belford, the youngest sister of the old duke, and a high stickler if ever me's seen one." The cook resumed beating the batter with her wooden paddle. "She arrives today for a visit."

Odd that no one had mentioned to Virgie that the

duchess was arriving. "Will she be here long?"

"Her message didn't say, but she always stays at least six weeks."

The dowager clearly liked the castle considerably more than Virgie did. "Does she come often?"

"Used to, but a year it's been since she's left Belford Manor. Traveling's difficult for her these days. She suffers terribly from the rheumatism. Me'd like to know what brings her now."

The cook pushed the batter she'd been mixing into a large baking pan. "Lady Albert hoped she wouldn't come, but a message arrived last night that she'd be here afore noon today."

Virgie buttered a piece of warm brown bread. "Why did her ladyship not want her to come?"

"They hate each other. All the Chartwells, most particularly the old duke and his sister, tried to stop the present duke's papa from marrying Lady Albert."

"Why was that?" Virgie took a bite of her brown, nut-flavored bread.

"No one 'cepting her husband thought her worthy to be a Chartwell. And once he were shackled to her, him changed his mind quick enough. But too late it were then. Poor man."

So Max had not exaggerated how unhappy his uncle Albert had been after he'd married Daphne. "He soon regretted his choice?"

"*Everyone* did," Cook said succinctly, not looking up from the batter she was scraping into the pan. When she finished, she called to the scullery maid to wash the bowl.

"Wish the message said how many people be coming with the duchess," Cook said fretfully. "Of course, there'll be Isabel Lake. Her Grace never goes anywhere without her."

"Who is she?"

"Her Grace's companion, and as nice and quiet a young lady as ever you'd want to meet."

"She must be many years younger than the dowager." Virgie took another sip of her coffee.

"Aye, Isabel's the age of young Duke Esmond." The cook sighed. "What will become of the poor girl when Her Grace passes on? The duchess were the only one who'd take her in after her pa fled to France in disgrace, leaving her without a pence. And her only seventeen and such a sweet thing too."

"How could a father do that?" Blessed with a loving, caring father herself, Virgie found such behavior beyond her comprehension.

"Her pa were the son of Belford's younger brother and the black sheep of the family, a wild and spendthrift cove and a gambler, too. Thought of nothing 'cepting his own pleasures. Fortunately, poor Isabel takes after her mama, as fine a woman as e'er lived."

Even though Virgie had not yet met Isabel, her heart went out to her, and she looked forward to having the company of another woman nearly her own age. She could not help wondering, though, how her stepmother and the dowager duchess would get along. Not well at all, Virgie suspected.

She finished her breakfast and drank the remains of the coffee in her cup, then bid the cook and her minions good-bye.

She went up to her bedchamber, where she curled up on the sofa by the window to read more of *Ma-*

dame Bovary in the original French edition that she'd found in the duke's library.

Several chapters later, she heard her stepmother's maid awakening Rowena in the adjoining bedroom. Virgie closed the book. Taking it with her, she silently left the suite to escape her stepmother.

When she was halfway down the great stone staircase, the knocker at the front entrance sounded. The butler, who was hovering in the hall as though awaiting this summons, opened the heavy door.

Hearing feminine voices, Virgie guessed the dowager duchess must have arrived, and she shrank back into the shadows of the staircase to watch the scene below.

A thin, old woman leaning heavily on a cane stepped inside, helped by a solicitous girl who must be Isabel Lake.

Duke Esmond came slowly into the hall, appearing uncertain of how he should greet the elderly visitor. He settled on a stiff bow. "Welcome to Castle Penrose, Your Grace," he said without enthusiasm.

A moment of awkward silence followed as the dowager looked him over, a frown on her face.

He twitched nervously, clearly intimidated. The quiet grew oppressive.

Finally, he asked, "Did you know that Max is here?"

"He is?" The dowager gave the duke a shrewd, speculative look that reminded Virgie very much of Max.

At that moment, he strode into the hall. When he saw the dowager, he broke into a wide smile. "Why, Aunt Elizabeth, what a marvelous surprise." Unlike his cousin, Max sounded as though he truly meant his greeting. "No one told me you were expected. What has finally lured you away from Belford Manor?"

"I want to talk to you, Max."

"Surely that is not what brought you here."

"Certainly not. I did not know you were here until Esmond told me a moment ago, but I am pleased that you are."

The dowager took an unsteady step forward, and Isabel went instantly to her side.

"Your Grace, you must have a nap before you do anything else," the young woman said firmly. "You arose very early this morning, and you told me only a few minutes ago how tired you are."

"Yes, I must," the dowager agreed with a docility that surprised Virgie. She suspected the old woman was rarely so pliant.

Virgie silently backed up the grand staircase so she would not be caught eavesdropping. She was almost to the top when the dowager said, "Max, attend me in my rooms in two hours."

It was a command, not a request.

Virgie paused in her backward climb and peeked over the balustrade at Max. He looked amused, as though he was used to the duchess's imperiousness. "Certainly."

Leaning heavily on her cane, the dowager made her way toward the great staircase, Isabel hovering protectively at her elbow.

Max at once took the old woman's other arm. "Allow me to escort you upstairs, Aunt Elizabeth."

Her withered face crinkled into an affectionate

smile for him, and he returned it with equal fondness.

Virgie hastily retreated into the upper hall. Why
was the dowager duchess so anxious to talk to Max?

Chapter 7

After seeing Aunt Elizabeth to her rooms, Max stopped at the estate office to pick up the ledger in which the castle's domestic expenditures were recorded.

When Esmond had first become duke, Daphne had attempted to hide her extravagant personal expenditures by disguising them as household expenses. She had failed, however, to fool Max.

Now, Daphne no longer tried to sneak her bills past him, but the moment he relaxed his vigilance in examining the ledger she would endeavor to do so again. So, much as he hated the tedious job of going over the accounts, he did so regularly.

In her most egregious effort at subterfuge, Daphne had listed the price of several new gowns for herself as the cost of a fictitious tenants' day banquet. Although this annual dinner for the castle's tenants and their families was a tradition while the old duke lived, it apparently had died with him.

Recently, Grigsby had reported to Max the tenants were complaining that the new duke took no interest in them and thought himself too good even to talk to them.

And that was not true. It was his mother, not Es, who thought herself above entertaining or even speaking to them.

Yes, her son had gone along with her refusal to hold the traditional dinner, but like his father before him, he never acted counter to her wishes. Furthermore, Max suspected in this case Es had been relieved to comply with her wishes because he was so shy and ill at ease with people he did not know well.

Although Max hated to admit it, that lying witch Virg was right. Es did need Max's help to become a man—and even more important, to become his own man.

Max was still seething at Virg. He prided himself on being a sophisticate, able to see through all the faces of deceit a woman wore. It stung that she had not only lied to him but—most unforgivable of all—had managed to dupe him into believing her.

He left the office wing for the castle's library, where he could go over the ledger in quiet solitude.

Before he reached that sanctuary, however, he was waylaid by Rowena Blair.

"Yes?" he asked curtly.

"The duke is courting my daughter, Virginia."

"Is it not the other way around?"

Mrs. Blair ignored his question. "And she intends to marry him."

"Does she now?" Max longed to wipe that smug expression from Mrs. Blair's face.

"Yes, she has already ordered her wedding gown." She raised a rolled-up paper that she carried in her hand. "I have a sketch of the design here. Do you wish to look at it?"

This additional confirmation that Virg was part of the bribery fueled Max's anger, and he said through his teeth, "No, and I advise you not to mail out the wedding invitations yet."

"You can do nothing to stop their marriage." She stalked away.

Stupid woman. She would soon find out how wrong she was. So would her damned stepdaughter.

Max went into the castle's Gothic library. He had always loved the way the light passed through its stained glass windows, turning the rays into a multitude of lovely colors. He paused just inside the threshold to admire it.

A movement on a sofa in one of the corners caught his eye. Virg was curled there with a book. She looked up and smiled at Max, clearly happy to see him. An involuntary wave of desire washed over him.

Well hell, what was the matter with him? How could he feel anything but contempt for this woman who had deceived him with her damned lies? His brief encounter with her stepmother a moment ago had added fresh fuel to his ire. Max could not remember when he had been so angry at anyone as he was at her.

He had been so strongly attracted to Virg that his good sense had been addled, something he had never let happen before. He had allowed himself—

indeed, *wanted*—to believe that she was innocent of bribing Daphne and that she was telling the truth when she said she would find being a duchess boring.

The title-hungry jade had not only lied to him but even wanted to demolish this grand room in which she sat.

He hid his fury beneath a cold, sardonic tone. "What a surprise to find you in the library, Virg."

The smile vanished from her face. She swirled her legs out from under her and planted them firmly on the floor, revealing in the process a pair of ankles so shapely that Max wished he could see more of her legs.

That made him even angrier. What the hell was the matter with him? He knew what she was.

"Why?" Her voice now was almost as cool as his. "Does it surprise you that we Americans know how to read?"

"I thought you preferred to spend your time with horses."

"I am a woman of many interests, my lord." She closed the book she had been reading and laid it beside her on the sofa.

"And which of those many interests brought you to the library?" His voice fairly dripped with sarcasm.

"I came for the solitude. No one uses this library, and I treasure the peace and quiet it offers. Why are you here?"

Actually for the same reason she was. "The library is my private hideaway when I am at the castle."

"And you are angry because I have invaded it?"

Ignoring her question, he picked up the book she had put down. "What are you reading?" He glanced at the title. "Good God, *Madame Bovary*."

"You sound shocked."

"I am shocked."

"Why? Have you read it?"

"Certainly, and it is not fit reading for a lady."

Virg smiled sweetly at him. "But you've already pointed out to me that I'm no lady."

"And the book is in French, too."

"Frenchmen generally write in French," she said tartly.

"Surely you do not speak French."

"Surely I do. Why do you look so surprised? You must think we are uneducated savages in America."

Although he said nothing, his expression apparently betrayed that this was exactly what he thought.

Virg snatched the book from him. She looked to be struggling to keep from bashing him over the head with it. She whirled and left the library with a quick, determined stride.

Lady Priscilla would never dream of walking with such unladylike speed.

Precisely two hours after Great-aunt Elizabeth's arrival at the castle, Max knocked lightly at the door of her apartment. Isabel Lake answered.

"Is my aunt awake yet?" he asked in a whisper, not wanting to disturb her if she were still sleeping.

"Yes, she is waiting for you."

"I should have known." His aunt was punctual to a fault—and expected everyone else to be so, too.

Isabel stepped back from the door, and Max entered the apartment's sitting room.

Aunt Elizabeth occupied a large green wing chair, a quilt covering her lower body. The chair had been turned so that she could see through the mullion windows, which looked down on the quadrangle enclosed by the castle's four wings. How weary and frail she looked.

"Isabel dear, please leave Max and me now." The dowager dismissed her young companion with a wave of her hand.

When the door shut behind the girl, Aunt Elizabeth said, "Isabel is the sweetest thing. She deserved so much better than that selfish, wastrel father of hers."

"So did her mama," Max said. "Somehow, though, I do not think you called me here to discuss Isabel's travails."

"No, you are quite right." She gestured at a chair facing her own. "Sit down there."

After he complied, she asked, "Why are you here, Max?"

"Must I have a reason for visiting the castle where I was raised?" he parried.

"No, but knowing how you feel about Daphne, you would not be here without good reason."

"Nor would you. This is the first time in months that you have stirred from Belford Manor, and I know the journey here was arduous for you."

"I suspect we are both here for the same reason, Max. Esmond wants to marry that American girl, and his dreadful mother is encouraging the match."

"It is worse than that, Aunt. Daphne was bribed to persuade Esmond to marry Miss Blair."

Aunt Elizabeth's mouth puckered as though she'd just bit into a sour green apple. "Disgusting! If it were anyone but Daphne, I would not believe it. That stupid woman. We must put an end to any possibility of his marrying the chit."

"I intend to do that, but it will not be easy. Es is much smitten with Miss Blair."

"What do you think of her, Max?"

"She is a charming, lying vixen. One cannot believe a word she says."

"Just as I thought. Can Esmond not see how absolutely unworthy she is to be his duchess? Surely, he cannot be impressed that her father is one of the richest men in America."

"Is he that rich?" Max asked dubiously. He had thought of trying to prove to Daphne that Virg's father could not possibly pay her that magnificent allowance she had been promised month after month.

"Oh, yes, richer than Midas. Leonard Blair owns railroads, shipping lines, factories, stores, and a large amount of highly desirable real estate."

Aunt Elizabeth could be counted on to have the facts right. Still, the extent of Blair's wealth surprised Max. For a former miner, Virg's father had done amazingly well for himself. He must have discovered the mother lode itself.

"I have a plan to cure Esmond of his infatuation, Max, and it will work."

Knowing his redoubtable aunt, Max was certain it would. "What do you propose?"

"You must seduce this American female yourself—the sooner, the better."

Max's body responded to his aunt's plan in a way that irritated and embarrassed him. Nevertheless, her proposal was unthinkable, however tempting it might be.

"I cannot do that, Aunt. Es believes himself in love with her. He would be heartbroken."

"Better heartbroken for a few weeks than to spend the rest of his life in the misery his father did," his aunt said sternly. "Besides whatever else Esmond lacks, he has the Chartwell pride. Once he discovers the American has betrayed him, he will hate her."

"True, but he will also hate me." And Max had too much affection for his cousin to want that.

"Oh, perhaps for a time." Max's aunt dismissed his concern with an airy wave of her hand. "But Esmond will soon come to realize you saved him from a terrible mistake. More important, no matter how greedy Daphne is, she could not bear for her son to marry a woman who had been *your* lover, Max."

His aunt was right. Daphne's hatred of him would outweigh even her greed.

"So you see, Max, it is absolutely necessary that you seduce this Miss Blair. The Chartwell family honor and lineage is at stake. While you are doing that, I shall do everything I can to drive Mrs. Blair from Penrose."

"What about my honor?" Max would feel like a scoundrel seducing Virg simply to keep her from marrying his cousin.

"You do not think it is honorable to save your poor spineless cousin from a woman totally unworthy of him? From an ambitious creature who will undoubtedly make his life as unhappy as his mother made poor Albert's? You owe it to the boy to rescue him from his mother's greed. The duke of Penrose deserves better than that."

Es deserved better. Max was less concerned about the family's honor than about his cousin's future happiness.

After observing Virg with Es, Max was convinced she did not care a tinker's damn about the duke—only his title.

Aunt Elizabeth's expression was stern and unbending. "I never thought you were a man who would go back on his word."

"What are you talking about?" Max asked, much offended. "You know full well I have never done so."

"Not yet, but you will be breaking your solemn promise to your grandfather that you would save Esmond from such foolish mistakes."

Yes, his grandfather on his deathbed had extracted that promise from Max. And it would be a terribly foolish mistake for Es to marry Virg.

Max did want to save his innocent, amiable cousin from a marriage poor Es would regret as bitterly as his father had rued his to Daphne.

Aunt Elizabeth was right. Max should have no scruples, when the three women involved in the bribery had none. Nevertheless, he did, and he silently weighed the dilemma he faced.

Finally, he concluded the most honorable course— or, more precisely, the less dishonorable one— would be to rescue his cousin and teach those two crass Americans that Es was not for sale to the highest bidder.

Yes, Max owed it to Es to save him from a lifetime of misery. If seducing Miss Blair would do that, Max would not shirk his duty.

An image of Virg in her chaps flashed into his mind.

And he would damn well enjoy doing it.

Chapter 8

When Virgie returned that evening to the suite she shared with her stepmother, Rowena was loudly berating her long-suffering maid Olive about how unsuitable the gowns were that the poor servant was presenting for her mistress to wear to dinner.

Curious, Virgie went to the open door to Rowena's bedchamber. The room looked as though it had been ransacked. Elaborate, expensive gowns littered the bed, the sofa, and every chair.

Her stepmother sat at a large dressing table, pawing through the jewelry dumped on top of it. So many necklaces, bracelets, and rings set with precious gems had been piled on the table that it looked like a jeweler's rummage sale.

"I told you I must look my very best tonight," Rowena said irritably. "The famous dowager duchess of Belford is here." Rowena could not have said

Queen Victoria's name with more awe.

"Why is she famous?" Virgie asked. Until today she had never heard of her.

"Your ignorance is abysmal, Virginia. The duchess is legendary for her beauty and wit. She was a great heartbreaker, who was pursued by many of the most illustrious men of her time. It is most important that we impress her."

"Why is that important?"

Rowena gave Virgie a contemptuous look. "You would know, if your understanding were not so inferior."

Virgie forbore retorting that, unlike her stepmother, she understood a good many more important things than *DeBrett's Peerage* and the English aristocracy.

"Now, get ready for dinner, Missy, or you will keep us all waiting."

That would be the day. Virgie turned and went into her own room.

As she bathed, try as she might, she could not push from her mind the way Max had acted in the library. What had prompted his cold, sarcastic attitude toward her, especially after he'd tried again to rescue her earlier that morning?

She selected one of the simplest wool gowns that she owned. Like the one she had worn the previous night, it had none of the puffs and bows that were so fashionable. Its color, a bright orange that few women could wear, compensated for its lack of decoration.

Her only jewelry was a single strand of creamy pearls around her neck.

When Virgie left to go down to dinner, Rowena

was still trying to decide which of her gowns and jewels to wear. By now, every gown in her wardrobe littered her room. Dinner would be delayed at least an hour, waiting for Rowena.

Virgie feared it would be a long night, especially if Max continued to act toward her as he had earlier in the library. His abrupt change in manner still hurt.

When she reached the withdrawing room, the duke and Max were already there, standing near the window she had closed the previous night.

After her confrontation with Max in the library, she expected him to ignore her altogether or to subject her to more sarcasm. She did not intend to give him the opportunity to do either, and she remained by the door.

The duke was talking to Max with more animation than Virgie had yet seen him display. Max listened with an indulgent expression and what appeared to be deep affection in his eyes.

He looked away from Esmond, and his gaze settled on her. He gave her an intriguing smile. "Ah, Virg, I did not see you come in." His voice took on a husky, sensual quality that elicited an odd ache deep within her. "You look lovely tonight."

The last thing she'd expected from Max was a smile and a compliment.

"Let me second—" Esmond broke off as the dowager duchess of Belford appeared in the doorway wearing a simple black wool gown. Her only jewelry was an unusual pin shaped like a sprig of flowers and set with diamonds. The gown set off her perfectly coifed white hair.

The dowager's face was still handsome, and her

pale skin was remarkably unlined for a woman of her years. She must, indeed, have been a great beauty in her youth.

Virgie saw Isabel hovering behind the dowager, all but invisible in her shadow.

As Esmond went to his great-aunt, her gaze settled on Virgie. "Well, well, Esmond, whom have we here?"

The young duke glanced at Virgie, and his face softened with affection and pleasure. "I am honored to present to you the most charming and lovely of women, Miss Virginia Blair."

Isabel Lake's face crumpled in pain.

Virgie almost gasped. Isabel was clearly in love with Esmond.

The young duke was looking at Virgie and did not notice Isabel's reaction. Virgie cast a quick sideways glance at Max, but he was watching the dowager.

The duke took Virgie's arm and led her to the old woman.

"Let me present you to my great-aunt, the dowager duchess of Belford."

"I am honored, Your Grace."

The old woman's gray eyes were the same shade as Max's—and just as penetrating. She studied Virgie with unmistakable hostility. Why should the dowager dislike her, when they had never met before?

Virgie turned toward Isabel, but the girl had faded back into the shadows of the hall. Tears trickled down her cheeks. Virgie wanted to greet the girl, but doing so would call attention to her tears and needlessly embarrass her.

Isabel was pretty in a shy, quiet way. Her eyes were a soft brown. So was her hair, but unfortunately it had been pulled back into a tight knot that would have been more fitting on a woman of the dowager's years.

The girl's figure in her plain, simply cut gray gown was slender and pleasing, but the somber color did nothing to enhance her complexion. She'd garner far more approving attention in the vivid colors that Virgie wore.

Seeing Isabel's obvious love for Esmond set Virgie to wondering. Had anyone else truly loved him in his short life? His mother was far too absorbed in herself, and his father had died when he was a baby.

Kind and amiable Esmond deserved to be loved for himself. Isabel might make him the perfect wife he needed. If only Virgie knew more about the girl.

Isabel belatedly came in from the hall and stood by herself, all but fading into the background in her gray dress. No one but Virgie seemed to notice her. Poor Isabel gave poignant definition to the term wallflower.

Seeing an opportunity to learn more about the girl, Virgie went over to her with a friendly smile.

"Hi, we've not been introduced. I'm Virginia Blair."

Isabel was obviously astonished that Virgie had approached her. "I am Isabel Lake, Her Grace's companion."

Virgie felt Max's gaze on her, but she focused her attention on Isabel, noting her pinched, weary countenance. "You look exhausted."

"I am surprised you observed that. Most people

do not notice me at all." Isabel sounded forlorn rather than bitter. "I fear I am not a very memorable person."

"Nonsense. You are very pretty." And she would be still prettier with a little assistance.

Isabel regarded Virgie as though she'd taken leave of her senses. "You are the first person, I am certain, who ever thought me pretty."

"You are much too modest. You have been to Castle Penrose before?"

"Yes, a number of times. When Her Grace's brother, the old duke, was dying, we were here for several months. We have not been here for some time now, though. Her Grace finds traveling very difficult, and she prefers to remain at Belford Manor. Even there, she rarely cares to have visitors any more." Isabel sounded wistful.

Sympathy for Isabel swelled in Virgie's heart. How constricted and lonely her life must be as companion to an old woman who no longer wanted people around her.

The dowager was still talking to her two greatnephews, but Max watched Virgie suspiciously, as if he suspected her of corrupting his aunt's companion.

The clock on the mantel chimed the dinner hour.

"Where is Daphne?" the dowager demanded irritably. "It is time to go into the dining room."

Another minute or two ticked by before their missing hostess swept in on the comte's arm.

"You are late," the duchess informed her. "It is most rude to keep your company waiting." Her tone was that of an adult reprimanding a particularly errant child.

Daphne reddened in anger.

The dowager turned toward the door of the dining hall. "We will go in to eat at once."

"We cannot," Daphne countered. "One of our guests, Mrs. Blair, is not here yet."

"It is even ruder for a guest to keep his hosts and the rest of the party waiting," the dowager said. "We shall not wait for such a mannerless person."

"You are quite right, Aunt Elizabeth," Max said, the hint of a smile playing at the corners of his mouth. "No reason to wait for her at all, is there, Esmond?"

The duke stole an uneasy glance at his great-aunt. "No, Max." Turning toward Daphne, he declared, "We will go in now, Mama."

Although Mama looked as if she wanted to strangle both Max and the dowager, she kept her mouth closed. Her expression betrayed how difficult this silence was for her.

So Lady Albert was afraid of the dowager as well as of Max.

"You may take me in, Esmond," the dowager announced.

From his expression, the young duke would rather have escorted the menagerie's lion, but he dutifully said, "Yes, ma'am," and took her arm.

He looked hopefully at Virgie. "Please, may I escort you too?"

His request brought a stricken expression to Isabel's face.

Seeing it, Virgie was about to suggest that he escort Isabel, but the dowager said sharply, "Come, come, Miss Blair. Do not keep us waiting."

Virgie took the duke's other arm.

When they passed the butler, the dowager said to him in an undertone, "After we go in, Jenkins, lock the door to the withdrawing room and do not let anyone who is late into the refectory. Tell them they are to eat in the kitchen."

Although the dowager used the plural, this instruction was clearly meant for Rowena, who was the only one still missing.

The startled butler murmured, "Yes, Your Grace."

As he turned away, Virgie saw a smile he could not entirely suppress.

Virgie could barely stifle her own smile. The dowager's edict would eliminate the grand entrance Rowena had spent so many hours planning.

Truly poetic justice.

In the refectory, all the covers were laid at one end of the long table, but Virgie noted with amusement that Daphne had not left the seating to chance. Each cover sported a name card.

Esmond seated the dowager at his right and Virgie on his left. Isabel was assigned to sit next to her employer, but the dowager insisted that Max take the chair instead, relegating poor Isabel to the lowest seat at the table.

Virgie nodded to the empty seat beside her. "Since my stepmother is not here, Miss Lake, won't you please sit beside me?" This would give Virgie a chance to get to know Isabel better. "I should so enjoy talking to you."

Max studied her with lively suspicion, but his great-aunt said, "Yes, Isabel dear, do sit there."

Virgie saw the butler take one of the liveried footmen aside for a whispered conversation.

Then, looking as though he'd just been ordered to the guillotine, the footman went into the withdrawing room. The butler closed the door and unobtrusively turned the key in the lock.

They had finished their soup and were eating the first course of entrees when Virgie heard Rowena's piercing voice in the withdrawing room.

"How dare you tell me I can't go into the dining room? I'll see that you're fired for your insolence, young man."

The footman's answer was too low to make out his words.

"Eat in the kitchen!" Rowena's voice rose to a high C. She sounded as outraged as if she'd been told to wallow in a pigpen. "I most certainly will not. Step away from the door."

Apparently the footman did not obey her order, for a few seconds later, she screeched, her voice still an octave higher than normal, "I said get out of my way!"

The doorknob twisted and rattled violently, but to no avail.

"Unlock the door!" Rowena screamed. "What is the meaning of this?"

"Whoever that rude creature is banging at the door, ignore her," the dowager ordered in a loud voice obviously intended to reach Rowena's ears.

"Yes," Max agreed in a voice of equal volume. "Dinner is far more pleasant without her company. She is the most ill-mannered, the *most uncouth* woman I have ever met."

As he said this, Max winked at Virgie across the table. He had deliberately turned back on Rowena the insult she had given her stepdaughter the previous night.

Virgie could not help smiling, but she was baffled by the difference between Max's cold, sarcastic manner earlier in the library and his friendliness toward her now.

He returned the smile, his gray eyes lidded and sensual, and Virgie felt a clenching in her belly that had nothing to do with hunger or food.

The damned man was positively dangerous.

When they finished dessert, the dowager rose. "The ladies will retire to the drawing room and leave the gentlemen to their brandy."

Recalling how Daphne had refused to do that the previous night, Virgie stole a sidelong glance at her. Her lips were drawn into such a tight, grim line that they'd all but disappeared, but she said nothing and followed the dowager from the room.

Isabel and Virgie trailed the two older women into the drawing room.

The dowager settled on a sofa and pointed the gold head of her cane toward a crimson wing chair across from her. "You, Miss Blair, sit there."

Virgie complied just as Rowena stalked into the drawing room, looking like a green sea dragon about to explode in fury.

The gown she had finally chosen to wear was a voluminous green satin. Its bodice sparkled with brilliants, and its full skirt could have tented a small circus.

Apparently choosing her jewelry had proved to be an impossible task, for she looked to be wearing almost every piece she possessed.

A diamond tiara that would have made Queen

Victoria jealous graced her head. A choker necklace with six strands of perfectly matched pearls encased her short neck up to her several chins. Below it sparkled another necklace with an intricate web of diamonds. And below that, a many-carat diamond nestled in Rowena's generous décolletage.

A half dozen bracelets graced each arm. Rings set with precious gems glittered on every one of her fingers. Only her thumbs had no ornaments.

She looked like a gaudy, overly trimmed Christmas tree.

Virgie longed to hide in embarrassment at her stepmother's display of wretched excess.

Rowena marched up to Daphne. "I . . . I . . . can't believe you would bar me from the dining room and eat without me." Rowena was so angry that she could hardly spit out the words.

Before Daphne could reply, the dowager said in an awful voice that could have driven a regiment into retreat, "You have nothing to blame for that but your own exceedingly ill-bred rudeness and lack of basic consideration in expecting everyone else to wait long past dinner time for you."

That deflated even Rowena. "But I—"

The dowager cut her off. "There can be no excuse, absolutely none whatsoever, for your shamefully vulgar, boorish behavior."

Rowena looked so apoplectic that Virgie feared she might have a seizure. Her stepmother contemptuously scrutinized the dowager's plain black gown and the delicate diamond pin that was her only jewelry, then touched the huge diamond nestled between her own breasts. "And you, I see, are another poor relation of the duke's."

Virgie could hardly keep from laughing. Rowena failed to recognize the famous dowager duchess of Belford, thanks to her tasteful garb.

The color vanished from Daphne's face, and she said hastily, "Let me present—"

Cutting her off, Rowena addressed the dowager. "I am Mrs. Leonard Blair." Her tone indicated that she expected the old woman to be greatly impressed.

The dowager gave an audible sniff of disdain. "Your name means nothing to me, although your atrocious voice and accent tell me you are one of those crude, barbaric Americans that have invaded our country like a swarm of locusts, hunting for titled husbands for their daughters."

Rowena choked on her anger. "Why, I have never been treated with such discourtesy. I have a good mind to leave for London."

"Please do so," the dowager retorted. "At once."

Rowena's mouth hung agape, and her eyes bulged like a shark's brought up too swiftly from the depths.

The dowager turned away from Rowena as though she were an annoying but insignificant insect, unworthy of attention.

Radiating fury, Virgie's stepmother stalked from the room. The duke's mother ran after her, pleading in a low voice, "Please, I beg you, do not . . ."

Daphne's voice faded away, and Virgie could not hear for what her ladyship begged.

"Their company, such as it is, will not be missed," the dowager said. "We are most fortunate to have them leave us."

Isabel hid a yawn behind her hand.

"Poor Isabel, you are exhausted." Both the dowager's tone and expression softened, indicating her affection for her companion.

That in itself spoke very well for Isabel. The old woman would not be easy to please.

"Go up to bed, dear."

Isabel's eyes told Virgie she was torn between duty and fatigue. "You may need help going upstairs, Your Grace."

"If I do, I will enlist Max. Goodnight, Isabel."

After the girl left the room, the dowager turned to Virgie. "Why did you come to England, Miss Blair?"

Virgie decided against telling her about Eden Valley. Instead she said, "My stepmother persuaded my father that the trip would give her and me the opportunity to get to know each other and become friends."

"Has it accomplished that?"

"It has the first objective," Virgie answered honestly. "We know each other better, but that makes the second objective impossible."

The dowager leaned forward with sudden interest. "So you and your stepmother are not friends, only accomplices."

"Accomplices?" Virgie echoed, baffled. "In what?"

"You know very well in what," the dowager said with a withering stare.

"No, I don't."

"Miss Blair, I cannot abide liars."

Insulted and outraged, Virgie stood up abruptly. "And I refuse to remain in the company of someone who falsely accuses me of lying. Goodnight."

"Sit down," the dowager ordered.

Virgie walked out of the room.

She wanted to go up to the apartment she shared with her stepmother and change into the old clothes she wore when she fed Lionel. Fear that Rowena would be there in a towering fury, however, kept Virgie from doing that. Bitter experience had taught her that she would instantly become the object of her stepmother's rage, no matter what its original cause.

So Virgie opted to hide out in the library for an hour or so to give Rowena's temper more time to cool.

In the refectory, Max stifled a yawn—and his impatience to join Virg and the other women in the drawing room.

Before leading the women from the refectory, Aunt Elizabeth had whispered to him to keep Esmond and the comte at the table with their brandy for as long as possible. Max suspected she wanted to question Virg without the men present.

Having faced Aunt Elizabeth's inquisitions himself as a boy, Max almost felt sorry for Virg.

Almost but not quite.

The interest Virg had displayed in his aunt's companion puzzled him. Virg had managed repeatedly to draw the quiet Isabel into the dinner table conversation by directing questions to her or seeking her opinion. Max had rarely heard Isabel speak at a meal before, and her intelligent answers had raised his already good opinion of her even higher.

He lifted the heavy crystal brandy decanter and poured still more of its contents into the Comte de

Beaucaire's glass. Thanks to Max's attentiveness, the Frenchman had already imbibed a considerable amount.

"The Comte d'Orley is an old friend of mine." Although Max affected an air of casual indifference as he poured, he watched Beaucaire intently. "You must know him and his lovely wife, Daniella, Comte."

"*Mais oui*, we are the dearest of friends." Beaucaire took another swallow. "Daniella is a great beauty, is she not?"

Yes, she was. But her name was Michelle, not Daniella. Max had deliberately used the wrong name to see whether her "dearest of friends" would correct him.

This was not the first such deliberate error Max had made and Beaucaire had failed to catch.

Max had become well acquainted with the remnants of the French aristocracy during his service as a British secret agent in Paris, but he had never heard of the Beaucaires. Suspicious of the comte's origins, Max had devised an impromptu test for him.

So far Beaucaire had failed it abysmally.

Max took a taste of brandy from his own glass. As he swallowed, an image of Virg in her damn "shaps" flitted into his brain.

And stayed there.

The drafty dining room suddenly seemed hot to him. He ached to run his hands down those luscious curves, to caress her breasts, to . . . yes . . . seduce her. He wanted to do so not only to save Es but because he hungered for her.

He stood abruptly, driven by the heat in his lower

region. Like it or not, Aunt Elizabeth had had as much time with Virg as Max would allow her. "Let us join the ladies."

He stepped back to allow the duke to lead them from the dining hall. The comte followed Es, with Max bringing up the rear.

When he reached the drawing room door, Max noticed a flash of bright orange down the hall. He turned in time to see Virg disappear into the library.

What the hell was she up to now?

And why was she not in the drawing room with the other women? Then he saw Aunt Elizabeth sitting alone there, looking very sour indeed.

Max turned away and went to the library. That quiet, secluded room would make an excellent setting for furthering—and perhaps accomplishing—his goal of seducing Virg.

When he reached the library door, she was perusing the contents of a bookshelf across the room, her back to him.

He paused for an instant to admire the lovely shape that the fitted top and flared, yet clinging, skirt of her gown revealed. His mouth grew dry with desire.

To ensure privacy, Max quietly shut the ornate carved oak door behind him and turned the key in the lock.

Chapter 9

In the library, Virgie studied the section that was reserved for scientific writings. She plucked a very old volume of Isaac Newton's *Principles of Mathematics* from the shelf to see if it could be a first edition.

A voice behind her asked softly, "What are you up to now, Virg?"

She'd thought herself alone in the library, and she started. The book nearly slipped from her fingers as she whirled around. Max stood very close behind her.

Too close. Her heart beat triple time.

Rather than stepping back, he closed his hand over hers—the one that held the book. Her breath caught at the warmth his nearness and his touch generated in her. He turned her hand so he could read the leather bound volume's title.

"Learning to multiply and divide?" He grinned, clearly teasing.

"No, to add and subtract," she retorted. The mercurial changes in his manner toward her were baffling. He had started the day trying to save her. Then, when he'd found her here in the library earlier, he'd acted as though she disgusted him.

But before and during dinner he'd been charming to her. And now he looked at her as though he intended to kiss her. She did not understand him at all. "Why did you sneak up on me?"

"Sneak?" Max sounded offended. "Not I. I fear you were too engrossed in arithmetic to notice me. I must warn you this book of old Isaac's is difficult reading."

"I read it in college."

Max looked at her blankly. "In college?"

"What you call university."

"You attended university?" He sounded incredulous. "You mean in America they send girls to university?"

"They send both men and women."

He frowned. "Males and females in the same classroom, studying the same subjects?"

"Yes."

"Good God!" Max was so clearly confounded by the idea of coeducation that Virgie could not help smiling.

She recalled what Rowena had said about the duke's mother fearing Max. Perhaps Lady Albert's reason for doing so would give Virgie a clue to understanding him.

"Rowena says the duke's mother fears you. Why is that?"

"I would not presume to speak for Daphne. She is the only one who can answer that question." Max smiled slyly at Virgie. "I encourage you to ask her. I am certain you will find her answer most illuminating."

He clearly wanted Virgie to question Daphne.

"Now I have a question for you," Max said. "Why were you so interested in Isabel Lake tonight?"

Virgie wanted Max's opinion of Isabel to see if it matched her own impressions. "I could not help but be. She is such an intelligent and pretty young lady."

"Pretty? Isabel?" Max's dark brows raised in surprise, then puckered. "I never thought about it, but I guess she is. Certainly, she is intelligent. And I thank God for her."

"Why?"

"You may have noticed how strong-willed Aunt Elizabeth is. Isabel can handle her as no one else in the family has ever been able to do, and she does it so unobtrusively that my aunt fails to notice." Max smiled wryly. "My aunt's late husband would be dumbfounded and most envious if he could see it."

"You think highly of Isabel?"

He nodded. "She has taken over much of the running of Belford Manor and does it very well. I do not know what Aunt Elizabeth would do without her."

"Isabel sounds as though she would make a wonderful wife for some lucky man." *Like Duke Esmond.*

Max shrugged. "Not that Isabel is ever likely to be married."

"Why do you say that? I understand one of her grandfathers was a duke and the other an earl. I thought such exalted bloodlines were much sought among the aristocracy."

"They are. She is well born, but the problem is her father, Belford's younger brother and an irresponsible wastrel. He was forced to flee England in disgrace, badly tarnishing Isabel as a marital prospect. Worse, she has no dowry."

"Neither that nor her father's sins are her fault."

"True, but between the scandal surrounding her father and her lack of dowry, she is all but unmarriageable to a man of her class."

"What if she and the man loved each other very much?" Virgie asked slyly.

"I told you last night that love has nothing to do with marriage."

"And I told you, it has everything to do with it."

"Perhaps in the wilds of America, Virg, but not among the English aristocracy. Too much depends on marriage to trust the fickle whims of the heart."

That ignited Virgie's temper. "Just because *your* heart is fickle, don't presume to speak for the rest of humankind."

She returned the book she held to the shelf and went to the door, only to find it locked. She whirled on Max. "Why the devil did you lock the door?"

He did not answer, only looked at her with the most peculiar expression on his face. Virgie turned the key and opened the door. As she went into the hall, she looked back at him.

"The problem with you and the rest of the English aristocracy, my lord, is that you're too restrictive in whom you condescend to marry. The inbreeding has sadly affected your intelligence."

Pleased at the angry flush her final salvo brought to Max's face, Virgie shut the library door hard behind her.

She started down the hall, then stopped abruptly. What was she to do now? She refused to go back to the drawing room and the dowager. Nor would she go up to her apartment, where her stepmother was certain to take her temper out on her. And now she had been denied her one cherished haven, the library.

Damn it, even though she'd probably ruin her gown, she would feed Lionel. She hurried to the kitchen, where the lion's heavy bucket of gruel was waiting for her.

Going outside with the bucket in one hand and a lamp to illuminate her way in the other, Virgie discovered that thick clouds blotted out both moon and stars. The promise of imminent rain hung in the humid air.

Virgie made her way carefully along a path that led past the kitchen garden toward the menagerie.

She had not gone very far when she heard an alien noise among the sounds of the night. A woman was weeping quietly on the other side of the bushes in the kitchen garden.

Virgie could not bear to hear someone crying without trying to offer comfort. For an instant, she contemplated leaving the bucket of gruel on the path and going directly to the poor woman. But Virgie had kept Lionel waiting too long for his dinner already. She would feed him first, then find the woman.

When she reached the lion's cage, the elderly beast pushed his jaws between the bars.

"Good evening, Lionel, here is your dinner." She unlatched the small barred gate near the bottom of the cage and pushed the bucket inside.

Virgie usually stayed with Lionel, talking to him until he finished eating and then removing the bucket. Tonight, however, she left him while he was still eating. She would come back later for the bucket.

At the entrance to the kitchen garden, redolent with the scents of basil, rosemary, and thyme, she heard the woman still crying in a dark corner. Lifting her lantern in that direction, she saw Isabel Lake huddled on a small bench among large tufts of thyme.

Virgie went to the bench. Placing the lantern on the ground beside it, she sat next to the weeping girl and put her arm comfortingly around her.

"What's wrong, Isabel?"

"Noth-nothing." The pale light from the lantern illuminated her tear-ravaged face for a moment before she buried it in her handkerchief.

"You are much too intelligent a woman to be weeping like this about nothing. And I am too intelligent to believe that you are doing so. Now tell me—why are you crying?"

"Please, do not ask me. I . . . I fear I have an unhappy disposition."

Given Isabel's circumstances, she had every right to be unhappy, but Virgie suspected the girl's tears were over Esmond.

Still puzzled by Max's behavior toward her today, Virgie wondered if Isabel could tell her more about him. "When Her Grace arrived today, she seemed very eager to talk to Lord Chartwell."

"Yes, Chartwell is her favorite, just as he was his grandfather's." Something that could have been anger or bitterness flickered for an instant in Isabel's eyes. "How unhappy they were when it became clear that Esmond, instead of Chartwell, would inherit the dukedom."

"Why did they not want Esmond to become the duke?"

"Everyone in his father's family dismisses him as stupid, yet he is not," Isabel said with passionate certainty.

"I agree with you, and I don't blame you for being so distressed on the duke's behalf."

"Why should I be distressed?" Isabel's attempt at nonchalance failed miserably, and her voice quavered.

Even though they were obviously alone, Virgie lowered her voice to a whisper so no one could possibly overhear her.

"Because you are in love with Esmond."

Isabel gasped, then stiffened and straightened her shoulders. "Please, Miss Blair, do not say anything to anyone about your ridiculous supposition I am in love with the duke," she pleaded in an urgent, agitated tone.

"It's a fact, not a supposition, but I promise that I won't say anything to anyone. You can't make me believe you're not in love with him." In the weak lantern light, Virgie saw Isabel's brows knit in an unhappy frown. "I know you are."

"Yes, I am," Isabel admitted, wiping at her tears, "even though it is beyond presumption of me."

"Beyond presumption? What on earth are you talking about?"

"He is so far above me." Isabel's voice pulsated with her misery. "He is a duke, and I have no title, no dowry, nothing, except a father who disgraced his family."

"Don't be ridiculous. You're not to be blamed for what your father did."

Virgie studied Isabel in the pale light of the lantern. The girl might be quiet, but she was intelligent, kind, and caring. Furthermore, from what Max had said, Isabel was highly competent.

Most important of all, however, she loved Esmond.

Contrary to what Max and his other relatives thought, Esmond deserved better than a loveless marriage. Virgie began plotting how to promote a romance between the duke and Isabel.

"Nor is it in the least presumptuous of you, Isabel, to love him. I think you'd make the duke a fine wife. And I intend to help you become his duchess."

"Help me?" Isabel stammered in obvious astonishment. "Why would *you* help *me*, Miss Blair?"

Why did Isabel sound so amazed? "Because I like you very much, and the duke deserves a sensible, capable woman like you who loves him."

And Virgie would see that Esmond got what he deserved.

Chapter 10

 ⌒⌒○○⌒⌒

Max awoke early the next morning with a powerful yearning to see Virg in her chaps. In the hope of satisfying his desire, he got up and stood on tiptoe to look out the high, narrow slit that served as his window.

Dawn was not beautiful this morning. At least not from his north-facing window, which revealed an overcast sky. All he could see on the ground was that damned lion's cage.

A flash of color in front of Lionel's cage caught Max's attention: Virg in a bright red jacket and those enticing chaps.

For once, Max's gaze did not linger on her derriere but fixed on her hands. He could not believe what he was seeing.

She was unlatching the door of the cage.

Christ, she's going into the lion's den!

The damned woman truly was stark raving mad.

His heart in his mouth, Max grabbed his pants. He was fastening them as, barefooted and bare-chested, he ran out of his room into the hall and past two astonished maids.

His room was closer to the back stairs, and he used those, taking them two at a time. In his haste to get outside, he nearly knocked down another maid and two footmen who were using the staircase.

Was there anything Virg would not do?

Thank God, Lady Priscilla would never dream of indulging in such maniac stunts. She was a lady through and through. Priscilla would swoon, as any proper lady would, at the mere thought of bearding a lion in his den.

In fact, no woman in her right mind, lady or not, would walk into a lion's cage.

Max dashed out of the castle and ran toward the cage, his heart pounding.

Virg was standing inside the cage beside Lionel, talking softly to him and rubbing his ear as though he were an overgrown house kitten.

"What the devil do you think you are doing, Virg?" Max's voice came out raspy with fear for her.

She and Lionel looked toward him.

Virg smiled.

Lionel snarled.

She turned back to the beast and said in her most soothing voice, "It's all right, Lionel."

Like hell it was!

The beast turned and presented his ear for Virg to scratch again, and she complied.

For the first time in his life, Max found himself jealous of a damned lion. And terrified for Virgie.

"Virg, why are you in the lion's den?"

"Lionel and I are good friends."

Max snorted in disbelief. "And the moon is brighter than the sun, too!"

The lion, his amber eyes glittering, snarled at Max again.

"Don't come any nearer," Virg warned. "Lionel doesn't like you."

"The feeling is mutual."

"Lionel senses that. Now if you would put aside your hostility toward him."

"How about his toward me?" Max demanded, hanging on to his patience by a thread. "Let him make the first move."

"If you keep acting like you are, he'll do just that, and it won't be nice. His claws are deadly."

Max's patience snapped. "Then get out of that damned cage," he roared.

Lionel thrust his powerful jaws through the bars of the cage and roared back at Max. Virg made no move to leave the lion.

"I said get out of the cage, Virg."

She flashed him a malevolent glare. "Have you English aristocrats ever heard of the word please?"

His eyes narrowed, but this was not the moment to argue. "All right, damn it, please."

Virg gave Lionel a final pat on his ear, retrieved a bucket from the floor of the cage, and stepped outside with it.

The cage door clicked shut after her. She was safe.

Max's racing heartbeat slowed to only quadruple its normal speed. He was so relieved that, hardly knowing what he was doing, he grabbed her and hugged her to him. The scent of orange blossoms drifted over him, and her body against his felt so good, so right, that he bent his head to kiss her.

Lionel snarled at him again through the bars, ruining the moment, and Virg pulled away from Max.

He felt like snarling back at the damned lion.

"You are a raving lunatic," he told her with strong conviction.

"You're the one who's raving," she replied calmly.

She had not pinned her dark hair up, and a light breeze blew it about her. Max smothered a powerful desire to bury his hands in the dark strands and feel their silky texture.

Virg's gaze dropped to his bare chest, and a slow smile turned up the corners of her mouth. "Why, you're not even dressed."

"No, I am not, thanks to you."

Her smile widened. "Saving me again, my lord?"

"Something like that. You would think I would learn," he grumbled. "It will not happen again."

"Good."

"Ungrateful wench!"

Her gaze returned to his chest and stayed there. Her eyes betrayed her appreciation for what she saw.

Now was the time for Max to launch his campaign to seduce her. He would start with a teasing kiss, which he intended to be the first of many that he would lavish on her. Then he would progress to far more intimate arts.

As his head dipped toward her mouth, a chorus of twitters drew his attention to the castle. Half of its servants appeared to be staring at them from every available opening.

He gnashed his teeth in frustration. He wanted more than anything to kiss those luscious lips, but he could hardly do so in front of this audience. He released her and took a step backward. "What did you think you were doing in there?"

Virg held up the bucket she had carried out of the cage. "Retrieving Lionel's bucket."

"Why in God's name would you do that?"

"So I could feed him."

A niggling headache threatened at Max's temple. She was the most impossible woman.

"He has a keeper who does that, Virg. In fact, now that I think about it, you are the one on this estate who most needs a keeper."

"Well, Lionel needs a new one. His current keeper is cruel and incompetent. I can't abide cruelty to an animal, no matter what his species."

Neither could Max, but that had nothing to do with this infuriating woman. "What are you talking about now?"

"Poor Lionel has lost all but one of his teeth. Anyone who paid the least attention to him would know he can no longer chew bones and joints of tough, raw meat. Yet that's all that wretched man will feed him."

Max raised a brow. "I am astonished you did not point that out to him."

"Oh, I did, but he was very rude to me and continues to do as he always has. He hates the lion and, I think, was deliberately trying to starve him."

"So you have been feeding him something he can eat?"

"Yes, a nice gruel full of pulverized bone that does not require teeth. I give it to him twice a day."

"Twice a day," he echoed, stunned that she had risked her life to go into that cage so often. Now he knew why Lionel looked so much better. With such devoted attention from Virg, Max would too.

"But I forgot his bucket last night, and I had to get it before I can feed him this morning."

"I will see that Lionel gets a new keeper immediately. I promise you will not have to worry about him any more."

Her grateful smile and shining eyes sent a fresh surge of desire through Max. He looked toward the castle. Instead of disappearing as he had hoped, their audience had grown.

He balled his hands into fists and turned away before he made a fool of himself and an enemy of Es by kissing that irresistible mouth in front of all those gawking servants.

If he were to do so, the tale, much embellished, would be all over the estate and the entire shire by nightfall, if not sooner.

But damn, it was hard to walk away from her without tasting her lips.

Nevertheless, by sheer force of will, he did.

After breakfasting in the kitchen, Virgie went up to her bedchamber, where she sat down on the chaise longue, her legs stretched out before her.

This morning was the third time in as many days that Max had thought her in danger and tried to save her, and she was feeling more kindly toward him.

Much more kindly.

After she'd left Lionel's cage, she'd thought Max

was going to kiss her. She was nonplussed at how much she'd wanted him to do so and how disappointed she was that he hadn't.

When other men had tried to kiss her, she had been disinterested, bored with the entire idea. The few who had succeeded had left her wondering what her girlfriends found so thrilling about a man's kiss.

But when Max had lowered his head toward hers, she'd waited with breathless anticipation and a strange aching for his lips. She'd wanted to feel the warmth of his sensual mouth on hers, had hungered for something she could not name.

When he had drawn back, it had taken every bit of determination she possessed to keep from throwing her arms around his neck and kissing him. Now, for the first time in her life, she wondered at the pleasures of an even more intimate act.

A rapping on her door startled her. Heat rose in her cheeks as though someone had read her thoughts. She opened the door to find Daphne's maid.

"Lady Albert wishes to see you at once, Miss Blair. Please come with me."

Virgie could not fathom why the duke's mother would want to see her, but she followed the maid to her ladyship's apartment. The meeting would give Virgie an opportunity to ask Daphne why she feared Max.

When they entered Daphne's apartment, she was sitting at a dressing table swathed in pink silk. Hammered silver pots, brushes, and combs were spread across the top of the dressing table. Her face had already been made up, but her blond hair hung down about her shoulders. She was studying herself intently in the mirror.

"Leave us, Marie," she instructed the maid. Daphne did not invite Virgie to sit down, leaving her to stand by the dressing table.

As soon as Marie left the room, Daphne said, "You clearly find Chartwell very interesting, Miss Blair. I must warn you how much he hates my son."

Virgie recalled the protective, affectionate note in Max's voice whenever he spoke of Esmond, and she hastened to assure his mother, "Oh, I am certain his lordship doesn't dislike the duke."

"Chartwell carefully conceals his hatred of my son from outsiders." Daphne's voice was colder than the ices that had been served at dinner last night. "But we in the family know how deep and dangerous his hatred is."

"Why would he hate the duke?" Even if Virgie had not detected Max's affection for Esmond, he was so much more impressive a man than his young cousin that she could see no reason for it. If anyone's hatred seemed deep, it was Daphne's for Max.

"If it were not for Esmond, Chartwell would be the duke of Penrose now. His loathing for my son is so intense that I fear for Esmond's life."

Virgie gasped in shock. "Are you saying you think Lord Chartwell would kill your son? I can't believe that!"

"You do not know Chartwell. Even before my son became duke, Chartwell several times maneuvered Esmond into such perilous situations it is a miracle that he survived."

"What did his lordship do?" Virgie still could not believe her.

"I have not the time to tell you all the incidents now, but believe me, when he learns of my son's decision to marry, he will do anything he can, even murder, to prevent the wedding." Daphne picked up a comb from the table and absently rubbed her thumb along its teeth. "So long as Esmond does not wed and father a child, Chartwell remains first in line for the title."

Was that why Max had seemed so disinterested in freeing Esmond from his mother's apron strings and guiding him to manhood? Still, Virgie could not believe that Max would harm his cousin.

In fact, she would have thought the strongest opposition to Esmond's marrying would come from Daphne herself. The duke's mother would not easily surrender her position as doyenne of Castle Penrose nor her control over her son.

"From what you say, I gather your son has chosen a bride." Poor Isabel's heart would be broken.

The comb Daphne had been fingering fell unheeded to her dressing table. "I thought the duke had told you!"

"No, he hasn't. Who is his bride to be?"

"My son must be the one to tell you. He would be so angry at me if I were to betray his plans before he announces them. Until he does, you must not say anything to him and most particularly not to Chartwell."

"Are you pleased with your son's choice?"

Daphne smiled. "Of course I am."

Virgie's heart sank for Esmond. If Daphne was not opposed to his marriage, he must be wedding some quiet, dutiful daughter over whom his mother could run roughshod. It would be one of those bloodless, loveless marriages that Max seemed to think was necessary for a British aristocrat.

How disappointed Rowena, who hoped to promote a match between Virgie and the duke, would be that he was marrying another woman. Perhaps when her stepmother learned of his betrothal, she would finally leave the castle and return to London with Virgie.

Except the thought of leaving while Max was here no longer held as much appeal to her.

Whoever Esmond's bride-to-be was, Virgie pitied her deeply. She did not doubt that Daphne would make her daughter-in-law's life miserable. And Esmond, tied as he was to his mother's apron strings, was not likely to intervene on his wife's behalf.

"I must warn you that you are not safe from Chartwell either," Daphne said. "Any woman he suspects the duke of having the smallest interest in is in danger."

Virgie found that hard—indeed, impossible—to believe, even though that would help explain Max's strange, contradictory behavior toward her, first attempting to rescue her, then treating her with hateful, insulting sarcasm. Yet, if he wanted to be rid of her, why would he keep trying to rescue her?

By now, Virgie was so confused she did not know what to think.

Daphne picked up the comb she had dropped and looked slyly at Virgie. "I knew you would want to know about Chartwell's true character and his hatred of my son."

"Is that why you fear Lord Chartwell?"

"Yes, I could not bear to lose my son." Lady Albert dabbed with theatrical delicacy at her eyes. "And I am terrified Chartwell will kill him. Max is an extremely dangerous man."

Chapter 11

~~~oOo~~~

Since the library was clearly one of Virg's favorite places in the castle, Max checked there and found her.

Virg glanced up from the book she was reading, clearly irritated to see him. "Yes?" she said coldly.

Why the hell should she be irritated with him now? "I thought you would want to know that Lionel has a new keeper, one who will take better care of him than the last one."

Max expected her to be pleased that he had acted so quickly, thus aiding in his seduction of her.

Instead she said coolly, "It would be impossible for the new man to take worse care of poor Lionel than Raffe did."

"Perhaps you will want to instruct the new keeper to make certain that he measures up to your standards."

"Yes, I will."

Max sat down beside her, and she slid away as though she could not stand to be near him.

"What is the matter?" he asked.

"Lady Albert told me this morning why she feared you."

So Virg knew now that he controlled the duke's estate and could veto her marriage to Esmond.

Could—hell, he would. She could count on it.

But that was hardly reason for her to look at him as though he were an ax murderer.

"I gather, Virg, you were shocked."

"Horrified far more accurately describes my reaction." The look she gave him was so fiery it would have melted an iceberg. "I couldn't believe it."

So Virg did not think he would stop Es from marrying her. "Believe it," he told her. "It is true."

"Dear God, and I thought you were fond of the duke."

"I am." Did she think Max's affection for his cousin would outweigh his intelligence, and he would allow Es to marry her? "That is precisely why I will not allow him to wed a female totally unworthy to be his duchess."

She regarded him as though he were a cockroach. "And you consider no female worthy of that honor?"

"I am not *quite* that particular."

"Aren't you? Then tell me what woman would pass muster with you?"

Her question caught Max by surprise. He opened his mouth to answer, then realized he had never thought about what young lady would make Es a good duchess.

"Just as I thought. Not a single woman meets your exalted standards, does she, my lord?"

Actually, one did. Lady Priscilla, but she was Max's intended.

Virg slammed shut the book on her lap, jumped up from the sofa, and headed for the library door.

The American's petulant reaction surprised and disappointed Max. It seemed childish and out of character. He would have thought her intelligent enough to try subtly to change his mind about permitting the marriage, instead of acting like a spoiled brat.

"Where are you going, Virg?"

She paused at the door and turned. "Out of your company. You appall me."

Her look of contempt and disgust flabbergasted Max.

"Furthermore, I warn you that I'll be watching you. Don't you dare do anything, even the smallest thing, to hurt the duke."

Virg whirled and walked out of the library, leaving Max sputtering in outrage.

Dressed in riding clothes that were considerably more feminine and fashionable than those she'd worn to ride Black Lightning, Virgie went in search of Esmond.

She had left Lady Albert's room that morning with her thoughts in turmoil. She would not—could not—believe Max would harm Esmond. But then Max himself had told her it was true.

Certainly that explained why he refused to help guide his cousin to becoming a man.

So Virgie, never adverse to a challenge, would train Esmond herself.

The duke often took refuge in a circular room at the top of the castle's south tower, and she went to look for him there. She suspected he used the room often to escape his mother.

Virgie found him staring out a narrow grated window at the countryside around the castle. He reminded her of a prisoner locked away in a tower, and, in a way, he was.

"Your Grace, could I convince you to show me your estate?" She held her breath, for she knew he did not care much for riding.

But he smiled, surprising her. "I should like that."

A half hour later, they rode away from the castle with Esmond on a brown mare that was considerably gentler than the one Virgie rode. This was the first time she'd seen him on a horse, and now she understood why he rarely rode. He was nervous and uncomfortable with horses.

"Shall we start with the park?" he asked.

"No, I want to meet some of your tenants. Will you introduce them to me?"

He stiffened in the saddle. Virgie's request clearly dumbfounded and unnerved him. "But I do not know any of them."

She was dismayed that he was so isolated from his own dependents. "Then let's meet them together." She gave him her warmest, most encouraging smile.

"Well, we can if that is what you truly want," he said dubiously.

"It is," she assured him.

Virgie let Esmond set the pace, and it was so

sedate she feared they would not reach the first tenant's home before suppertime.

White cloud puffs rolled across the sky, but the temperature was still cool. Everywhere Virgie looked, the leaves had turned to the gold and scarlet of fall.

They rode for several minutes in silence, Virgie's mind still reeling from Max's confirmation that Daphne had profound reason to fear him.

"You are very quiet today," Esmond finally observed.

"I was wondering about Lord Chartwell." Virgie intended to find out everything she could about him and his relationship with the duke. "He told me he earned his title but not how he did so. Do you know?"

Esmond's head swiveled toward her. "I am surprised he said that much. He has never told anyone, not even Grandfather, about his work. The title was Max's reward for being a superlative secret agent."

"Is he still one?"

"No, when Grandfather first got sick, he begged Max to resign and come home to help him, and Max did."

"But you said he did not even tell your grandfather about his work?"

"He did not. The queen told Grandfather, and he told me what she'd said. He was fairly bursting with pride."

Noting Esmond's wistful expression, Virgie asked, "Surely your grandfather was proud of you too."

"No, I never did anything to make him so. He—and all of the Chartwells—wanted Max to succeed him. And I cannot blame them. Max would have made a far better duke."

Esmond looked so forlorn that Virgie wanted to cry for him. "When you say all the Chartwells, does that include Max, too?"

Her question clearly startled the duke. "I never thought about it before, but no, I do not think so."

They rode past a tenant's small, whitewashed cottage, but Virgie saw no sign of life there. She was looking for one with a resident outside. In the face of Esmond's reluctance, that would make it easier to stop casually and talk.

"Max is the only Chartwell who paid any attention to me," Esmond confided. "He used to write me wonderful letters. I would wait for the post every day in the hope one would be there. Although he was rarely in England, whenever he was he would come to see me in Cornwall." Esmond's face lit at the memory. "How I loved his visits."

That did not sound to Virgie like a man intent on murder, unless perhaps he was trying to win his victim's trust. "How did your mother feel about his coming to see you?"

"Oh, Mama liked Max then—except when I was eighteen and he insisted on teaching me to ride. He said I should have learned long before that . . ."

Indeed, you should have.

". . . but Mama did not want me on a horse. She even accused poor Max of trying to kill me."

Could that have been one of the incidents Daphne had had in mind this morning? "Why doesn't she like Max now?"

"Well," Esmond said slowly, "it began when Grandfather was dying. Max insisted I come to the castle to stay, but Mama was not allowed to come with me. She blamed Max for that, but it was actually my grandfather's edict. He disliked her."

"Did Max tell you why he wanted you here?"

"He hoped Grandfather and I would grow fonder of each other."

Had that truly been Max's motive? "Did you?"

Esmond shook his head, his expression sad. "Unfortunately, no."

"After you came to the castle, did you and Max spend much time together?"

Again Esmond shook his head. "He had said that we would, but then he was too busy. Grandfather wanted Max with him constantly."

"You must have been terribly bored."

"No, but only because Isabel Lake was here. Dear Isabel was a godsend."

Virgie recalled what Isabel had said about spending several months at the castle during the old duke's final illness. That must have been when she had fallen in love with Esmond.

They had ridden past several tenants' homes before Virgie saw one with an adult outside. A woman, her back to the road, was hanging laundry on a line strung between the house and an outbuilding. Two small children played near her. The whitewashed cottage was well kept, with newly painted shutters at its windows.

After Virgie and Esmond dismounted, he said shyly, "I will stay here with the horses."

"I wish you would come with me so we can both talk to her."

"What would I talk to her about?" He both looked and sounded panicked.

"You might ask her how her family is or how many children she has. Or whether she and her husband were pleased with their harvest this year."

Esmond listened solemnly, obviously mulling over her suggestions.

"If you can think of nothing else, you can talk about the weather."

He appeared tempted, but then he said, "Still, I prefer to remain here with the horses."

It was all Virgie could do to keep from groaning aloud, but she decided against cajoling him further.

She went through the gate in the front fence, which was lined with rose bushes that, unfortunately, were out of bloom.

The older of the two children, a girl of about four, pointed toward them. "Look, mum, they's comin' here."

"What?" The woman looked in the direction her child was pointing. When she saw her visitors, her eyes widened in surprise, then narrowed in suspicion.

Virgie strode quickly toward her with a friendly smile. "Hello, I'm Virginia Blair, and I'm visiting here. I'm sorry I'm too late to see your roses in bloom. Your yard must be lovely then."

"Aye, 'tis," the woman replied proudly.

Her daughter, a thin little girl with curly brown hair and a spattering of freckles, eyed Virgie critically. "You talk funny."

"Addie," her mother cried, reddening with embarrassment, "you're not to say such things to visitors."

"Well, her does," Addie said defiantly.

Her mother gave her a sharp, reproving look. Addie looked down and fiddled with the cloth of her faded, worn homespun dress, clearly a hand-me-down that was too big for her.

Smiling, Virgie bent down to Addie. "I talk funny because I come from another country than yours, and that's the way we sound. If you went there, we would think you talked funny too. It's all in what you're used to hearing."

From the corner of her eye, Virgie saw Addie's little brother watching them. After a moment, he toddled off toward Esmond and the horses.

"Where are ye staying?" the mother asked.

"At Castle Penrose. I'm sorry I didn't catch your name."

At the mention of the castle, the woman's manner toward Virgie changed from curiosity to deference. Clearly flustered, she made an awkward curtsy. "Mrs. Simpkins me name, ma'am, Nellie Simpkins."

"Have you lived in this pretty cottage long, Mrs. Simpkins?"

"Since I married me husband seven years ago." She hesitated, started to speak, then stopped.

Virgie flashed her friendliest smile. "Please, what is it?"

"What be the young duke like?" Nellie blurted.

Virgie started. Had the woman recognized her companion? "Why do you ask?"

"Is him as top-lofty as e'eryone says him is?"

"Oh, no, not at all," Virgie assured her. "He's most amiable. I don't understand why people would think him haughty."

"In the seven years I've been here, not once have I laid eyes on him. When his grandfather were alive, the old man were always ridin' about his land, talkin' to his people and seein' all were as it should be. Now 'tis not the duke, but Lord Chartwell who does that."

"Does he?" Why did Max do that? A cold shadow fell across her heart. Was it in anticipation of his becoming duke?

"Aye, and he don't even live here. He's not so grand that he's above talking to us like the duke is."

Poor Esmond, his tenants had misread his shyness and uncertainty as haughtiness.

"E'eryone wishes his lor'ship were the duke stead of his cousin."

Including Chartwell.

A movement caught Virgie's eye. She surreptitiously watched the little boy go up to Esmond. The child tripped and would have fallen had the duke not grabbed him and set him on his feet again. Esmond knelt on one knee so he could talk to the little boy at eye level.

Virgie would wager they weren't discussing the weather, either.

A minute later, the duke took the boy up in his arms and held him so he could pet the horses. Johnny chortled with glee as he timidly patted the nose of the mare Esmond had been riding.

His mother glanced toward the spot where her son had been standing. "Oh dear, where did Johnny go?"

"Over there." Virgie gestured toward Esmond. "Your son is in good hands."

"The gentleman likes children, does he?"

"Yes." Although Virgie suspected Esmond had

not been around children much, he was obviously enjoying Johnny.

To forestall the woman asking the duke's identity, Virgie inquired, "Do you have more children than these two?"

"Aye, a daughter of six and another son, Danny, still in the cradle."

"You must have your hands full," Virgie said with sympathy.

"Aye." Mrs. Simpkins managed a weary smile. "Thank heaven the baby is asleep now."

"May I see him? I promise not to wake him."

Clearly surprised, Mrs. Simpkins said, "If you want, but I warn you me house's not at all grand, not like the castle."

Thank God. It might even be warm and cozy.

And it was.

In its homey kitchen, a baby's cradle rested near a hearth in which a warming fire blazed. Virgie observed ruefully that the fireplace in this tenant's cottage was considerably more efficient than any she had discovered in Castle Penrose.

They went to the cradle, and Virgie looked down at the plump, pink-cheeked baby, who was sleeping soundly.

"Danny's adorable," she whispered.

His mother smiled proudly.

Virgie turned away from the crib. A big trestle table in the center of the room had a bench along each of its long sides.

"May I sit for a minute?" she asked.

"If you wish, m'lady."

"I'm not a m'lady. I'm an American." She sat down on the end of one of the benches. "We have no use for aristocracy in our country. Please call me Virgie."

The woman looked askance at her. "Nay, I couldn't."

"Certainly, you can. I insist upon it. May I call you Nellie?"

The woman nodded.

The outside door opened, and Esmond came in with Johnny hanging on his right hand and Addie grasping his left.

"Mum, this here's Es. He don't talk as funny as the lady does."

"Addie, I told you you're not to say things like that!" her mother exclaimed in mortified accents. "Won't you have a seat, sir?"

"Thank you." Esmond settled on the bench beside Virgie.

Danny began to squall, and Nellie hurried to the cradle to pick up her crying son. Holding the infant in her arms, she tried in vain to soothe him.

A minute later, the infant glanced toward the duke and stopped in mid-shriek.

Esmond was making faces at the infant. Little Danny began to laugh while tears still coursed down his cheeks.

Soon the baby was flinging his arms about glee-fully as Esmond entertained him with a variety of expressions.

The oldest child, Ellie, came in to join Addie and Johnny. The trio whispered among themselves and sent furtive glances toward the duke.

When their mother went outside to fetch some-thing from the root cellar, Addie asked him, "Will you play hide-and-seek with us, Es?"

He looked acutely embarrassed. "I am afraid—"

Addie interrupted him. "Puh-leeze," she begged. "We wants you to."

"Why don't you go outside and wait for us," Virgie interjected, seeking a moment alone with Esmond so she could discover what had flustered him. "We'll be out in a minute."

The three children did as she asked. When they were out of earshot, she said, "I take it you don't like hide-and-seek."

"I do not know." Esmond's cheeks reddened. "I have never played it."

Virgie could scarcely believe her ears. "You never played it when you were little?"

Esmond looked down sadly at his polished riding boots. "Mama never allowed me to play with other children."

That dreadful woman! No wonder he looked forward so to Max's visits. "Why not?"

Esmond's flush deepened.

Virgie said hastily, "Never mind. Here's how you play the game."

"Where will I find Miss Blair?" Max asked the butler.

So far, Max's quest to seduce her had been a resounding failure. However, Max suspected Virg would swallow her pique now that she knew he had the power to veto her marriage to Es. Once her anger cooled, she would try to charm him any way she could, erroneously thinking that would win his approval for the marriage.

"She has gone riding with His Grace."

"What?" Max asked in surprise. Es never willingly climbed on a horse.

"Miss Blair persuaded the duke to show her the estate," Jenkins said tonelessly.

Why the hell had she done that? Given all of her galloping about, Virg surely must know the estate better than Es by now. So why had she asked him?

Perhaps Max was not the only one with seduction in mind. Did Virg intend to seduce Es in some quiet, wooded spot in the park, which offered many places for a tryst?

That thought eased Max's conscience a little. In seducing her, he would only be turning her own game back against her.

It was no more than she deserved.

Max rode in the direction Es and Virg had gone but found no sign of them in the park, even though he checked every romantic bower that he had ever discovered there.

Frustrated, he left the park behind and rode past rolling green pastures, newly harvested fields, and neat cottages where the estate's tenants lived. In a few of the fields, men were still finishing up the harvest, racing against a sky that grew more threatening by the minute.

Twice he passed men walking along the road, whom he greeted by name. Like his grandfather before him, Max knew every one of the estate's tenants and their families.

At last, Max sighted the two mares Virg and Es had been riding tethered to the gate of Joe and Nellie Simpkins' whitewashed cottage.

He stopped by his quarry's horses and tied his

own mount next to the mares. What the hell was Virg up to now?

Walking toward the house, he heard children's shouts coming from behind the dwelling. Max recalled the Simpkins had four children, one still a babe in arms.

The upper half of the cottage's Dutch door was open. Peering inside, Max saw no one. The adults must be behind the house with the children.

As he went around the cottage, he heard Virg counting loudly and slowly, "Three, four, five . . ."

She and Nellie Simpkins stood in the backyard, their backs to him, watching a game of hide-and-seek in progress. Max stopped behind them, wondering where Es was.

The game's "it" was a small boy, too young to know how to count. He covered his eyes with his hands and leaned his head against the trunk of an English elm while Virg counted for him.

"Ten," she cried. "Here I come, ready or not."

The child dropped his hands from his eyes and ran from the tree trunk.

He tried to catch a girl of perhaps six, but she easily eluded him and touched the trunk of the elm. So did another girl, a couple of years younger than the first.

Max thought the little boy would be "it" again.

Then Es popped up from behind a bush near the back fence. He ran toward the elm so slowly that the little fellow had no trouble tagging him.

"You's it!" the boy shouted at the duke, clapping his hands.

Seeing a grown man—especially the titular head

of the Chartwell family—playing a game for small children dismayed Max.

Damn it all, a duke did not forsake his dignity like that. Although Max was pleased to see Es out among his people, playing games with their children was carrying sociability too far.

"Your husband is so good with children," Nellie Simpkins said to Virg.

Was she already passing herself off as Es's wife? That was too much for Max's frayed temper.

"He is not her husband, Mrs. Simpkins," Max said with such fierce emphasis that both women turned and stared at him. *And he never will be.*

"My lord!" Mrs. Simpkins exclaimed, clearly flustered and confused by Max's anger. "What be wrong?"

He gestured toward Es. "He is not this woman's husband. He is His Grace, the duke of Penrose."

Mrs. Simpkins gaped at Max. "My lord, you're hoaxing me."

"No, I am not."

Looking horrified, she opened her mouth, but no sound emerged.

The duke saw his cousin and hurried to him. Max could not remember ever having seen Es look so happy and excited.

"Why, Max, I did not expect to see you here."

Max nodded toward the children, who had suspended their play to watch the grown-ups. "I am happy, Your Grace, that you are getting to know your tenants," he said more coolly than he intended.

The brightness faded from Es's face. "Why are you angry at me, Max?"

"I am not angry at you. Why does Your Grace think I am?"

"You have never addressed me so formally before."

"But we have always been in a family setting, where informality is permissible."

"Max, do you know Mrs. Simpkins?" Virg interjected.

"I have known Nellie since the day she became Mrs. Simpkins." Max smiled at the befuddled woman. "Grandfather and I attended her wedding."

"You did?" Es exclaimed in surprise.

"And you both danced with me." Mrs. Simpkins glowed proudly at the memory.

"And a fine dancer you were."

Thinking Max would inherit Penrose, his grandfather had trained him to carry on the practices that had made the old duke's tenants both respect and revere him.

Foremost among these had been his genuine interest in his tenants, considering them all part of Castle Penrose's family and himself its patriarch. He had never missed a wedding or a funeral, sharing his dependents' happiness and sorrow, and he had always taken Max with him.

Grandfather had known everything that occurred on the estate, and as long as Max was responsible for it, he would, too. One of Grigsby's most important duties was to keep Max informed.

"I understand you have a fourth child now, Nellie, a second son named Danny," Max said.

"Aye, m'lord," Nellie said, clearly pleased that Max knew of her baby's birth and his name.

Virg's head swiveled, and she looked at Max as

though she suspected him of fathering the baby.

Well, she was wrong. Max was not one of those careless, irresponsible aristocrats who spread their seed among their tenants and servants.

Nellie turned reproachful eyes on Virg. "Why didn't you tell me him was the duke 'stead of lettin' me think him were yer husband and lettin' me say . . ."

She clamped her mouth shut in mid-sentence and cast a frightened glance toward Max and Es.

"I thought you'd be more comfortable having the duke play with your children if you did not know who he was," Virg said. "He so enjoyed it. Didn't you, Your Grace?"

"Indeed, I did," Es assured Nellie. "I hope you will let me visit again."

For a moment, Nellie could not seem to find her voice. Then she blurted, "Anytime Yer Grace wants to, yer most welcome." She dropped an awkward curtsy to him.

"Thank you," Es said.

Max consulted his watch and was dismayed at how late it was. "We must return to the castle, or we will be late for dinner. I do not advise that with Aunt Elizabeth there."

Es took Virg's arm, and they followed Max to their horses.

When Max tried to help her mount, she pulled away from him. "I do not require your assistance, my lord."

"Let me help you, Virgie," Es said eagerly.

"Certainly."

Max swore under his breath. Was the damned vixen trying to play him and his cousin against each other? Max turned his mount toward the castle, and Es fell in beside him. Virg, however, held her mare back.

"Come, Virg, we must get back to the castle."

"I prefer to ride back alone."

The glint in her eyes told Max she objected to his company, not his cousin's. "Fine, do as you please, Virg."

"But—" Es started to protest.

Max cut him off. "Do not try to change a woman's mind when it is made up, Es. It is a futile task. Come."

"Please, Your Grace, go with your cousin." She gave Es an entreating smile.

He heeded her plea and went with Max.

In deference to Es's nervousness on a horse, Max set a slow pace for their ride to the castle.

"I did not know you were so fond of hide-and-seek that you still liked to play it."

"I never played the game before today. When I was little, Mama would not permit me to play with other children."

Max turned his head and stared in astonishment at his cousin. "Why not?"

"She said I was too frail to be out of doors and that the children where we lived were all beneath us and not worthy to associate with us."

Max was horrified at how terribly circumscribed his cousin's childhood had been. No wonder he was so shy and uncertain of himself. When their grandfather had banished Daphne from Penrose, he should never have allowed her to take Es with her.

"What a marvelous day it has been," Es burst out, his face glowing.

"Why?" Max inquired. "Because you finally played hide-and-seek?"

"No, although that was great fun." Es smiled bashfully. "I confess I have always avoided visiting my tenants because I did not know what to say to them. I had no difficulty today, though, thanks to Virgie. She made it easy for me."

"How did she do that?"

And what the hell were Virg's true motives in doing so? Was she trying to make the countryside think that she and the duke were already betrothed?

"She suggested questions to ask them. And if all else failed, she said I could talk about the weather." Es beamed proudly. "But I did not have to resort to that."

"Good for you."

"Max, I want to meet all my tenants."

And past time it was for Es to do so. Although Max questioned Virg's motives, he had to applaud the results.

"Perhaps I can persuade Virgie to ride with me again tomorrow so I can talk to more of the people."

"Oh, I am certain you will persuade her, but even if she refuses to accompany you, you should go anyway."

"By myself?" Es looked as though Max had suggested he walk alone through a black cavern filled with murderous monsters.

"If she declines your invitation, I will go with you."

"Would you? Oh, Max, I would like that."

So would Max, although he had no doubt that Virg would be the one to accompany Es.

But maybe he would go along, too.

Chapter 12

When Virgie returned alone to the castle, she met Isabel in the hall. The poor girl's dowdy, gray gown was even uglier than the one she had worn the previous night.

"You mustn't wear that gown again, Isabel. It isn't in the least becoming."

Isabel's mouth turned down sadly. "But it is no worse than my other two."

"What color are they?"

"Gray."

"You have only three gowns, and they are all gray? You must love the color."

Isabel shuddered. "I hate it! But a lady's companion is not permitted to call attention to herself."

"Thank heaven, we're almost the same size. You can wear some of my gowns. You are a little bigger than I am, so we may have to alter them."

"Oh, I could not allow that," Isabel protested.

156

"Yes, you can. You must win the duke's attention and admiration, and we must do everything we can to ensure that you do."

Hope shone in Isabel's soft brown eyes. Her quiet looks would require enhancing, too, but Virgie could easily take care of that. "Come to my room, and we'll find a gown for you to wear to dinner."

"You are much too kind, but it would be a waste." Isabel's courage was clearly faltering. "His Grace will not even notice me."

"Oh yes, he will, I promise you! What fun this will be."

An hour later in Virgie's bedroom, she stepped back and admired the transformation she had wrought in Isabel. Virgie had not yet permitted the girl to see herself in the mirror. "Now you can look."

Isabel hurried to a full-length mirror in a mahogany stand. When she saw her reflection in the glass, she gasped. "Why, I scarcely recognize myself."

Virgie had taken the girl's hair from the unbecoming knot at the back of her head and arranged it in an intricate style atop her head, with soft brown tendrils about her face.

After that, Virgie had touched Isabel's cheeks and lips with a little color that called attention to her soft brown eyes and elegant cheekbones.

The gown of emerald green velvet that she had loaned Isabel was simple but elegant. It was high necked, with a bow around the collar, but the fitted bodice emphasized the girl's slender curves. The gown's color accentuated her pale, flawless complexion.

Isabel's excitement at how she looked faded into nervousness. "I do not know what Her Grace will say when she sees me."

"She will say you are beautiful, and you are." Virgie prayed that the dowager would not be so cruel as to demand Isabel wash her face, pull back her hair, and change into one of her ugly gray gowns. "The duke will not be able to resist you, Belle."

Isabel started at Virgie's using the diminutive of her name.

"May I call you Belle?" Virgie asked. "It fits you very well. Don't you like it?"

"Oh, I like it very much, but only my mother ever called me that." She smiled shyly at Virgie. "I must go back to Her Grace. She will be most upset if I make her late to dinner."

Anxious to see the reaction of the men, especially Esmond, when Belle made her appearance, Virgie dressed quickly and hurried down to the withdrawing room. She hoped that Esmond would be there, and he was.

So was Max. He immediately came up to her. Placing his hand on her arm, he caressed her arm gently, almost imperceptibly, as he asked, "Would you like me to escort you into dinner tonight, Virg?"

Yes. NO! Reminding herself what kind of man he was, she pulled her arm away, and said in the most disdainful tone she could muster, "No, thank you."

His hand dropped to his side and his smile lost its warmth, no longer reaching his hard, gray eyes. "Why not?"

"I prefer other company."

"I see," he said sardonically. "As you Americans

say, 'you have bigger fish to fry tonight'?"

"What are you—" She broke off at the sound of a cane tapping on the threshold, signaling the arrival of the dowager and her companion. Virgie craned her neck to see Belle through the doorway. She still looked as she had when she'd left Virgie's room. Thank heavens, the dowager had not made Belle change.

Virgie turned so she could observe Esmond's face. The young duke blinked in surprise and then confusion at the new Belle.

Even Max was clearly taken aback, but he recovered first. "Isabel, I have never seen you look lovelier than you do tonight."

She fairly glowed at his compliment. "Thank you, my lord."

"So it is you, Isabel," Esmond said. "I did not recognize you at first."

The glow vanished from Belle's face like a bright lamp suddenly extinguished.

Virgie longed to give Esmond a good, swift kick. All that saved his ducal backside was the look of dazzled wonder in his eyes as he gazed at Belle.

"I can scarcely comprehend how different you look tonight, Isabel," he said. "Max is right. You are positively lovely."

"Yes, isn't she," Virgie said quickly. "You truly are beautiful, Belle."

Max watched Virgie with narrowed eyes and a baffled expression.

When the dowager began discussing some bit of Chartwell family history, Virgie seized the opportunity to take Belle aside and ask her what the dowager's reaction had been to the "new" Isabel.

"She said I was far prettier than she had realized."
Belle smiled at the recollection.

The duke came up to them. "Shall we go riding
tomorrow afternoon, Virgie?"

"Yes. Won't you come with us, Isabel?"

"Oh, I could not. Her Grace—"

The dowager interrupted her. "Her Grace wishes
you to go, Isabel."

Belle smiled shyly. "Then I should love to do so."

Tomorrow Virgie would find some last-minute
reason for not going riding with Esmond and Isabel.

Daphne and the comte came in. Both of them
stared at Belle—Daphne with surprise, the comte
with undisguised lechery.

Only a second or two later, Rowena followed
them in. For the very first time since she had been
at the castle, she was on time for dinner. She cast
a venomous glance toward the dowager, who did
not deign to notice her.

When the clock struck, they promptly went in to
dinner. Esmond seated his great-aunt at his right,
then looked over at Virgie and Belle. "Please, will
you lovely ladies sit at my left again?"

"Certainly," Virgie replied and contrived to place
Belle between her and the duke.

"This is your chair," Belle protested in a low
voice.

"Don't be silly. Besides, I want to talk to the
comte." Virgie gave a silent prayer that God
wouldn't strike her dead for such an outrageous lie.
She could think of no one with whom she'd less
rather converse than the Frenchman.

Max studied Virgie with suspicion, while the
comte looked at her as though her sudden interest
was no more than he deserved.

As it turned out, she was too busy making sure that conversation did not lag between Esmond and Belle to pay the comte any attention. Whenever silence threatened, Virgie hastily asked the duke or Belle a question designed to keep the talk between them flowing.

And flow it did. By the time dessert was served, they were so engrossed in talking to each other that they had no need for Virgie's intervention. Nor did they seem to notice anyone else.

She was well pleased with the budding success of her scheme.

Max studied her with a baffled expression. His great-aunt also perused her with speculative eyes.

Tonight the dowager said nothing about leaving the men to their brandy, and everyone went together into the drawing room.

In the drafty hall, the duke guided Isabel to a corner, where they were soon deep in a private conversation. Virgie smiled in delight.

"What are you up to now, Virg?"

She jumped at Max's low, suspicious question very near to her ear.

She affected a look of pure innocence. "I don't know what you're talking about."

"Oh yes, you do."

"Well, since you seem to be omnipotent, you tell me."

He regarded her silently with narrowed gray eyes.

Virgie turned and walked away from him without a word.

A few moments later, she slipped out of the hall and went up to her bedchamber.

*   *   *

As Virgie sat at her dressing table, brushing out her hair before going to bed, Belle came to her room.

Virgie put down her brush and turned from the mirror. Belle dropped to her knees beside Virgie. "I came to thank you again for what you have done for me."

Virgie gripped Belle's hands in her own. "I think you will soon be betrothed to the duke. He's smart enough to recognize the perfect wife for him."

"If only the Chartwell family thought as you do, instead of thinking him stupid."

"Why do they think that?"

"They have never given him a chance to show them otherwise." Isabel's voice throbbed with the certainty of her conviction. "They hated his mother. After his father's death, the old duke banished her and Esmond from the castle. If only His Grace had kept Esmond here and trained him as he did Lord Chartwell, Esmond would be just as capable as his lordship is and able to take over the estate."

That confused Virgie. "But Esmond has taken it over. He is the duke."

Isabel's face puckered unhappily. "In name only."

"What do you mean?"

"Lord Chartwell controls all of the Penrose estate until Esmond is thirty-five. The duke cannot even marry without his cousin's consent."

"That's the most outrageous thing I've ever heard." Poor Esmond. Between his relatives' lack of trust and confidence in him and his mother's isolating and hog-tying him with her apron strings, of course he was uncertain of himself.

"You did not know that?" Isabel seemed surprised.

"No, and furthermore, I don't understand how it's possible. Esmond has reached his majority. I can't believe Max can legally deny him permission to marry."

"But he can, and I fear he will never permit me to marry Esmond when I have no dowry."

With a sinking heart, Virgie recalled what Max had said about Isabel's lack of dowry keeping her from marrying. Virgie hid her concern from Isabel behind a smile. "Let me worry about the dowry. Everything will work out fine, I promise you. Now get some sleep."

After the door closed behind Belle, Virgie tried to make sense of what she'd learned.

If what Belle had said was true, why had Daphne told Virgie that she feared for Esmond's safety should Max learn her son intended to marry?

That made no sense. All Max would have to do is refuse his permission, and Esmond could not marry. Chartwell would not have to resort to murder to prevent the duke from fathering a legitimate son.

Unless Max thought, as Virgie did, that the stipulation was open to legal challenge.

She longed to confront him immediately, but the hour was too late. Virgie would have to wait until morning.

Chapter 13

A t dawn, Max awoke from a dream in which he had been chasing Virg in her shameless "woollies" across the meadow where they had first met.

He'd had no more success with her in his dream than he had been having in reality. Even in his nocturnal fantasy, she was too fleet afoot for him to catch her.

His body ached with unrequited lust. He craved seeing the real Virg in her chaps more intensely than he had ever craved chocolate as a child.

She loved the dawn, so perhaps she was on her way down to the stable now.

That thought instantly propelled him out of bed. Max peered through the high, narrow slit, looking toward the stable. He caught only a brief glimpse of her woollies as she disappeared inside.

He pulled on his riding clothes in record time,

went outside, and took the path to the stable. It had rained hard during the night, and the leaves dripped with wet mementoes of the storm.

Dawn had painted the clouds on the eastern horizon gold and orange. Max inhaled deeply of the clean, wood-scented air. He found it so aromatic and refreshing that he drew in another long breath. Maybe, he thought grudgingly, Virg had a point. Dawn could be beautiful.

At the stable, Max found no one, not even Pauley, the stableboy whose job it was to be there. The boy's absence annoyed Max almost as much as not finding Virg there in her woollies.

Wherever she had gone, she had not done so on Black Lightning. The stallion was still in his stall.

He went through the door on the opposite side of the stable, looking for Pauley. Max heard noise coming from behind the hedgerow that hid the corral used to segregate difficult horses and ran through the opening in the thick tangled bushes. Vesuvius was snorting and pawing the ground in the corral.

And there, in the very middle of the pen, calmly stood Virg with her back to the angry horse.

Max's heart stopped beating. What was she doing now?

Getting herself killed, that's what. Again!

His heart resumed beating erratically. He would have vaulted the fence, but it was too high, and he had to take the time to open the gate and enter that way.

Max had never known such a reckless woman. By God, if he managed to get her out alive, he was going to lock her in the empty cage next to Lionel's.

The noise of the gate slamming after Max alerted

the stallion to his presence. If Vesuvius had been angry before, it was nothing to what he was now. He snorted and reared wildly.

Virg whirled angrily on Max. "What are you trying to do, get me killed?"

"No, damn it, to save you from getting *yourself* killed!"

He grabbed her and tried to pull her toward the gate, but she jerked away from him.

Damned female was as contrary as Vesuvius.

"Get out of here," she cried. "You're upsetting Vesuvius."

"And you, Virg, are upsetting me." Max dodged the stallion's flailing hoofs and backed away. "What the hell do you think you're doing in here?"

"Taming him."

"You idiot!" he cried, masking with derision his fear for her life—and, yes, his affection for her, which baffled him.

Vesuvius bolted for the fence and galloped around and around its inside perimeter at a speed that would surely win the Derby.

"Don't you know anything about horses?" she countered.

Max prayed for patience. "That is not how you break a horse."

"I do not *break* horses." Her words rang with disgust. "That's a barbaric practice."

"Well, maybe you should try it before this one kills you."

"He'd have been fine if you hadn't butted in and upset him."

Max swept her up in his arms, grumbling, "I wish

to hell you would add the phrase 'thank you' to your limited vocabulary."

He wished, too, that her lovely body didn't feel so seductively small, soft, and enticing against his own.

When Max headed toward the gate, Virgie began struggling to free herself, and it was all he could do to hang on to her.

"Dammit, Max, put me down! I thought you were a man of your word."

That stung. Max prided himself on being just that. "I am," he said through clenched jaw.

"No, you're not. You said you wouldn't try to save me again, and now you are."

He looked at Vesuvius. He was still circling the fence and posing no danger to either Virgie or Max.

"How terrible of me! What a cad I am!" Max dumped her unceremoniously on her feet. "Very well, save yourself."

Belatedly, he noticed Pauley and two other stable hands perched on the corral fence, watching the spectacle. As he stalked toward the gate, they scrambled down and nearly tumbled over each other in their haste to open it for him.

Once outside the fence, Max turned to the three stable hands. "If any one of you permits Miss Blair in there again or in any other place where Vesuvius is, your employment at this estate will terminate instantly."

This statement—as Max had anticipated it would—brought her running out of the corral after him.

Before she could speak, he said, "You are not to go in that corral again, Virg. That is an order."

Her aquamarine eyes sizzled with anger. "I don't take orders from you! I'm going to tame Vesuvius."

"Like hell you are." He turned back to the gaping stable hands. "I will tell Mr. Grigsby what I just told you about the condition of your employment here."

She put her hands on her hips and glared at him. "They should not be punished for what I do! That's not fair!"

He returned her glare. "Apparently it has escaped your notice, Virg, that life is not fair."

"Very true—especially in England if one is not born a male aristocrat like you. You consider it your birthright to order everyone else around."

"That blasted tongue of yours is a lethal weapon," Max growled.

"Unfortunately, *you* don't seem to be wounded. However, I *thank you* for the lovely compliment."

"You are very welcome," he retorted through his teeth. Why the hell did she always regard his insults as compliments?

Max took Virg's arm firmly in his own. She tried to pull away, but he held her fast. She glowered at him so hotly it was a wonder her eyeballs didn't melt.

"What do you think you're doing now?" she demanded.

"I am taking you back to the castle with me, so I can talk to Grigsby."

"You don't need me for that."

"No, but I will know you are not getting into more trouble."

Virg tried to pull her arm from Max's hold again. "I won't go with you."

He promptly hoisted her into his arms again. She was so light that he wondered if she weighed even a hundred pounds.

"No, dammit, put me down! I'll walk."

"I thought so." He dropped her on her feet.

Her decision to walk did not surprise Max, but it mightily disappointed him. Never mind that he wanted to throttle her for putting herself in danger and frightening him half to death—he still ached to hold her tempting body against his own.

The mere thought had such a pronounced effect on him that he was thankful she struck out ahead of him, moving with her rapid, no-nonsense stride along the path through the grove of English oaks.

Max followed a half dozen paces behind her, mesmerized by the rhythmic sway of her hips above those woollies.

They walked like that for several yards before Virg turned to face him so abruptly that he nearly stumbled into her. He took a step backward, and his foot snagged in a small forked branch that had fallen to the ground.

"I want to ask you a question, my lord."

Max untangled his foot from the branch. "Yes?"

"Isabel Lake told me that you control Penrose, that you are the duke in all but title, and that you can veto Esmond's marrying if the match does not please you. Is that true?"

"Certainly, it is true," Max said impatiently. Daphne had already told her that. "Why are you asking that now?"

"Because I don't understand why, if you have the power to keep Esmond from marrying, you would kill him to prevent his doing so."

For a moment, Max thought he must have misheard her. "What the devil are you insinuating? Clearly, it has escaped your notice that I am very fond of Es. Why the hell would I want to kill him?"

"But you admitted to me that's what you want to do."

"I did *what*? You are out of your mind!"

"No, after Lady Daphne told me you would kill Esmond to prevent him from marrying and fathering a legitimate child, you insisted that what she'd said was true."

"Daphne told you that I would murder her son?" Much agitated, Max ran his fingers through his thick black hair. "Christ, I cannot believe this!"

"I couldn't either," Virg confessed, "but you told me to believe it, that it was true."

Max was so enraged that he grabbed up the fallen limb that had caught his foot and snapped it in two. Too bad the branch was not Es's mother. "If I murder anyone, it will be that lying witch Daphne."

"Then why did you tell me to believe her?"

"Because I thought she told you the truth. I should have known better than to expect that from her."

Max angrily tossed away the two halves of the broken limb.

"What is the truth?" Virg asked.

"Daphne fears me because I must approve all her son's expenditures, including the foolish, extravagant ones she wants for herself. I can also prevent him from marrying if I do not approve of his choice of wife."

"Who gave you that power?"

"My grandfather." A drop of water fell from an

oak leaf overhead onto her cheek, and Max could not resist wiping it from her soft skin.

She absently brought her own hand up to touch lingeringly the spot where his fingertip had brushed away the drop. "Why?"

"It is a long story."

Virg smiled and sank down on the thick trunk of a recently felled oak. She patted the bark next to where she sat. "Then sit here and tell it to me."

He settled beside her on the log. Her scent of orange blossoms perfumed the air around him, and he breathed deeply of it. Her dark hair, as willful as she was, had escaped its restraints, and teased at her cheeks.

Max longed to put his arm around her and smooth back the hair from her face with his other hand, but he reluctantly restrained himself.

"Daphne was the second wife of Es's father," Max began. "He was married to his first wife for nearly twenty years, and they had no children."

"So your grandfather thought his eldest son would die childless."

"Yes. He and the rest of the family assumed that I would be his heir. After my parents were killed, he raised me, all the while training me to take over his duties."

Max picked up a long twig and began drawing absently in the leaves and dirt on the ground in front of him. The quiet lent an air of intimacy to the secluded pathway—intimacy that could be used for other than conversation. Intimacy for which he longed. He tried to push that thought from his mind—and failed.

"But then Uncle Albert's first wife died," Max

continued. "He met Daphne, who was determined to be the next duchess of Penrose. She wasted no time in getting my uncle to marry her over the strenuous objections of Grandfather and everyone else in the family. Esmond was born when I was thirteen."

"And cost you the dukedom. You must have been terribly upset."

"Not I. No longer being the heir allowed me to lead the life I wanted."

"As a secret agent?"

He spun around to look at her beside him. "How the hell do you know about that?"

"I inquired how you had earned your title."

"I might have known. Promise me you will keep that to yourself."

"I will. Do you miss that life now?"

"Not as much as I thought I would. It is a young man's game."

"And you are so old," she teased. "So you truly were not upset to no longer be the heir?"

"No, but Grandfather was. He continued to train me as though I were still his heir. My cousin was a frail child, much plagued by ill health. Grandfather was certain Es would die before he reached adulthood, and I would inherit the estate after all."

Virg listened intently to him, her small, slim fingers absently toying with a leafy frond on a fern growing beside the downed trunk.

Max wished her lovely little hands were on him instead of that damned plant.

"Why did your grandfather exile his heir to Cornwall?"

"Actually, it was Daphne he banished, and for good reason." Max forced his gaze from Virg's hands and resumed drawing aimlessly on the ground with his stick. "But Grandfather allowed her to take Es with her."

"What was your grandfather's 'good reason'?"

"My uncle hid from him Daphne's wildly extravagant expenditures that had put him deeply in debt. When Uncle Albert died unexpectedly, all of the worried creditors descended on Grandfather, insisting he pay Daphne's exorbitant debts."

"Did he?"

"Yes, but he announced publicly that he would not pay another farthing of any new debt she incurred."

Max threw away the stick he'd been using to draw on the ground. It landed with a soft thud on a bed of leaf mold beneath a tree, startling a sparrow from one of the upper branches. Max watched as the sparrow disappeared above the trees. "That cut off Daphne's credit."

"But not her extravagant tastes?"

"No, and to get what she wanted, she resorted to the tactics that had worked so well on her husband—tears and temper tantrums."

"I gather they did not work on your grandfather?"

"Oh, they worked," Max said wryly, "but not in the way she intended. He soon could not stand the sight of her and sent her away."

"I've had the misfortune of seeing two of her tantrums." Virg's voice echoed the sympathy in her expression, and she shuddered. "I don't understand, though, why he gave you so much control over the duke?"

Max sighed. "Grandfather had no patience with Es. He considered him a pea-brain, incapable of running anything. In his will, Grandfather made clear that only primogeniture and the entail, which tied his hands, kept him from leaving his title and his entire estate to me. He had to settle for leaving only the unentailed portion, which was substantial, to me."

Virg picked up a brown acorn that had fallen to the ground and rubbed it lightly between her fingers. "What a horrid insult to Esmond."

"Yes, it was," Max agreed. "Grandfather stipulated all of the entailed property be placed in trust for Es with me as the sole trustee. In effect, Grandfather gave me control of the estate and made me my cousin's de facto guardian until he is thirty-five."

"That must have pleased you."

"Good God, no! How could you think that?" Max demanded hotly. "Es was twenty when Grandfather died and is only twenty-two now. I will be saddled with this unwanted responsibility for the next thirteen years. I have my own estate to look after, not that it is nearly the time-consuming responsibility that Penrose is."

Virg's forehead furrowed in thought. "Then why did you accept this burden your grandfather imposed on you?"

"To shield Es from his mother's extravagant and incessant demands. He is so amiable and good-hearted that he would not be able to withstand her pleas. He would indulge her until she ruined both him and the estate. I, however, am as deaf to her demands as Grandfather was, much to her fury."

Virg tossed the acorn back and forth from one

hand to the other as though she were weighing what Max was telling her.

"Considering what Daphne must subject you to, you must hate to come here."

He gave Virg a surprised, appreciative smile. "You are very perceptive."

"Why, thank you."

This was the first time she had accepted either a compliment—or an insult—as he intended it. Her glowing smile drew Max's attention to her lips, and once again he had the damndest time restraining himself from kissing her.

"Your grandfather was wise to require your approval of expenditures, but he was dead wrong in his estimation of Esmond as an incapable pea brain." Virg tossed the acorn away. "The duke's not stupid."

"No, he is not, but my grandfather did not spend enough time with him to discover that. Why do you look so surprised? I told you I am very fond of Es."

"If you are, why, when I asked, wouldn't you help to free him from his mother's apron strings?"

"Why should I? So you can then tie him to yours?"

"No! Why would I want to do that?"

"So he will marry you."

"That's ridiculous. What a terrible thing to say."

The reproach and hurt in Virg's aquamarine eyes made Max want to wrap her in his arms and comfort her. He steeled himself against his softer inclinations. Were her emotions real or feigned?

"The truth is sometimes terrible, Virg," he said coolly.

"Well, that's *not* the truth! How can you think I want to marry Esmond?"

"It is easier than you think."

"Why on earth would I want him to marry me, when I don't love him?"

"Because you would love to be a duchess."

She looked at him as though he had escaped from Bedlam. "I can't think of anything I'd *less* rather be!"

"Then why did you bribe his mother to convince him to marry you?"

Chapter 14

$$\sim\!\!\!\bigcirc\!\!\!\bigcirc\!\!\!\sim$$

"**W**hat!" Virgie cried, horrified. "Tell me you're teasing me."

"No, I have never been so serious in my life." Max's grim expression confirmed his words.

"You think I . . . I can't believe it." She jumped up from the trunk of the fallen oak and began pacing back and forth. After three or four turns, she stopped abruptly in front of Max and glared down at him.

"I did no such thing! What kind of terrible person do you think I am? I would not bribe anyone for any reason, least of all to make a man I don't love marry me."

His gaze met hers unflinchingly, and she saw a fleeting sadness in his, as though he would like to believe her but could not.

She started to pace again, then stopped and gave

him a murderous look. "You're the one who's stark, raving mad."

If anything, Max's face turned grimmer. "I know you do not love Es, but that has rarely stopped an ambitious woman from marrying a rich and titled man."

"I told you I'd never marry a man I didn't love!"

"And you told Daphne your father would pay her a huge sum each month if she gets her son to marry you."

Virgie would have called Max a liar, but he clearly believed what he was saying was true.

"No, dammit, I did no such thing! Nor would my father ever, ever, *ever* agree to such an outrageous bargain."

"Would he not?" Max asked with deliberate irony. "I wish I could believe that."

"You would if you met my father." She resumed pacing, her boots sinking into the soft blanket of leaf mold beneath her feet.

"Then he had better inform his wife of that."

Dear God, Rowena! After nearly four months in England with her stepmother, Virg knew Rowena was fully capable of claiming her husband would do such an awful thing.

With growing dread, Virgie froze and faced Max. "On what, my lord, do you base the notion that Lady Albert was bribed?"

He jumped up from the log. "Hell's fire, it is not a notion, and you damned well know it."

He towered over her, but if he thought he could intimidate her, he had the wrong woman. She held her ground, even leaned forward to show him he could not scare her. "I know nothing of the sort."

"Rowena was overheard offering the bribe to the duke's mother. Greedy witch that Daphne is, she naturally accepted."

Virgie's stomach churned. She was thankful she had not yet eaten this morning, for at that moment, she would have lost it.

"Who supposedly overheard this?" she demanded hoarsely, terribly afraid that what Max claimed was true.

"I do not betray my sources."

"How do you know this mysterious source of yours is reliable?"

"He has proven himself to be so on many previous occasions."

And no doubt he would prove to be again this time. Damned Rowena! "I was certain she was trying to promote a match between Es and me, but I never imagined she would do anything as terrible as this."

Max watched her silently, his expression giving no clue to his thoughts.

"You said *I* told Daphne." Virgie's heart ached with the pain his allegation had inflicted on her. "How can you possibly think I would be a party to such an evil scheme?"

"Because you too bragged you were going to marry Es. You even ordered your wedding gown."

"I never did either one! I don't want to marry him. I want him to marry Isabel. Isn't that perfectly obvious?"

"The truth is sometimes more subtle than the obvious," Max said quietly.

"Not this time! Who told you I said I was going

to marry Es? That I had ordered my wedding gown? I want to confront the liar!"

"Grigsby related what you said when he asked you when you and the duke would be married."

Virgie's stomach somersaulted as she recalled that conversation. "Damn! He made me so angry with that knowing smirk of his! I decided to tell him what he wanted to hear. I said I would marry His Grace as soon as my conditions were met. Then I made up a list of impossible demands, including that Penrose Castle be demolished. But I never told him I'd ordered my wedding gown."

"He told me you wanted the castle destroyed."

"And you believed I was serious?" Her eyes narrowed scornfully. "How could you? I thought you were smarter than that."

She expected an angry, cutting retort from Max.

Instead he said quietly, "When it comes to you, Virg, I seem to be uncommonly stupid."

Her heart skipped a beat at that, and she looked up at him. Their gazes met and held in a way that took her breath away. She saw apology and admiration and something else—could it be affection?—in his eyes. For a moment, she thought—hoped—he would kiss her, but he disappointed her.

"You know what troubles me most, Virg? If you are not a party to the bribe, why the hell do you remain here with your stepmother? I know how much you dislike her, so it cannot be the pleasure of her company that keeps you here."

"I must stay. Too much is at stake."

"What is at stake if it is not marriage to the duke?"

"The thing I want most in the world. Eden Valley

in California that I told you about, the place where I want to live."

Max frowned. "I must be unusually witless today, but why does that valley you love in America keep you here in England? If anything, I would think it would send you back to your own country."

"It is a long story."

"Go ahead." He sank on the downed oak again and leaned back against the trunk of another oak that was still standing. "You listened to mine earlier. I have all the time in the world to hear yours now."

"I don't want to bore you," she said dubiously.

"I doubt it is possible for you to bore me, Virg, but please try. I promise to let you know if you succeed."

He patted the trunk beside him where she had been sitting earlier, and he smiled. "Come, sit and tell me."

She could not resist his crooked smile, and she sat down. If only he would put his arm around her, but he didn't.

Virgie picked up another acorn from the ground and absently squeezed it with her fingers. She had never tried to explain her father's child-rearing theories before, and she chose her words carefully.

"My father believes in making his children prove their mettle. After my three brothers and I came of age, he challenged us to do whatever was hardest for each of us for six months. If we succeed in sticking it out for a half year, he rewards us with whatever we most want."

"And what you find most difficult is to be with your stepmother? I can easily understand that."

"Not exactly, but close enough," Virgie said, unwilling to confess the truth.

"I'm not interested in close enough. Let me hear exactly."

She hesitated, nervously fingering the acorn.

"Come on, Virg," Max prodded. "What happened to that candid tongue of yours?"

"Well," she said slowly, "growing up, I was a terrible tomboy. My father's challenge to me was to be a lady for six months."

For a moment, Max looked at her incredulously. Then he threw his head back and laughed.

Virgie dropped the acorn on the ground. She would have preferred words, no matter how scathing, to his merriment. She bowed her head and stared down at her hands in her lap.

"I know you think I've failed miserably." Her voice quavered.

Max's hand, warm and large, instantly covered one of hers. Shivering at the gentleness of his touch, she looked up at him from beneath her lashes.

"Do not presume to read my mind, Virg."

His voice was low and husky, and a strange ache throbbed within her.

He kept her hand in his. "You are a much better lady than you are a mind reader."

Max bent his head and kissed her, his lips lightly brushing hers with a sweet tenderness that surprised and thrilled her. The warmth of his lips lingered on hers and stoked that aching within her.

It was nothing like other kisses she'd experienced. When Max lifted his head, disappointment stabbed her with surprising sharpness. She hadn't wanted the kiss to end.

He smiled, his gray eyes soft and smoky, and she lifted her mouth toward his, inviting another kiss. He put his arms around her and drew her into his embrace.

Once again, his lips covered hers, and their mouths melded in a long kiss that began almost teasingly and grew more intense as she returned it with the same fervency that he gave it.

When the kiss ended, she was breathless and aching for more.

Max, however, withdrew his arms and stood up. "I think we had better go back to the castle."

Virgie noticed his breathing sounded ragged too. She ignored the hand he had extended to help her up. "Could we not sit here a little longer?"

For the first time since she'd met him, Max—usually so decisive—appeared uncertain.

Finally, he said, "Very well." He sat down again on the log, but not as close to her as she would have liked.

"One thing puzzles me about your father's challenge, Virg. Why did you come to England? You could have been a lady in your own country."

"England was Rowena's doing. She told my father how much better and easier it would be for her to teach me to be a lady—"

Max snorted. "How could *she* teach *you*? A whorehouse madam is more of a lady than she is."

Virgie laughed. "Perhaps I will tell her that the next time she subjects me to a barrage of criticism. In her eyes, I can do no right. As I was saying, she convinced my father she should take me to England"—Virgie imitated Rowena's harsh, nasal accent—"'where manners are infinitely more refined and Virginia will be removed from her brothers' bad example.' "

"That sounds so much like your stepmother my ear hurts. Why does your accent and hers sound so different? I would swear you came from different countries."

"My mother came from Virginia, and she never entirely lost her southern accent. Not only were we very isolated at the ranch, but I loved her so much I wanted to be exactly like her, and I mimicked her speech. Rowena sounds like a typical New Yorker."

"Remind me never to visit New York. So you must remain in England for six months with your stepmother?"

Virgie swallowed the lump as big as an orange that rose in her throat. "I'm afraid so."

"How long have you been here?"

"Nearly four months. In her company, it seems like an eternity."

Max took one of Virgie's hands in his and squeezed it sympathetically. "I am certain it does."

They sat for a moment in companionable silence, his large, dark hand warming her smaller, pale one. Virgie had never felt so comfortable and content, so happy with a man before. She wished that he would kiss her again.

Instead he asked, "If you do not want to marry Es, why did you ask me to help him?"

"Because he desperately needs it. He needs an example of what a man should be."

"And I am?" He grinned, a teasing light in his eyes. "I am honored."

"You should be," she retorted in amusement. "As nearly as I can tell, Es's mother isolated him from most normal human contact as he was growing up. And his Chartwell relations have made it clear that they think he is stupid. He is not, although if one is told he is stupid often enough he comes to believe it even if it isn't true."

Max still held her hand, and she placed her other hand over his. "Please, Max, I think the duke will quickly learn to run this estate if only you will take the time to teach him."

Max was silent for a minute, clearly mulling over what she had said. "I think you are right, Virg."

She grinned at him. "What? You admit a woman—and an American one at that—is right?"

Max chuckled. "Shocking, is it not?"

"Please then, would you do that for your cousin?"

"Is that why you kissed me? To persuade me to do so?"

Max's question shattered the rapport that had blossomed between them.

"No!" She rose with ladylike dignity and headed for the castle, then turned and said, "Besides, you were the one who kissed me."

Chapter 15

~~∞~~

Max watched Virg stride away from him, her dark hair flying about her. She was gorgeous when she was in a snit.

"You kissed me back," he called after her to see whether that would stop her.

She kept walking. "Did not!"

"Did too!"

Virg did not bother to answer him this time.

Max jumped up from the log and went after her. "I see only one way to settle this argument."

Virg turned and waited for him to catch up with her. "What's that?"

"Do it again."

"No, thank you!"

Despite her reply, Max pulled her into his arms and kissed her anyway. After a second or two of halfhearted resistance, her ardor sparked, and they

186

were lost in a long, passionate kiss—to his great delight.

He loved the taste of her lips, loved the scent of orange blossoms that enveloped him, loved her soft, sweet body against his.

When the kiss ended, her aquamarine eyes were as warm and sparkling as a pristine tropical lake in the summertime. Her lips curved into a smile. "Yes, I believe you were right after all. Another kiss was the answer."

He laughed, and they walked hand in hand down the path, the camaraderie restored between them.

"Why do you want Es to marry Isabel?" Max asked.

"She will make him an excellent wife." *And she loves him.*

"What makes you think that?"

"You ask me that when you're the one who told me what a fine job she does running Belford Manor?"

Yes, Isabel did, and Max had no doubt she would run Castle Penrose with equal skill. Furthermore, having watched her and Es together, he thought they would deal very well together. "I never thought about it before, but I think you are right."

"Of course I am," she retorted with a mischievous smile.

"And modest too," he teased, tucking her arm beneath his own. He kept his pace to a saunter to prolong his time with her, and she fell into step with him instead of striding ahead.

"What about you, Virg? Do you think you can

make it another two and a half months in England, masquerading as a lady?"

Virg's chin tilted upward in proud determination. "I must. I want Eden Valley so much. Nor could I bear to be the first of my father's children to fail his challenge."

As they walked on, her shoulders suddenly slumped for a few seconds, then she pulled them straight again.

Max stopped, turned to her, and put his hands gently on her arms. "What is it, Virg?"

At first, he did not think she would tell him, but then she confessed, "I am terribly afraid that even if I succeed in being a perfect lady, it won't matter. I know now what a spiteful liar Rowena is, and I'm afraid, no matter what I do, she'll tell my father that I failed."

Max suspected Virg was right, but he did not want to add to her worries. He squeezed her hand. "It is too early to convict your stepmother of that."

"I suppose," she said dubiously.

Max tried to divert her thoughts from Rowena. "What did your father ask of your brothers?"

"My oldest brother Leo was required to run my dad's mercantile store in San Francisco."

"That does not seem as though it would be such an unpleasant task."

"Except Leo loves horses and ranching more than anything except his wife and son. He despises cities, especially living in one, and wearing a suit and collar every day."

"What was his reward?"

"He's running the family ranch and will inherit it when my father dies."

A flock of large black crows flew overhead, beating their wings and delivering a raucous chorus of "caw, caw, caw."

Virg looked up at them. "Those are the biggest crows I have ever seen."

Max could barely hear what she said above the caws. "And the noisiest too. What was required of your second brother?"

"That he spend six months as a crew member on a yacht that was sailing to the Far East."

"That should have been his reward, not his challenge," Max observed dryly.

"Except that poor Mark could not even look at water without getting violently seasick."

"Did he survive the six months?"

"Better than anyone expected. He came back so enamored of the sea that now he manages Dad's shipping interests."

The wind was rising, blowing the leaves of the oaks and sending a miniature shower of drops cascading down on Virg and Max.

As he wiped them away with his handkerchief, he asked, "And your third brother?"

"Scott was the wild one, with a gunslinger's fast draw and a gift of gab that could con anyone out of anything. A real lady's man, too. Dad was very worried that he'd end up an outlaw. Scott spent his six months in a monastery, where the monks were not allowed to talk to each other."

Max burst out laughing. "Do not tell me he became a priest."

"No, a U.S. marshal."

"What is that?"

"A federal lawman."

"Your father sounds like a wise man. Why on earth did he marry Rowena? Surely not for love?"

"Yes and no."

Max raised a mocking eyebrow. "Why, Virg, are you equivocating? I did not think you knew how!"

"No, I'm not," she retorted, clearly insulted. "I'm answering your question as honestly as I can. When my father was very young, Rowena was his first love. I have seen a portrait of her then, and she was breathtakingly beautiful. You would not recognize her as the same woman now."

"But your father did not marry her then?" Max glanced up at the sky. The clouds were growing thicker and darker. At their slow pace, they might not reach the castle before the rain began. Yet he was so loathe to forfeit Virg's company sooner than he must that he did not lengthen his stride.

"No, Dad went away to college, intending to wed her after he finished school, but while he was gone, she rejected him for a man who had more money."

"Your father should have counted his blessings."

"Perhaps, but he was devastated. After he finished college, he left his native New York and went west, vowing to make himself so rich that Rowena would regret not marrying him."

"And he obviously succeeded. Your father must have discovered a remarkably rich vein of gold."

"Oh, he was never a miner. He reached California in the waning days of the gold rush and opened a store in San Francisco that was very successful."

"But he never forgot Rowena?"

"Oh, but he did. He fell wildly in love with my mother and married her. She was the daughter of a rancher who had come west from Virginia. I was named for the state where my mother was born."

A sharp gust of wind hit them, scattering golden oak leaves on them. One caught in Virg's hair, and Max gently plucked it off.

She looked at him with startled eyes.

He showed her the leaf. "Go on with your story."

"After my parents were married, Dad bought a large ranch in the foothills of the Sierra Nevada."

"Ah, yes, the real mountains, as opposed to our ersatz ones," Max said with a smile.

"My three older brothers and I spent most of our time growing up on the ranch. We were so happy— at least until I was twelve."

She sounded so wistful that Max's heart went out to her. "What happened then?"

"My mother died suddenly and unexpectedly. She came down with a terrible sore throat that turned into scarlet fever. We were all devastated, especially my father. By then both the ranch and his store were doing very well, and he parlayed the profits into other successful businesses, becoming far richer than even he'd once dreamed of being."

Max and Virg emerged from the oak wood. By now, the air was misty with suspended moisture.

"When did Rowena come back into the picture?"

"About eighteen months ago. Dad got a letter from her. She wrote that she was now widowed. Although they hadn't seen each other for thirty-four years, she professed that she had never forgotten him and she still loved him more than any other man." Virg's lips tightened. "What she loved was his wealth."

"But your father believed her?"

"Yes, I think because he wanted to. He had been

so lonely since my mother died. He never found a woman to replace her in his heart, and Rowena had been his first love. I think when she wrote him, he hoped that she would ease his pain and loneliness. He answered her letter, they continued to correspond, and he finally wrote proposing to her."

"Naturally she accepted."

"Of course. My mother used to say that when people grow old, their character defects often become their character."

"Is that what happened with Rowena?"

Virg nodded. "Money and status were always important to her, but now she is obsessed with them. When we went to New York for the wedding—although Dad never said anything—he was clearly horrified by the woman she'd become."

"Then why did he marry her?"

"My dad's a man of honor and integrity. He'd committed himself to marrying her, and he would not go back on his word, even though she had changed so much he no longer loved—or even recognized—her."

"Ah, yes, the dreams of youth. They are best buried and never resurrected."

They were crossing the drawbridge to the outer curtain gate house, and their footsteps sounded hollowly on the wood planking.

"I wager that by now your father regrets he did not cancel the wedding."

Virg stopped and faced him, challenge in her eyes. "Why? Because he no longer loved her? That from you, the man who would never marry a woman he loved?"

"I refuse to marry for love, but I would take care

to ascertain the character and temperament of the woman to whom I intended to shackle myself."

"What if you are surprised when the honeymoon is over? Like your Uncle Albert was?"

"But he proves my point. He married for love, and see what a disaster that was."

"Yes, but he married a woman who did not reciprocate his love. A couple should marry only when their love is mutual."

Virg resumed walking, and they passed through the outer curtain entry.

By the time they approached the steps of the castle, the misty moisture had become heavy sprinkles, and Max was surprised when she stopped again.

"Before we go into the castle, I have a favor to ask of you."

"What?" Max was always suspicious when a woman asked him for a favor.

"Will you promise to tell Daphne and Rowena that you will never, never, ever permit the duke to wed me?"

He could not help chuckling at the irony of her asking him to do that.

"With pleasure, Virg. With pleasure."

Chapter 16

A man of action, Max took Es out after breakfast that very morning to begin instructing him on running the estate. By early afternoon, Max judged he had given his cousin enough to absorb for one day, and they rode home.

Besides, Max had something else to do that afternoon. He had been considering its feasibility ever since learning that Virg had not known about her stepmother's bribe.

If what Virg had said about her father was true, he would be no happier than she was to learn of Rowena's bribery.

Nor did Blair sound as if he was the kind of man who would allow his wife to carry out such a scheme. No matter what his wife might promise, Daphne would never get the money.

Max would inform Virg's father of his wife's treachery, and not by letter, which could take weeks. Instead Max would ride to Ipswich, which had a telegraph station, and cable him.

But when the cousins returned to the castle, Jenkins told Max that the dowager duchess wanted to see him in the library.

He went there immediately. She was watching the play of light through the stained glass windows.

"Where have you been?" she asked when she saw him.

"Teaching Es what Grandfather should have taught him."

"How is your seduction of Miss Blair coming?"

"We were wrong about her, Aunt Elizabeth. She was not a party to the bribery."

"How can you be certain?"

"I accused her of bribing Daphne, and she was so shocked she clearly knew nothing about it. She also made me promise to tell both her stepmother and Daphne that I would never permit Es to marry her."

"What a scene that will be," Aunt Elizabeth said with relish. "I insist on being present. I do not understand, however, why Miss Blair does not want to marry the duke of Penrose."

"She intends to marry for love."

"And here I thought she was intelligent."

Max was a little surprised at how much that slur irritated him. "Miss Blair is very intelligent, make no mistake about that!"

His aunt gave him an odd look, and he could swear the corners of her mouth twitched as though she were fighting a smile.

He was anxious to leave for Ipswich, and he stood up. "I must go now. I have an errand to do."

She waved her hand in dismissal. "Go."

Max went immediately to his chamber, where he wrote out the message he wanted to send to Virg's father.

When he finished the cable he decided he might as well send a second message to France to check on the "Comte" de Beaucaire's credentials. He wrote that out too, then departed on horseback for Ipswich.

When he reached the town an hour later, he went at once to the telegraph office on a side street, two doors down from the corner of High Street.

The office, a narrow cubicle, was squeezed between a large tack shop on the corner offering everything an equestrian could possibly want and a bakery with petit fours and an elaborately frosted gateau decorating its window.

Max handed the telegraph clerk, a scrawny, gray-haired man with a squint, the two messages he had written out. The one to France was on top.

The clerk looked at the first without comment, but he frowned when he saw the second.

"It is very long, my lord."

"I know. I wrote it."

"It will be very expensive."

"No matter. I will be happy to pay whatever it costs."

"Yes, sir." He looked down at the message again. "It is to go to Mr. Leonard"—the clerk paused, clearly surprised—"*Blair*?"

"Correct." The man acted as though Blair were a difficult name. "I do not have his exact address in New York. Will that be a problem?"

"No, my lord."

"Are you certain?"

"Very, my lord."

Apparently, the clerk was more knowledgeable about America's richest men than Max was.

When he left the telegraph office, delicious odors wafted from the bakery next door. Giving in to temptation, Max bought himself a petit four covered with chocolate glaze.

As he left the bakery, a flash of royal blue farther down the side street caught his eye. A woman had come out of a shop in the next block and was walking toward High Street.

Her bright walking dress and quick, determined stride told Max that she must be Virg.

What was she doing in Ipswich? And how had she gotten here?

Max frowned. Into what trouble would she plunge herself here? Although he could think of none, trouble was her middle name.

Then he noticed that Virg was not alone, although no doubt she thought she was.

A burly man was skulking along behind her. A second later he grabbed Virg from behind and tried to rip her reticule from her.

Max dropped the petit four on the street and broke into a run toward them.

Before he reached them, though, an agonized howl rang out. The robber sailed through the air over Virg and landed hard on the street.

When Max ran up to them, the man still lay there, gripping his groin in agony. Virg stood over him, pointing the derringer Max remembered all too well at the footpad's heart.

She told the robber crisply, "Don't even think about getting up."

The footpad froze, still clutching himself, but trying not to move.

Since Max was not the derringer's target this time, he could enjoy the scene, especially since the thief was getting no more than he deserved.

Max told the footpad, "Do exactly as she tells you. She is a crack shot, and I assure you she will not hesitate to pull the trigger on you. Do not make the fatal mistake of thinking she suffers from any of the usual feminine qualms or weaknesses. I can assure you she does not."

He stole a sideways glance to see her reaction.

She gave him a brilliant smile. "Thank you, Max, for the compliment."

He looked at the burly man on the ground. "By the way, her favorite target is the part of you that you are presently so vulgarly hugging."

Clearly terrified, the man clutched even more desperately.

Max turned to Virg. "What did you do to him?"

"Stopped him from stealing my reticule," she said calmly. "I'll guard him while you fetch the police or sheriff or constable or whatever it is you call your cops here."

"W-w-w-ouldn't the mister rather guard me," the footpad stammered nervously.

"I will do whatever you wish, Virg." The scoundrel deserved to sweat a little.

"I'll guard him."

"If it's all the same to you, mum, me'd rather have the mister guard me." The footpad's voice quavered. "Meaning no offense, mum."

A crowd was gathering around them and growing larger by the minute. After all, it was not every day—or, for that matter, *any* day—that a man lay in broad daylight on an Ipswich street, clutching his privates, while a lady, expensively dressed in the first stare of fashion, stood over him, pointing a gun at him.

More people hurried toward the scene, including Constable Twitchel. Max glanced down at the footpad. The scoundrel also recognized Twitchel and appeared delighted, no doubt for the first time in his life, to see the constable.

Hurrying up to Max, the constable asked, "My lord, what happened?"

"This man attempted to relieve my lady friend of her purse."

Virg raised one of her charming eyebrows. "*Lady* friend?"

"A mere figure of speech," Max muttered to her.

"And then what happened?" the constable asked.

"Good question." Max was still uncertain himself what the answer was. "My friend here likes to handle such matters in unusual ways. You will have to ask her."

The constable looked inquiringly at Virg.

"I simply protected myself and my reticule."

"Protected, me arse," the footpad grumbled from the ground. "Damned near killed me, ye did."

"On your feet," the constable ordered. "Off to the gaol, you go."

The footpad staggered to his feet. After an apprehensive glance at Virg, he went docilely with the constable.

Max took Virg's arm and guided her through the

gaping crowd. He finally appreciated just how lucky he was to have survived whole and unmaimed his attempts to save Virg. She was a greater threat to a man's well-being than he could have imagined.

And to his heart.

When they reached the edge of the crowd, Max asked under his breath, "What did you do to the footpad? I have never seen anything like that."

"I merely used a self-defense maneuver to protect myself."

"If that's what you do to defend yourself, Virg, I would hate to see you on the offensive. Where did you learn that—er, maneuver?"

"From an Oriental man in San Francisco. He taught me a number of other maneuvers too."

"Thanks for the warning!"

"Would you like me to demonstrate them for you?"

"On me? No, thank you," Max said with great politeness.

Her eyes gleamed with amusement. "You might like to learn them."

"From you? I don't think so."

"Coward!"

"A man of my advanced age must maintain his dignity."

"Perhaps we should buy you a cane before we return to Penrose," Virg teased.

"I can manage to hobble without it."

They passed the bakery near the corner of High Street, and Max saw what little was left of his trampled petit four lying in the street.

"What brought you to Ipswich, Virg?"

She looked away. "I—I wanted to shop."

Max recognized evasion when he saw it. "For what?"

"Various things."

"Did you find them?"

"Yes. Some ornamental combs and a hat for Belle."

They turned on to High Street. "How did you get to Ipswich, Virg?"

"The coachman brought me in the coupe."

"Where is he, and why are you wandering the streets by yourself?"

"He was thirsty. I told him he could stay in the pub, and I would come for him when I was ready to go back. See, there's the coupe in front of the pub."

As they approached the conveyance, Virg said, "You must see what I bought. I never thought to find one in England."

"One what?"

"Saddle."

"I did not see you riding bareback at Penrose," he said dryly.

"But those were English saddles. This one is a real saddle." Virg threw open the coupe's door. "Look."

Taking up most of the seat was a large, oddly fashioned saddle. Of tooled leather, it had thick stirrups and a large knob sticking up from the front.

"Isn't it beautiful?" Virg breathed.

Max wished she would gaze at him with a quarter of the appreciation she was showering on that damned saddle. His chagrin prompted him to say, "What is that ridiculous knob at the front?"

Virg reached out and caressed the object in a way

that made an important part of Max's anatomy beg for similar attention.

"This is the saddle horn, which is one of the principal reasons that our western saddles are superior to yours."

Max was less interested in the saddle than in the coupe. It had only one seat inside, just wide enough for two. He would trail his horse behind the vehicle and enjoy a cozy ride inside with Virg. "Are you ready to return to Penrose?"

She nodded.

"I will collect the coachman." Max turned into the pub, hoping the man was still sober enough to drive them without incident.

After the pub door shut behind Max, Virgie climbed into the coupe. Her unexpected meeting with him in Ipswich disturbed her considerably more than her confrontation with the footpad.

Indeed, she had not yet fully recovered from her encounter with Max that morning in the oak wood, especially from the powerful effect of his kisses.

Virgie had avoided telling Max the real reason she had come to town. She had cabled her father, telling him about Rowena bribing the duke's mother in the hope he would order his wife home immediately.

Max emerged from the pub, and the coachman, still buttoning his coat, ran out behind him. While the coachman scrambled up on his perch, Max opened the coupe's door.

"I will tie my horse behind the coupe and ride with you," he announced to Virgie.

The thought of how snugly the two of them

would fit on the seat during the lengthy journey to Penrose unnerved her. So did the possibility he intended to continue what they had started that morning.

Even though her heart wanted that more than anything.

But her head told her she would be a damn fool to go down that path with a man who would not marry for love.

She hid her anxiety and uncertainty behind a cool voice. "I'm sorry, but my new saddle leaves no room for you."

"We will put it on the roof."

"No!" she cried so emphatically that he stared at her in surprise.

"Why not?"

Virgie forced herself to take a deep breath while she tried to come up with a reason.

"I'm afraid it will fall off, and I'll lose it." She was pleased—and a little surprised—at how calm and reasonable she sounded. "Or it will be ruined in the fall."

"It will be firmly tied down. It will not fall off."

Max reached for the saddle, but she grabbed the horn. "No, I refuse to take the chance."

Which was true, but the chance she was avoiding involved Max, not the saddle. She already cared too much for him, and she had to protect her heart.

He frowned at her, making no attempt to conceal his irritation. "You insist I ride my horse back?"

She nodded and then winced as he slammed the coupe's door shut.

A minute later, the conveyance jerked forward,

and she leaned her head back against the seat, trying to make sense of her roiling emotions.

Virgie had never been drawn to another man as strongly as she was to Max, had never been as happy and content as she was with him. The more she learned about him the more convinced she became that he was exactly the kind of strong man she had dreamed of meeting—and marrying.

But she would only marry a man whom she loved and who loved her in return.

Max had made it clear to her that love would have no place in his marriage. He cared only that his wife be a proper British lady from an aristocratic family of wealth and connections. An American like herself had nothing to offer that would tempt him into marriage.

Yet she was falling in love with him. And that was the biggest mistake she could make because he would only break her heart. Even though she knew that, she could not help herself. The more she was with him, the more she cared.

Her only hope of saving herself from heartbreak was to keep him at a distance and avoid him whenever possible.

And, she vowed, that's what she'd do.

That night, Max planned to keep his promise to Virg to tell her stepmother and Daphne that he would not permit Es to marry her. Daphne, however, was feeling unwell and did not come down to dinner.

So it was the night after his trip to Ipswich that he informed Daphne and Mrs. Blair that he and his aunt wished to meet with them in the withdrawing room off the refectory.

"I haven't the time," Mrs. Blair said.

"What nonsense," Aunt Elizabeth told her. "What else, pray tell, do you have to do? Nothing! Besides, it will be a very brief meeting."

As soon as the door closed on the four of them, Max said, "I know that Mrs. Blair has bribed you, Daphne, to convince your son to marry her step-daughter."

All color bleached from Daphne's face, and she looked as though she might faint.

Mrs. Blair, however, attacked. "I did no such thing! How dare you accuse me of such a thing?"

Max outlined the exact terms of the bribe, including the amount of money Daphne was to be paid each month.

He concluded by saying, "Perhaps you Americans do not call that a bribe, Mrs. Blair, but no one in England would consider it to be anything else."

She sneered at him. "And you can't do a thing about it."

"Oh, but I can, and I am. I forbid Es to marry your stepdaughter."

"You can't do that!"

"Oh, yes, he can," Aunt Elizabeth interjected. "Is that not true, Daphne?"

Es's mother, apparently so stricken that she could not find her voice, merely nodded her head in confirmation.

Max gave Mrs. Blair a nasty smile. "So you had better start looking for another duke whose title you can buy. This one is not for sale."

Chapter 17

Wh   hen Max and Es returned to the castle after
                    the day's lesson on managing the estate, the
sun was sinking low in the sky.

For the past two weeks, Max had taken his cousin
about the estate every day, instructing him and introducing him to his tenants. Prior to each meeting,
Max gave Es a brief history and description of the
tenant. By now, the duke had met all of them.

Es's innate amiability and kind heart were so ap-
parent that their longheld belief that he harbored no
interest in them or their problems quickly faded.

The duke was proving to be a far better student
than Max had expected, and he was gratified by his
cousin's progress and by Es's growing attachment
to Isabel, who clearly loved him.

What would it be like to have Virg look at him
the way Isabel gazed at Es? If only he could find

out. That seemed unlikely, though, the way Virg was acting toward him.

Since that day in Ipswich, she avoided Max whenever possible. If she could not, she was polite but cool to him.

Max wanted more kisses like the ones they had shared in the oak wood. Hell, he wanted more period, not the cold shoulder he was getting from her.

Beaucaire had become increasingly bold and overt the past few days in his attentions to Virg, and she was *not* avoiding him.

Max and Es turned their horses over to a groom waiting at the foot of the castle steps. For once, Max was eager to get inside the cool castle. After a string of chilly, often rainy days, the weather had turned unseasonably hot today.

Jenkins opened the great, iron-strapped door for them. As Max stepped over the threshold, he heard Daphne in one of her tantrums, loudly berating a servant. It was almost enough to make him plunge back into the heat.

"What happened?" he asked.

"Lady Albert is displeased about preparations for the shooting party." The butler's face was devoid of expression. "The guests arrive tomorrow."

Damn, Max had forgotten about the shooting party.

"Come, Max, we will go to my apartment at once," Es said, clearly anxious to get out of range of his mother's voice as quickly as he could.

Each afternoon, after they returned to the castle, Max accompanied Es to his rooms in the east wing to discuss estate problems, both real and hypothetical, and how best to deal with them.

As they walked up the stone staircase, Es said, "Jenkins told me you are leaving for London soon. Is that true?"

"Yes, I have a commitment there."

"Please," Es begged, "stay here through the shooting party."

"I will try." Max knew that Es, shy and uncertain of himself, did not want to face the guests alone, but Max was due in London before the party would end.

When they reached the duke's apartment, the air in the sitting room was so close and stuffy that Max asked if he could open a window or two.

"Please do," Es said. "I leave them open in the morning, but Mama insists the maids close them. She is so afraid that I might catch a chill."

And that she will lose her meal ticket.

Max crossed to the windows that looked down on the quadrangle around which the castle was built. He swung one of the windows open wide and leaned out to fill his lungs with fresh air.

The leaves on the paper-bark maple that grew on the quadrangle near the entrance to the west wing had turned to autumn crimson, attracting Max's attention.

He nearly tumbled out of the window.

The comte stood beside the maple, embracing and kissing a woman with a passion that was best left to the bedroom.

Her cloud of dark hair shone with glints of red from the sun that was about to set. Her hair, her petite size, and the bright lemon color of her gown assured him the woman was Virg.

An intense pain, as though he had been stabbed in the heart, staggered Max. For a moment, he stared in speechless shock at the scene beneath him.

Then a bolt of fury ripped through him. Virg had told him she did not like or trust the comte. But damn her, she liked and trusted him enough to kiss him passionately—and in public, at that. Max clenched his hands into fists and turned away from the window.

"What is it, Max?" Es asked in alarm. "You look as though you want to kill someone."

Max did, but he was not certain whether he wanted the victim to be the comte or Virg.

Both, he decided.

"It is nothing," Max lied. "Come, we must get to work."

Max opened the rent ledger, but he had trouble concentrating on it. How many people besides himself had witnessed Virg kissing the comte?

No lady would participate in such a spectacle in a quadrangle surrounded by windows where people were virtually certain to witness her brazen, amorous conduct.

Lady Priscilla would be horrified at the mere thought of such behavior.

On the quadrangle, Virgie struggled against Beaucaire's unwanted embrace, but he had such a stranglehold on her that she could scarcely breathe, let alone fight him off.

She'd been crossing the quadrangle, using it as a shortcut between the east and west wings of the castle. As she'd passed the maple tree, he'd stepped out from behind its cloud of scarlet leaves directly into her path. He's been so close that she could not stop herself from walking into him.

Before she could recover from her surprise, he'd grabbed her as if to prevent her from falling, even though she'd been in no danger of doing so.

His mouth fastened onto hers. His tongue jabbed at her lips, roughly seeking to plunder her mouth.

How different his kiss was from Max's.

And even more different was her reaction. She had loved Max's. The comte's sickened her.

She clenched her teeth together and tried to push him away, but he held her too tightly against him.

"Let me go," she hissed through her teeth.

He drew his mouth back a fraction from hers. "*Cherie*, let me show you how beautiful love can be."

"Damn you, I said let me go!"

He clearly did not consider her demand to be serious. He nibbled her earlobe, then whispered, "Let me take you to paradise, *cherie*."

The only paradise Virgie wanted to visit was Eden Valley.

And not with Beaucaire.

Max, perhaps.

But the Frenchman? Never.

"I know you want me as much as I want you," he murmured.

"I'll show you how much I want you, you insufferable Casanova!"

Although Virgie could not move her arms, she still had her legs. She raised the heel of her half boot over his instep and ground down hard on his foot. Then she tried to bring her knee up against his groin. Unfortunately, she was too close to him to do much damage.

Nevertheless, he let out a strangled yelp and released her.

Surprise, pain, and reproach mingled in his dark eyes. "Why are you so cruel to me?"

"Because you won't leave me alone."

"I cannot." He managed a soulful look that no doubt had served him well with many of his conquests.

But not with Virgie.

"I cannot live without you, *cherie*."

"Well, I can live very well without you."

"My darling, you break my heart. I am madly in love with you."

She glared at him scornfully. "What you are madly in love with, Comte, is my fortune."

He clutched at his heart as though she had just broken it. "*Non, non*, you wrong me terribly."

"No, you wrong me—thinking me so stupid I would believe you love anything other than my money."

Virgie whirled and moved swiftly through the nearby entrance into the west wing.

She wished she would run into Max, which was ironic considering how she had been avoiding him for the past several days to protect her heart. Doing so had been the hardest thing she had ever done.

And futile. She had watched his patience with Es, and her heart had swelled with love for Max.

He was the one person at the castle in whom she could confide, and she needed to vent her anger at the comte. She also wanted Max to take her into dinner tonight so she would not have to sit next to the fortune hunting Frenchman.

Virgie did not see Max until she entered the withdrawing room before dinner. She approached him, but he deliberately turned and walked away from her. She drew herself up proudly, refusing to let him see how much his intentional snub hurt her, and she went to join Isabel and Esmond.

During dinner, Max continued to ignore Virgie. Once she directed a question to him, but he answered her so brusquely that she did not bother to do so again.

She reminded herself this was what she wanted.

But that didn't make her any less miserable.

Worse, her stepmother had chosen tonight to make her first appearance at dinner since Max's telling her he would never give permission for the duke to marry Virgie.

The refectory door opened as they were finishing dessert, and Jenkins came in, carrying a cable. He bowed and gave it to Max. "Pardon me for disturbing you, my lord, but I feared this might be too important to wait."

"Thank you, Jenkins." Max was already opening the message. As he read it, a wicked smile curved his mouth.

Virgie wanted to ask him what the message said, but given the silent treatment to which he'd subjected her tonight, she doubted he would answer.

Its arrival reminded her yet again that her father had not answered the cable she had sent him about Rowena bribing the duke's mother.

Virgie could not understand her father's silence,

unless her stepmother had somehow convinced him that his daughter was lying. Whatever the reason for his failing to reply, she feared it boded ill for her cherished dream of acquiring Eden Valley.

"What is your telegram about, Max?" the dowager inquired.

"Information I requested, but nothing of interest to anyone else."

Virgie didn't believe that. Max looked too pleased and triumphant.

In the drawing room after dinner, Max, who rarely drank much, consumed more brandy than he had during the rest of his stay at Penrose combined.

And, unlike other nights, he paid little attention to the conversation that swirled around him. He contributed even less.

He could not excise from his mind the romantic scene he'd witnessed between Virg and the comte under the crimson leaves of the maple tree. Max's hand tightened convulsively around his brandy glass, and he took another gulp.

His other hand patted his pocket, where he had stowed the cable he had received at dinner. It was the answer to the inquiry he'd sent to France about the comte. As Max had suspected, Beaucaire was no comte, merely a poor artist with a talent for ingratiating himself with rich women.

Max had never received a reply from Virg's father to the other cable he had sent, and that disturbed him. After what she had told him of her father, Max had expected to hear from him very quickly.

Even if Blair decided against replying to Max

directly, why had he not cabled his daughter to ascertain the truth about what Max had said?

Or had her father done so? Virg had been treating Max so coolly since their return from Ipswich that she might well not have told him.

Not until tonight had she demonstrated the slightest interest in him. Why tonight? Was she trying to conceal that she was launching an affair with Beaucaire?

Max took another gulp of brandy and looked around for the ersatz comte. He had withdrawn from the conversational circle ten or fifteen minutes ago on the pretext of examining a Turner seascape that hung on one of the walls. Now Max discovered that the Frenchman had disappeared from the room.

So had Virg. Was she with Beaucaire even now?

Max drained the rest of his brandy. Were they making love somewhere in the castle?

That maddening thought nearly propelled Max out of the room too.

Reining in his jealousy and impatience, he said, "Aunt Elizabeth, you look very tired. Shall I escort you to your apartment?"

"Thank you, Max. You are always so observant."

He took the dowager's arm and helped her up the stairs. As soon as he deposited his aunt at her apartment, he would check whether Virg was in her room.

When he and the dowager reached the top of the grand staircase, their ears were assaulted by Mrs. Blair's loud nasal voice.

"Olive, where is that wretched Virginia? She should be in her bedroom preparing for bed."

Max could not hear Olive's reply, but Mrs. Blair

demanded, "Why don't you know where she is?"

Since Virg was not in her bedroom, Max was spared having to knock on her door.

Was she in the fake comte's chamber?

At the door of his aunt's apartment, Max turned her over to Isabel and went to his own chamber.

He paced the floor, driven by anger and jealousy, an emotion to which he had thought he was immune until he'd met Virg. He tossed his jacket on a chair and opened his shirt.

Damn it all, he wanted to know for certain whether Virg was with Beaucaire. Well hell, why should he not knock on the man's door. Max had consumed enough brandy tonight to quell any reservations he might have over what he was about to do.

He did not take the time to put his shirt back on. Instead he pulled on a dressing gown to cover his bare chest and headed for Beaucaire's room.

When Max was still a half dozen feet from the Frenchman's door, he heard the unmistakable sounds of lovemaking coming from the room. The lady of the duo was clearly in the throes of a noisy climax embellished with panting, moans, and ecstatic squeals.

So Max's suspicions were right.

Never in his life had he wished so much that they were wrong.

If the noise Virg was making was any indication, Beaucaire must be as accomplished a lover as he thought he was.

A wave of intense fury hit Max with such force it was all he could do to keep from breaking the door down and accosting the lovers.

Damn them both!

But most of all, damn Virg and her lies to him about Beaucaire.

Max turned away from the Frenchman's chamber and stalked toward his own. As he passed Virg's door, he had a sudden idea. Why not wait in her room for her to return?

Let her try to explain her way out of this!

He quietly tried the door. It swung open without so much as a creak, and he glided inside.

The damned room was as dark as a mine tunnel five hundred feet underground.

The drapes were closed, allowing not the faintest light in. Nor had Virg left a single lamp or candle burning.

Feeling his way carefully, Max inched silently toward the bed. When he reached it, he discovered the heavy brocade bed curtains had been pulled shut—undoubtedly to conceal Virg's absence from her bed.

Clever of her.

But then she was a very clever woman.

Not, however, clever enough.

He smiled grimly. What a shock she would get when she climbed into her bed after her romp with the comte.

The *ersatz* comte. Max could hardly wait to see Virg's face when he told her that tidbit.

He kicked off his slippers, tossed aside his dressing gown, and parted the heavy curtains. As he climbed into the bed, he discovered Virg had taken the time to muss the bedclothes so it would appear she had been sleeping there.

He grabbed one of the pillows and propped it

behind him against the headboard, settling himself in until she returned.

The bed curtains dropped back into place. He was startled at how strongly Virg's fresh, unique scent of orange blossoms clung to her bed. It was almost as if she were here herself.

Max put his hand down on the bed and touched something soft and tantalizing. He curled his fingers around the object and discovered to his shock he was squeezing a woman's breast.

A small, firm, delectable breast.

He heard a gasp very close to his arm.

Bloody hell! Max's mouth went as dry as dust.

Guessing what would happen next, he moved with lightning speed. One hand closed over the source of that feminine gasp, sealing off any possibility of a scream following it. His other hand dropped to guard his family jewels.

Christ, how was he going to explain his way out of this mess? No one would believe his story.

Not that he could blame them. He would not have believed it either.

Feeling much injured, he demanded in a voice fraught with indignation, "What the hell are you doing here, Virg?"

Chapter 18

❦❦

"This is *my* bed," Virg told Max. "Where else would I be?"

Where else indeed? "In the comte's bedroom."

"Why would I be there?"

She sounded shocked. At least she was not screaming at the top of her lungs.

Max frowned. Why the hell was she not?

Lady Priscilla would have been.

Instead of waiting for him to answer her first question, Virg asked a second. "Tell me, my lord, what are you doing in my bed?"

A reasonable question, but not one he wanted to answer. "I, ah, became lost and blundered into the wrong room," Max improvised.

Her hypnotic scent of orange blossoms and the warm, inviting curve of her hip and thigh sparked his desire, and he surreptitiously edged closer to her. She did not seem to notice.

"I can understand why you would hardly know this castle," she said wryly, "having only lived here for what—fifteen or twenty years?"

"I have occasional memory lapses," he lied. "Please accept my most sincere apologies."

"Why don't you get out of my bed, and I'll think about that."

"Must I?" he asked, loathe to comply. He stroked her leg, slowly and rhythmically, moving a bit farther up her thigh with each sweep of his hand. "I promise you will enjoy my staying."

"Will I now? How very certain of yourself you are." With that, she flung back the covers, slipped between the brocade bed curtains, and disappeared into the darkness beyond.

Max made a grab for her and ended up with a fist full of brocade. He cursed himself. The last thing he had wanted to do was anger her. However, her lovely scent, combined with the softness and heat of her body next to him, had generated such a lusty response in him that his good sense had vaporized.

It was so damned dark in the bed he had trouble even finding the opening through which Virg had disappeared.

He listened anxiously for the sound of a door that would signal Virg was fleeing the room. He did not hear that—to his enormous relief.

Virgie stood between the draperies at the window, watching the fast-moving clouds play hide-and-seek with the moon and stars.

The cold and damp of the night penetrated the glass, and she shivered in her silk and lace night-

dress. She had not thought to grab her robe as she'd
jumped from the bed.

Virgie heard the thud of Max's feet as they hit
the floor. She looked toward the bed and saw that
he had lifted the curtains and slid out beneath them.

"Where are you, Virg?"

She said nothing, certain that the darkness, cou-
pled with her position between the draperies, would
prevent his seeing her.

Max stumbled around the room, clearly looking
for her. He hit his toe against a piece of furniture
and cursed softly.

Virgie shivered again, this time not from cold but
from excitement as she recalled the strange aching
hunger within her as he'd stroked her thigh. She was
shocked at how much she wanted to taste the pleasure he offered her.

Max did not know that the battle she was waging
was against herself, not him. She did not need him
to tell her how much she would enjoy his staying.
She knew. And she feared that.

What he wanted from her was pleasure.

What she wanted from him was love.

He would not know that he held her fragile heart
in his hand and could so easily crush it.

And he would do so, not deliberately, but because
he did not believe in marrying for love.

For her, no other reason existed.

Even if she somehow managed to convert him to
her view—and she had about as much chance of
that as she did of stopping the earth from rotating
on its axis—their situation would still be hopeless.

He'd made it clear he would reside nowhere but
in England. And she could not stand to subject her-

self to all the strictures that imprisoned an English lady like one of those awful crinoline cages they wore.

Nor could he live elsewhere, even if he wanted to do so. For the next thirteen years, he was responsible for the duke and his estate. Virgie knew how seriously Max took that duty.

Yet he was the one and only man that she could imagine marrying.

Would she ever find another?

Would she ever taste the sweet promise and wild passion that he offered her tonight?

Max's voice came to her from near the door. "Damn it, Virg, where are you? We must talk, and I am not going to leave until we do."

Were he any other man, Virgie would have remained silent, but this was Max. Although she would not admit it to another living soul, she loved him. With a sigh, she turned.

"I was under the impression talk was not what you had in mind. What is it we must talk about?"

He came to her at the window and stood beside her, so close she could smell his scent of soap and sandalwood, but he made no attempt to touch her.

Her perverse heart yearned for him to do so.

The clouds were momentarily blown away from the face of the quarter moon and some of the stars. In the pale light falling through the glass, she saw Max's sharply etched profile in silhouette.

He turned toward her and somehow managed to capture both of her hands in his own.

"I am sorry, Virg. I swear I would never hurt you." Max squeezed her hands gently as though to emphasize his words. "Nor would I do anything to you that you did not want."

That was the problem. Her heart and the rest of her body wanted too much from him. Only her brain, addled as he was making it, held her in check.

When she did not answer, he asked, "Do you not believe me?" He sounded hurt.

"I believe you." And she did, but she did not want to continue down that conversational path. She asked quickly, "Whose room were you looking for, my lord, Lady Albert's?"

"Good God, no! She is the last person whose room I would visit. How can you think? . . ."

"Because there are very few other ladies at the castle to call on in the middle of the night."

"I was not intending to call on any lady," he said testily.

"Oh, then you were coming here, since in your opinion, I am no lady."

"Virg, you have this all wrong."

"And how could you think I would be with Beaucaire?" she demanded indignantly. She wished she could see Max's expression, but the clouds had again hidden the moon. "There's not room for three of us in his bed. Even if there were, Lady Albert would not share him with me."

"You say Beaucaire is more than Daphne's art instructor?" His bland tone betrayed that he believed the same thing.

"I suspect you know very well, my lord, that the art he's teaching her has nothing to do with brushes and paints. Although I suppose they're often in the perfect position for him to explain the ceiling of the Sistine Chapel to her."

Max laughed. "I do enjoy your tongue, Virg, when its barbs are not directed at me."

"I assure you I have no desire to be part of a *ménage à trois* with any man—least of all Beaucaire. Believe me, Lady Albert is welcome to him. Do you know what that damned Frenchman did to me this afternoon?"

"What?"

Virgie was puzzled at how wary he sounded. "I was cutting across the quadrangle from the east wing to the west. He was hiding behind that lovely, big maple, the one with the leaves that have turned a beautiful scarlet. As I passed it, he jumped out, wrapped me in a suffocating embrace, and kissed me."

"And you sent him flying through the air just as you did the footpad in Ipswich."

She wondered again at Max's odd, ironic tone. "No, more's the pity. He was squeezing me too tightly for me to get the leverage I needed. He is stronger than he looks. It was . . ." She hesitated as though she were searching for the right word.

"Was what?" Max prompted.

". . . disgusting."

Max chuckled.

"It was not in the least amusing," she protested. "Here I was trying to struggle against him, and he was telling me he loves me and wants to take me to paradise."

"You do not sound pleased by his declaration of love."

The moon emerged for a few seconds from behind the clouds—just long enough for Virgie to see that Max was grinning hugely.

"I'm not so stupid that I believe him. As I told him, all he loves is my fortune."

For a moment, Max sounded as though he were choking. Then he asked, "Did that make him release you?"

"No, I had to grind the heel of my riding boot into his foot to make him let go of me."

More choking sounds came from Max, and she asked in concern, "What's wrong?"

It was a minute before he answered her. "Believe me, nothing is wrong."

The peculiar fervency of his tone mystified her.

"So, Virg, you think the comte is a fortune hunter?"

"Yes—if he is a comte—and I sincerely doubt that he is."

"What makes you think he is not?" Now Max sounded disgruntled.

"I've met too many frauds like him. I told you I neither liked nor trusted him."

A hard gust of wind rattled the window and seemed to push the cold through the glass and into Virgie. She shivered.

Max let go of her hands and moved his own up her arms. "Why, you are freezing." He pulled her against him and wrapped his arms around her, trying to warm her with his body.

He succeeded. His robe had come open, and his chest was bare. Virgie felt the heat of his skin and the hardness of his muscles through her thin gown.

She yearned for more light so she could see, as well as feel, his naked chest.

His hand lightly caressed her back and waist through her nightdress. Not only had he warmed her with his body but now he was overheating her.

"Silk and lace on a night as cold as this?"

She heard in his voice the frown that she could not see.

"No wonder you are cold, Virg. Why are you not wearing something warmer?"

"I don't have anything," she confessed. "I brought three heavy flannel gowns with me, but I think Rowena took them. She said only dried-up old women and peasants wore such ugly, unladylike nightdresses. I told her I would rather be a warm peasant than a frozen lady, but that very day the gowns disappeared."

Max muttered something nasty.

"It's not too cold in the bed if I keep the bed curtains drawn tightly," Virgie said.

The moon emerged from behind the clouds again. Max's expression as he looked at her was so tender that her heart leaped.

He cupped her face with his hand, and his lips brushed hers gently. She felt cherished, even though she told herself it was all a moonlight mirage.

Instead of deepening his kiss, Max moved on to lay a trail of kisses across her jaw and down her neck, tenderly exploring the sensitive spot below her ear, and finally visiting the small indentation at the base of her throat.

A bolt of excitement shot through her, and she moaned.

He brought his mouth back to hers in a heated kiss.

She moaned again, pushed her fingers through his hair, and held his head as she returned his kiss with as much fire as he'd given her. His hair, softer than she'd anticipated, curled around her fingers, snaring them as Max had snared her heart.

While their mouths blended, his hands caressed her, first down her back, then her thighs, and finally he cupped both cheeks of her derriere with his hands. He groaned.

Alarmed, she pulled her head back a little. "What is it?"

His hands tightened, sending another wave of excitement through her.

"I have been aching to do this since the first time I saw you in those damned 'shaps.' You know how to torture a man, Virg."

His lips settled on hers again. He lowered one of his hands to her stomach, lazily caressing it. Then he moved his hand upward, slipped it beneath the thin silk and lace of her nightdress, and cupped her breast.

Who was torturing whom?

During the long, passionate kiss that followed, he teased the tip of her breast with his thumb. Then he pushed her gown from her shoulders, and his lips replaced his thumb, licking and gently suckling her breast. Sharp waves of pleasure washed over her.

She moaned. He gently took her other breast into his mouth, and she moaned again. His hand caressed her belly and her thighs in wide, sweeping strokes.

While his mouth still suckled her breast, his hand stopped at her most secret place. "What are you doing?"

He stopped his attentions to her body. "You have never made love with a man before, have you?"

"No-o-o," she admitted.

"Afraid?" he asked softly.

She gulped. Blairs did not admit fear. "No." A tremor that had nothing to do with cold shook her.

"Are you certain about that, Virg?"

"Well . . . ah, maybe . . . a little . . . nervous."

He chuckled and pulled her into his arms, holding her tightly to him. He kissed her tenderly. "I understand."

"I wish I did," she whispered plaintively, more to herself than to him. "I ache so I don't want you to stop, yet I'm . . ."

She did not know how to explain her tumultuous feelings without admitting that she was afraid. Not of physical pain, but that he would break her heart. She wanted her first taste of love's pleasures with a man who loved her as much as she loved him.

And Max did not reciprocate her love.

Es had told her at dinner that Max must soon leave for London. Once he was gone, would she ever see him again?

He continued to hold her in the warmth of his arms, nothing more. She sensed that he was waiting for her to tell him whether she wanted him to stop or to continue.

Virgie tried to buy herself a little time to sort out her confusion. "The duke told me you leave for London soon."

Max's arms dropped away from her as though she had burned him, and he stepped back.

Virgie felt bereft. "What's the matter?"

"You reminded me of something very important that I had forgotten." He sounded shocked, even horrified, as though he could not believe that he had not remembered.

"What did you forget?" Given Max's reaction, it had to be serious.

Instead of answering her question, he kissed the tip of her nose and was gone.

As the door shut behind him, both her heart and her body, aching with a need she instinctively knew only Max could meet, cried out in silent protest.

Feeling like a scoundrel, Max made his way to his own room. Once he had discovered Virgie in her bed, smelled her scent of orange blossoms and felt the warm curves of her body, he had forgotten everything: Priscilla, the marital negotiations with Stonybrook, and his forthcoming journey to London to keep his promise to her ladyship to escort her to a ball.

How the hell could he have done so?

Whenever he was around Virg, he seemed to forget everything else, including his good sense.

He was deeply ashamed of himself, invading a virgin's bedroom and then, when he'd found her there, trying to make love to her. It had been one thing to seduce Virg when he thought her a lying, plotting jade, but now he knew the truth.

Thank God she had mentioned London before he had taken her. Still, he felt like a complete cad. For her first lover, Virg deserved better than a man who could not marry her.

And Max could not. His grandfather had instilled in him since he was a boy that marriage was far too serious a business—meant to connect and unite aristocratic families—for passion to sway a Chartwell's choice. One had only to see how unhappy Es's father had been to realize that.

Never before had duty seemed so onerous to Max.

Furthermore, he and Virg came from different worlds that could never meet. He could not leave England. Even if he wanted to do so—and he did not—he could not abandon his responsibility to Es and Castle Penrose.

Virg wanted to live in that California valley she so loved. Even if she would forsake that dream and agree to live in England, she would be making a grave mistake. He doubted whether a spirit as free and passionate as hers could survive being locked into the constricted life of an English lady.

After a long, cold trek to the Norman section of the castle, Max reached the chamber Daphne had allotted him. Had she been Beaucaire's noisy lover tonight?

Most likely, but Max discovered to his surprise that he did not care who the woman was in the Frenchman's bed as long as she was not Virg.

Chapter 19

~~~⌒⌒⌒~~~

Virgie awakened later than usual the next morning. After Max had left her, she had been unable to sleep for hours.

Would she have enough time to squeeze in her early morning session with Vesuvius? Despite Max's prohibition against her riding the stallion, she'd been quietly sneaking down to the corral each morning and working with him.

He had been mistreated by his previous owner and still bore the scars. By now, however, Vesuvius trusted her, and she was pleased with the progress she had made with him.

She scrambled out of bed, dressed quickly in denim pants and chaps, as well as the top half of her green riding habit, and headed for the corral.

Virgie no longer used the direct path to the stable. Instead she relied on the narrow, circuitous walk that wound through the oak grove where Max had kissed her.

The trees concealed her both from the house and from Pauley or any of the other stable hands. The latter were less of a problem than she had feared they would be. If no one from the castle appeared, the hands napped on a pile of straw inside the stable.

The hedgerow concealed the corral from their view, and the hands were so used to Vesuvius's commotion that they paid him no heed.

Virgie preferred to work alone with the stallion. With no one else around to distract him, she was taming him more quickly.

The first guests to arrive that afternoon for the shooting party were Viscount Horton and the earl of Rotherman.

Max knew both and liked neither. They were rotund gourmands and reckless gamblers who devoted their nights and a large slice of their immense fortunes to the dinner and gaming tables.

Max was certain Daphne had invited them because she thought them prospective rich husbands for herself, but she had miscalculated.

Horton, a lifelong bachelor, had never displayed any interest in women. Rotherman, now a widower, had married a great heiress and was rumored among the London clubs to have gambled away much of her fortune and his own. She had died two years before, and now he was looking for another very rich heiress to marry to replenish his depleted coffers.

Daphne, in a billowing gown of pale blue, her hair and makeup perfectly done, swept into the hall and greeted both men effusively.

To her obvious annoyance, however, their gazes quickly strayed from her to the staircase where Virg, dressed in a green riding habit that accentuated her slender, petite figure, descended the steps. A perky green feather crowned her matching hat.

"Why, it is you, Miss Blair," Horton said, clearly delighted.

Max's eyes narrowed. He had never seen Horton so happy to see a woman before. How the hell did Virg know this sybarite?

"So good to see you again, Miss Blair," Rotherman chimed in.

Max noted with satisfaction that Virg did not look nearly so pleased to see Horton and Rotherman. Daphne's furious expression betrayed that she would happily strangle Virg for stealing the two guests' attention.

"Since we last saw you in London, Miss Blair, we have been taking poker lessons," Horton said. "We demand a rematch tonight."

The arrival of another guest, Lord Yarwood, who was noted for his shooting prowess, spared Virg the necessity of answering.

A few minutes after that, the widowed earl of Kingsbury appeared with a surprise in tow—his eldest son, Lord Warwich, who had not been invited.

"Warwich loves to hunt, and he wanted so much to come," the earl explained to Daphne. "I knew you would not mind."

She clearly minded very much, extending only a

tepid welcome to Warwich, a heavyset young man
with a florid, yet handsome, face.

And so did Max. He suspected that Warwich's
eagerness to come had nothing to do with hunting
but everything to do with a desire to humiliate Es
in front of the other guests.

If Warwich succeeded, Horton—who loved to
spread malicious gossip as much as he loved to
gamble—would be certain to broadcast much embellished tales of Es's embarrassment, making the
duke the laughingstock of the polite world.

After exchanging pleasantries with the others in
the hall, Warwich said loudly, "What a fine afternoon for a ride, gentlemen. Let us not waste it."

He turned to Es. "Have you enjoyed riding Vesuvius? I miss him terribly. Such a fine animal, he
was one of my favorite mounts. I rode him all the
time."

Max would wager every farthing he owned that
Warwich, lying coward and bully that he was, had
rarely, if ever, attempted to mount Vesuvius.

All eyes turned toward Es, and his face flushed.

The room fell silent, waiting for his reply.

Virg saved him from having to answer. "Are you
Vesuvius's former owner?" she asked Warwich.

"I am."

Rage flashed for an instant in her eyes and then
was gone so quickly that Max wondered if he had
been mistaken.

She smiled demurely. "Vesuvius is such a gentle
horse that even I can ride him."

Warwich's mouth fell open, but no words came
out.

Max bit his lip to keep from laughing. *Bless Virg.*

She gave Warwich her sweetest false smile. Max suspected she was about to make the lying bully sorely regret that he had come to Penrose today.

"Since you have missed riding him so much, my Lord Warwich, you must not be denied that pleasure a moment longer," she said. "We will have Vesuvius saddled for you."

Warwich's Adam's apple moved convulsively. "Oh, I could not deny the duke—"

Virg cut him off. "Oh, but His Grace would not dream of being so rude as to deny you your wish to ride Vesuvius. After all, you are his guest. Come."

She headed for the door, and the men trooped outside after her.

Max looked to the north, where turbulent, black clouds swirled across the sky, moving ominously toward Penrose. If they rode for very long, they were likely to be soaked.

As the group started down the path to the stable, Max took Virg's arm. "What mischief are you up to now?" he whispered.

"No mischief. I can't stand the way that ugly, cruel, insufferable Warwich is baiting Esmond."

"You think Warwich ugly? Most women think him handsome."

"His face may be, but his character is decidedly ugly. To me that's all that counts. He abused poor Vesuvius terribly. I'm going to teach him a lesson he'll never forget."

Max hoped she succeeded, but he warned her, "Be careful. Warwich is a bastard and mean as hell."

At the stable, the hands were told to prepare the requisite number of horses.

"And one of them must be Vesuvius for Lord Warwich here," Virg said.

The stable hands looked at her as though she had just ordered them to run inside a house engulfed in flames. Each one hastily picked one of the other horses to saddle. Since there were more riders than hands, no one was left to tackle Vesuvius.

Never had Max seen stable hands work so slowly, each one trying to take longer than the others so he would not have to go near Vesuvius.

At this rate, the ride would get started at dawn tomorrow.

Max considered saddling Vesuvius himself, but he had about as much hope of succeeding as he had of flying across the sky above the treetops.

A few minutes later, Max turned to Virg, only to discover she had disappeared. Alarmed, he asked the other men, "Where did Miss Blair go?"

Rotherman gestured toward the hedgerow that hid the isolated corral. "I caught a glimpse of her moving in that direction."

Max immediately started toward the tangled greenery, followed by a smirking Warwich and the other male guests.

When Max passed through the opening in the hedgerow, he saw Virg cinching a saddle on Vesuvius. When she finished, she patted his nose and talked to him in soothing tones that were too low for Max to make out what she was saying. The horse whinnied softly.

Max glanced toward Warwich. The uninvited

guest watched Virg as though he could not believe his eyes.

She called, "Your steed awaits you, Lord Warwich. Come mount him."

Virg left Vesuvius and went out the gate as Warwich came in.

Emboldened by Virg's success, he swaggered toward the stallion, giving his audience a cocky smile.

As Warwich approached Vesuvius, the horse pawed the ground nervously. When Warwich put his foot in the stirrup to boost himself onto the horse's back, the stallion went wild, kicking and bucking, snorting and rearing.

Warwich tumbled to the ground. One of Vesuvius's flailing hooves struck him a glancing blow on the arm, and he yelped in pain. He scrambled gracelessly to his feet and ran screaming for the fence, his face a study in terror.

He tried to scale the wooden barrier, slipped, and fell again. He ended up slithering like the snake he was, belly on the ground, below the bottom rung of the fence to escape.

His father and Lord Yarwood grabbed his arms and pulled him to safety. Warwich lay on the ground, panting and half crying with fright.

"My lord, what did you do to this poor horse to frighten him so?" Virg asked.

Max looked up from Warwich. She was back inside the corral. Vesuvius trotted up to Virg, and she patted his nose again.

"Nobody could ride that beast!" Warwich cried.

"Don't be ridiculous." Virg continued patting his nose. "He's perfectly gentle."

"Gentle as a tiger," Max muttered.

All eyes were focused on Virg.

"As I said before, Vesuvius even lets me ride him."

"I will not believe that until I see it," Warwich yelled, his face purple with rage and embarrassment.

"Very well." Virg raised her skirt, thrust her foot in a stirrup, hoisted herself up, and threw her other leg across Vesuvius's back. Max saw she wore denim pants beneath her petticoats.

As the hunting party gaped at her, she rode the stallion slowly around the enclosure. She brought him close to the fence where the men stood. Everyone but Max hastily backed away.

"You see how gentle he is," she said with a beatific smile. "He lets even a small, weak woman like me ride him."

Max almost snorted aloud at that. Virg might be small, but he had never met a stronger, more fearless woman.

The ominous clouds were directly overhead now, and a raindrop hit Max's face, warning of worse to come.

Virg looked over at Warwich, still lying on his belly on the ground. "My lord, again I ask what on earth you did to this poor sweet horse to make him act as he did?"

Max choked. *Sweet!*

Warwich did not answer her, and she turned to the men along the fence. "As you all can see, dear Vesuvius is generally the most well-behaved of mounts."

"Indeed, he is," Horton agreed loudly.

Max suppressed a smile. Knowing Horton, he

could scarcely wait to return to London with a humiliating tale to spread far and wide—but Warwich, not Es, would be its subject.

Just as Virg had said she would, she had taught Warwich a lesson he would never forget.

Nor live down.

Chapter 20

⌒◯◯⌒

Max watched Warwich slink back toward the castle. He would be damned if he would let the snake escape so easily.

"The heavens are about to dump on us," Max said to the guests. "Unless you want to be soaked to the skin, you had better forgo the ride and return to the castle for some warming refreshment."

As he had known they would, the indolent members of the shooting party welcomed his suggestion with a chorus of approval.

Max looked toward Virg, but she shook her head, indicating she intended to stay with Vesuvius.

The men, with Max in their wake, tramped after Warwich toward the castle, subjecting him to a steady barrage of needling and bad jokes about his failure to stay on a horse that a frail little female rode so easily.

By the time they neared the castle steps, Warwich

snarled that he was returning to his father's estate at once, and he turned back toward the stable. Like most bullies, Warwich loved to dish out, but when the tables were turned, he could not take.

Seeing the joyful, relieved expression on Es's face at the uninvited guest's imminent departure, Max again blessed Virg.

At the castle, the guests rushed up the worn stone steps and inside, eager to get to the whiskey and brandy. Max, who did not like any of them, dropped back behind.

The blessed quiet that followed, however, was broken a minute later by the noisy arrival of a coach, top-heavy with baggage on its roof and still more bags strapped to the back.

Who the devil could be arriving at the castle with enough baggage to see him through a two-month stay?

The coach stopped a few feet from Max, and he recognized Lord Burland riding inside. His lordship had been attached to the British embassy in Paris when Max had been working there as a secret agent.

Burland's uncle had secured the embassy position, a superfluous sinecure, for his nephew, who suffered from the worst case of foot-in-mouth disease Max had ever seen. Burland had proved to be such a disaster at diplomacy that the ambassador himself had pleaded with the Foreign Office to order him home before he ignited a war between the two countries.

Burland lumbered down from the carriage. His substantial girth betrayed his continuing fondness for rich French food and wine. Popeyed with several chins, he reminded Max of an aging bulldog.

But a very rich bulldog.

Which was undoubtedly why Daphne had invited him.

"Lord Burland, what a pleasure to see you," Max lied.

"The same, Chartwell, the same."

"Let me show you into the castle," Max said. Burland, a snob of the first order, prided himself on knowing everyone in the British aristocracy and what remained of the French. Now if only they would run into Beaucaire.

They were crossing the Gothic entrance hall when Daphne swept in on the comte's arm.

"Lord Burland, you are here at last," Daphne exclaimed. "I was terrified that you had met with an accident on the road."

Burland bobbed a slight bow. "Sorry to be late. My apologies."

"No apology is necessary," she assured him with a flirtatious flutter of her eyes. "I am delighted to welcome you to Castle Penrose, my lord."

Max might as well have been invisible for all the attention Daphne paid him.

"My Lord Burland, let me present you to the Comte de Beaucaire, our guest from France," she said with another flutter of her lashes.

Burland's eyes bulged more than usual. "Thought I knew everyone left in the French aristocracy. Not heard of you, though, Comte."

Max told Burland, "You have not heard of the Comte de Beaucaire because he does not exist. This man is an impostor."

"What!" Daphne shrieked.

The color drained from Beaucaire's face. "You insult me, Chartwell."

Max raised a questioning eyebrow. "How can the truth be an insult?"

"*Non, non*, it is not the truth."

"Then let me refresh your memory about your past since you seem to have forgotten it," Max said. "You were born to a poor farmer in northern France, the third son of eleven children."

A gasp escaped Daphne.

"Farming was beneath you, however, and you went to Paris to study art. There you supported yourself by providing escort and other—er, services to wealthy older women." Max paused. "Shall I continue, Beaucaire?"

The Frenchman's expression betrayed his desire to murder Max in the most painful way possible, but he contented himself with hissing, "Damn you, damn you, *damn* you!"

Daphne looked at the Frenchman as though he had turned into a viper before her eyes. "Why, you . . . you . . ."

She apparently could not find a word that adequately described his iniquity, and she settled for telling him, "Get out of here."

"But *cherie*—"

"If you are not gone from the castle by dinnertime, I will have you thrown out bodily."

Not since Max's arrival at the castle had Virgie dreaded going down to dinner as much as she did tonight. She had met three of the new guests in London before coming to Penrose, and she was hard pressed to say which of them she most disliked.

When she entered the withdrawing room, Max was standing by the doorway. "May I escort you into dinner, Virg?"

"Yes." She gave Max her arm, recalling last night and wondering again why he had departed so hastily from her bedroom.

"Remember, Rotherman and I demand a rematch with you at the poker table after dinner, Miss Blair," Horton called to her.

"Yes." Rotherman smirked at her. "I hope you have enough blunt to cover your losses to us tonight."

Her only answer was an enigmatic smile. If these two titled fools persisted in playing poker with her, their pockets, not hers, would be empty at the end of the evening.

"What prompts your Mona Lisa smile?" Max asked.

"I don't know what you're talking about," she fibbed.

"I think you do. How is it that you know Rotherman and Horton?"

"We met at an excruciatingly boring London dinner party where I was seated between them. Unlucky me! The conversation turned to cards."

"It always does with those two," Max said.

"I told them the only game I played was poker. When they learned a gambling game actually existed that they'd never played, they insisted I teach them. I tried but . . ." she shrugged.

"But what?" Max prompted.

"Once they learned the rudiments of the game, they were convinced they knew everything—or at least more than a mere woman could possibly teach them."

"Did you meet any of our other illustrious guests in London?"

"Yes, Burland, and I do not like him any better," she said with her habitual candor.

"I share your dislike," Max admitted.

She smiled at him. "Thank you for offering to escort me in to dinner."

Max looked at her lazily, through half closed eyelids. "I had no choice. Daphne ordered me to do so."

"I see. You must be ordered before you will take me in," she teased.

Max's eyes seemed to turn to molten silver. "You're an intelligent woman, Virg. What do you think?"

His eyes held such heat and promise that a quiver of excitement ran up her spine. "Intelligent period? Or intelligent for a mere woman?"

"Period."

"Coming from you, that is a high compliment indeed."

"You think so?" His face was alight with mischief. "A proper British lady would consider it an insult."

"One more reason why I'm not a lady."

"Are you avoiding answering my original question?"

She recalled the pleasure he had brought her the previous night, which had ended with his departure, as strange as it was abrupt, from her bed, and she answered honestly, "I don't know what to think when it comes to you."

The dinner bell rang so loudly that she started.

"Nor I about you," he said so softly she was not certain she had heard him correctly over the bell's noise.

In the refectory, Daphne had again set out place cards. Her son was at the head of the table, with Horton at his left and the earl of Rotherman at his right. Daphne had put herself between Rotherman and the other earl, Kingsbury. She'd lined up Horton, Burland, and Yarwood in a row directly across from her.

Virg's stepmother was seated next to Yarwood. The two chairs next to Kingsbury, assigned to the dowager and Isabel, remained empty. Max was placed on the other side of the two empty chairs and Virg was next to him.

Max knew that Aunt Elizabeth had sent word to Daphne several hours earlier that she and Isabel would not be down to dinner. Daphne had deliberately isolated him and Virg.

"Is the dowager ill?" Virg asked him. "I had a message from Belle that they would not be at dinner tonight."

"No. Aunt Elizabeth does not care for Daphne's guests."

Actually, his aunt's comment had been more pungent than that: "I am too old and have too little time left to waste it listening to those stupid fools Daphne has invited."

"Sorry, Virg, but you will have to make do with my company tonight."

"I'm not complaining, I'm merely puzzled. I've

never seen three men seated in a row at a dinner party before."

"Daphne's male guests have been paying far more attention to you than to her, and she is jealous. So she did her best to put you out of conversing distance with them."

"What an enormous favor she did me."

Virg said this with such fervor that Max chuckled. "You do not appear to be properly awed by our impressive guests."

"Impressive, hah! They possess the qualities I most dislike in English aristocrats. They are indolent and indulgent, brainless and boring. Oh yes, and utterly useless. As far as I can tell, they have done nothing worthwhile in their lives. That would be beneath them."

Max could not argue with her cutting, but accurate, indictment of the guests.

Virg looked around the table. "Where's the comte tonight? I just realized he's not here either."

Max was delighted that she had not noticed Beaucaire was missing until now. "Ah, you have not heard. Daphne learned he is an impostor and ordered him gone from the castle before the dinner hour."

Virg's rippling laugh delighted Max.

"So my suspicion about him was correct," she said. "How glad I am to be rid of him."

Not as glad as Max was.

As the meal progressed, Daphne flirted shamelessly with the men she had invited to the shooting party. Apparently the dowager duchess's absence from the table freed Daphne from any constraint.

But her guests were more interested in touting their own accomplishments than in listening to her.

When Lord Yarwood modestly described himself as the best shot in England, Kingsbury immediately challenged him.

"That title is mine. Why, I killed seven hundred twenty-nine grouse one day last year at my estate in Scotland," Kingsbury bragged.

Virg flinched, and her expression reflected how appalled she was.

"Well, I have killed nine hundred forty-six birds in a single morning," Yarwood replied.

"How can they exaggerate so outrageously about killing poor innocent birds?" Virg whispered to Max.

He could not bring himself to tell her that he was certain the numbers, horrifying as she found them, were not exaggerated.

Max grew increasingly embarrassed and disgusted as he listened to the male guests and realized what they must sound like to Virg.

No wonder she had no use for the English aristocracy.

With examples like them, who would?

"Poor Esmond," Virg said softly, watching the duke. "He's hardly said a word all night and look at the way he's picking at his food. He is clearly miserable and no wonder. Except for you, every man here is old enough to be his father, and I doubt he has anything in common with a one of them."

Max lifted his wineglass in a mock toast to her. "Right again, Virg."

"Your Grace," Kingsbury boomed, "we depend

upon you to show us your best spots for shooting tomorrow."

Es looked up, startled.

Before he could answer, his mother trilled, "Oh, Lord Kingsbury, I fear that may not be possible. My poor son has contracted a severe inflammation of the chest and the most ghastly cough. If it rains tomorrow, he cannot jeopardize his life by going out."

Max had spent a considerable part of the past several days with his cousin. Not once had Es coughed. Nor had he mentioned feeling unwell.

"I don't understand why Lady Albert arranged this party for her son when she does everything she can to keep him from shooting," Virg whispered.

"The party is for Daphne, not Es."

Confusion flickered on Virg's face. "But you said ladies do not shoot. Does she?"

"No. You already noticed all the guests are her age, not his. They are also either bachelors or widowers, mostly the latter."

Comprehension dawned in her lovely eyes. "Lady Albert's husband hunting?"

"Undoubtedly." Max raised his wineglass toward Virg again. "Little do these fearless hunters know they are actually the hunted."

Virgie giggled, and that pleased Max.

When the party left the table after dinner, Daphne invited Rotherman and Horton to play whist with her.

"Sorry," Horton replied. "Rotherman and I have challenged Miss Blair to play poker with us."

"The gaming table, gentlemen, not shooting, is

my forte," Rotherman interjected. "I challenge any of you to try to best me there."

"I accept your challenge," Horton said promptly. "Neither you nor Miss Blair will beat me. Are you certain you dare play us tonight, Miss Blair?"

His smile was so condescending that Max was strongly tempted to use his fist to wipe it from Horton's face.

That Mona Lisa smile played at the corners of Virg's mouth again. "I'm terrified, my lords."

Right. About as terrified as she was of Lionel.

"But I will force myself to accept your challenge."

Max hoped she would defeat the two blowhards so decisively tonight they would never dare brag about their gaming skills again.

They went into the drawing room, which seemed colder and draftier than usual.

Daphne failed to recruit a single whist player, not even her son. The men all wanted to watch the poker game. She had invited these marital prospects for herself, and they were paying no attention to her. She had outsmarted herself.

Like Warwich, Daphne was getting what she deserved.

When the game began, each player contributed five hundred pounds to the pot and received a large mound of chips. The other guests gathered around the table to watch. Max positioned himself behind Virg's right shoulder.

He had never seen a poker game before, but he quickly discerned that Virg was by far the best player of the trio. She was particularly good at bluffing about her hand, almost always fooling her opponents. The pile of chips in front of her rapidly multiplied.

When she skillfully won yet another hand, Rotherman said sourly, "You have the devil's own luck, Miss Blair."

Both her opponents dismissed her many successes over them as pure luck, but they attributed their rare wins to their great skill. The damned fools were convinced that only luck could allow a mere woman to defeat their superior ability, which existed only in their imagination.

Max ground his teeth at their insulting, patronizing behavior toward Virg. He longed to stuff the cards down their throats.

Instead he contented himself with giving Virg's shoulder a sympathetic squeeze. She tilted her head, brushing his arm for an instant in acknowledgment.

Then something Max had said to Virg surfaced unbidden from his memory. *Your father must be a very generous man to finance your losses.* Remembering his own condescending statement, Max wanted to cringe. Now he was embarrassed for himself.

And deeply ashamed. Hell, he had been as big a fool as Rotherman and Horton were.

The men standing around the table were so engrossed in watching the game that they had scarcely a glance to spare for Daphne, and she was clearly furious at this neglect.

"We must make a short night of it, gentlemen," she said sharply. "You will want to be up early tomorrow for the shooting."

Horton looked up from his cards. "Right you are,

my lady. Stop after this hand. Mustn't be bleary-eyed tomorrow."

Both he and Rotherman had only a few chips left. Virg, however, could scarcely be seen behind the mountain she had accumulated.

"Will you accompany us tomorrow, Miss Blair, and watch us shoot?" Rotherman asked.

She looked up from the cards in her hand. "Perhaps I will."

"Yes, please join us," two of the other men chimed in.

Daphne cleared her throat loudly.

Trying to prompt a similar invitation for herself, Max thought.

But none of her guests offered her one. From Daphne's expression, had she known anything about shooting, Virg would have been dead.

After the trio finished the hand, Max accompanied Virg from the room. "I do not know how you managed to keep your temper with that insufferable pair."

She smiled at him. "They're not worth getting angry over."

As usual, Virg was right.

Chapter 21

❧◦◦◦❧

"Is this what you call hunting?" Virgie asked Max.

The shooting party was tramping through tall grass and weeds, which had faded from summer green to autumn beige, on a dew-coated meadow. Their destination was a narrow stand of deciduous trees, which had lost many of their leaves.

"Why are you asking?" he inquired warily.

"For one thing, we're making enough noise to wake the dead and alert every bird for miles. For another, why are all those people coming with us?"

Virgie gestured toward the small army of dog handlers and gun bearers that accompanied them. Never in her life had she seen such a production merely to hunt birds.

Although the sun had risen, its rays failed to penetrate the thick, lead gray clouds that blanketed the sky. The air around them was heavy with moisture, promising more rain to come.

Max was the only member of the party carrying his own weapon. Both Kingsbury and Yarwood had *two* gun bearers, each carrying two shotguns.

"Are these so-called shooters too lazy to carry their own guns?" Virgie asked Max.

"Probably."

The hounds flushed a covey of pheasants from the trees. The birds scattered among the grass and weeds in the meadow, but the brilliant plumage of the males against nature's beige background betrayed them.

The members of the shooting party grabbed their guns from the bearers and emptied them at the birds, then thrust the weapons at the bearers to be reloaded.

Virgie could scarcely believe what she was seeing. "Can't these so-called shooters even load their own guns?"

"Gentlemen generally prefer not to do so," Max said. "I am an exception."

Having two gun bearers and four guns each gave Kingsbury and Yarwood considerable advantage. While their bearers worked feverishly to reload their weapons, they blasted away with one gun after another. By the time they fired their fourth guns, the first ones were reloaded, and they began the whole process over again like mechanical automatons. The field was littered with dead and wounded pheasants.

Appalled and sickened, Virgie turned her back on the senseless slaughter. Max was watching her with an unreadable expression.

"This is not hunting," she protested on the verge of tears. "This is unjustified, sickening slaughter."

"Yes." He looked embarrassed.

"You have not fired yet, my lord."

"I do not care to contribute to the carnage."

His answer pleased Virgie, but she was still so angry at what she'd seen that she said vehemently, "I wish I could use Kingsbury and Yarwood for target practice."

"You *are* bloodthirsty today, Virg."

"I'm amazed these great white shooters can manage to pull the trigger without help. Their index finger is the only part of them that gets any exercise."

"Oh, I wager one other appendage is well exercised too."

Virgie's face grew hot and, she suspected, red as well.

"Sorry, Virg, I did not mean to embarrass you." Max sounded truly contrite. "Sometimes, though, when I am with you I forget I am talking to a woman."

A woman, not a lady. Still something about the soft, rueful timbre of Max's voice sent a shiver of longing through her. She ached to have him caress and kiss her again as he had two nights ago.

The rest of the party had moved ahead of them, and he said, "We had better catch up with the others."

"I'm going back to the castle. I refuse to watch any more of this ugly massacre."

"So do I." He took her chilled hand in his warmer one and squeezed it comfortingly. Suddenly, she felt better as they walked hand in hand toward the castle.

They had gone only a short distance when large raindrops splattered on them. The other men immediately abandoned their so-called sport, tossing their weapons to the gun bearers, and hurried to catch up with Virgie and Max.

As they passed through the outer curtain wall, Max saw Grigsby inside the gatehouse talking to the gatekeeper. The steward, a worried expression creasing his face, signaled to Max that he must talk to him.

Max reluctantly slipped his arm from Virg's. "Go back to the castle with the others. I must speak to Grigsby."

As soon as he relinquished her arm, both Yarwood and Rotherman hurried to take Max's place. Rotherman reached her first and claimed her arm. Her expressive face betrayed how offensive she found him, and she tried to pull away. The fool, obviously oblivious to her reaction, hung on.

He would be lucky not to end up in the same position the footpad in Ipswich had.

Max reluctantly dragged his gaze from Virg and stepped into the gatehouse. "What is it, Grigsby?"

"You remember Raffe, the former lion keeper, whom you ordered dismissed. He's been skulking around the castle grounds. I fear he is up to no good."

"Lied to me," the gatekeeper said. "Says 'im's been given other work here so I lets 'im in."

"He has been bragging at the pub in Penmoor that he will make your lordship regret letting him go," Grigsby said. "Frankly, I am worried."

So was Max.

*　*　*

Virgie yanked her arm from Rotherman's grasp and slowed to a tortoise's pace, hoping he would join the rest of the party rushing to reach the castle before the light rain became heavier. Instead he fell behind with her.

As they neared the lion cages, she heard the clang of metal hitting metal. A second later, a snarling roar that could come only from Lionel reverberated between the two stone curtain walls that had served as medieval fortifications.

Terrified shouts and shrieks of "Lion's escaped! Lion's loose!" accompanied by the pounding of running feet plunged the area into chaos. Among the fleeing people, Virgie noticed a man who looked like Lionel's former keeper hugging the perimeter of the outer curtain wall as he ran.

The members of the shooting party turned tail and fled, nearly trampling Virgie and Rotherman in their haste to get away. It was by far the fastest she had seen any of these men move.

Rotherman fled with the other men, leaving her to fend for herself. Evidently their hunting bravado only extended to helpless birds.

Virgie broke into a run too, but toward—not away from—Lionel's cage. The poor lion was so old and toothless that she doubted he would hurt anyone, and certainly not her.

She rounded a corner and saw Lionel standing alone in tawny majesty near his cage. Somewhere behind her, a gun blasted. A ball whizzed past her and Lionel, lodging in the curtain wall and pelting her with stone fragments. The lion snarled his displeasure.

Virgie looked back, trying in vain to discover
who had fired the shot. Lionel streaked past her toward the castle's gate and freedom. She ran after
him. By now a steady rain was falling, but she refused to let that deter her.

The lion bounded through the open gate of the
outer curtain wall, across the creaky drawbridge,
and vanished into the park.

When Virgie reached the gatehouse, Max stepped
out directly into her path.

"Stop right here, Virg." The steel in his voice told
her this was nonnegotiable. "You will *NOT* chase a
damned lion on foot through the countryside." He
gripped her arms hard with his hands. "Do I make
myself clear?"

She would have been angrier at him had she not
seen the deep concern—and something else—for
her in his eyes. *He does care for me, whether he
knows it or not.*

"You make yourself very clear, Lord Chartwell."

He raised one thick, black eyebrow. "How formal
we suddenly are."

"Please, let me go after him," she pleaded.

"No, I am considerably less worried about the
lion than I am about you. I will take care of his
recapture."

"How do you propose to do that?"

"Trust me for once, will you?" Max released one
of Virgie's arms, but he still held the other firmly
in his hand, and he pulled her toward the castle
entrance. "Where is the rest of the shooting party?"

"They ran away, but I have no idea where they
went."

"To their homes, if we are lucky," Max muttered.

* * *

But they were not so lucky.

Max with Virg in tow discovered the missing men gathered in the gloomy, drafty drawing room. They had pulled chairs into a half circle around the blazing logs in the huge stone fireplace.

Virg stepped up to the hearth and, with her back to the men, extended her hands. The flames silhouetted her petite figure. She was so small, not much bigger than a child, and yet so courageous. Max felt a surge of desire, admiration, and another emotion he could not name.

Although it was not yet noon, the male guests were downing copious amounts of brandy to quiet their shattered nerves. Three large crystal decanters on a small table by the group were already nearly empty.

"What are you gentlemen doing?" Max asked. *Besides getting drunk.*

"Discussing how best to kill that lion," Yarwood said. "We intend to go out shortly to do so."

After you have consumed enough brandy to shore up your courage. Max sneaked a glance at Virg. Yarwood, not Lionel, was clearly her candidate for annihilation.

Max turned to face the men. "It is not necessary to kill the lion."

That earned him a glowing smile from Virg that did more than the fire to warm him.

"Are you mad, man?" Horton took a gulp of brandy before continuing. "We have a wild, killer beast running free over the countryside."

"Of course the lion must be killed," Yarwood said. "When we told poor Lady Albert of the lion's escape, she swooned. Fortunately I was there to catch her."

"How very lucky for Lady Albert," Max said dryly. He doubted Daphne would have pretended to faint had Yarwood or another member of the hunting party not been standing handily by.

Max turned to talk to Virg but discovered she was no longer warming herself at the fire. He looked around the huge room for her and discovered she had disappeared.

He hoped she had gone to change her damp clothes, but knowing Virg, he strongly doubted she was up to anything as innocent as that.

Max quietly left the drawing room to question the servants on Virg's whereabouts, but it was nearly a quarter of an hour later when he finally found a maid who said she had seen Virg headed toward the stables.

Damn it, now what is she up to?

Rescuing Lionel. What else?

Max ran outside and down the path to the stable in time to see Virg gallop away on Black Lightning. The rain had stopped, but the gray sky promised the respite would only be temporary.

When he reached the stable yard, a groom was leading a black gelding, already saddled, out of the stable.

Max ran up to him. "I must have this horse at once."

"Yes, my lord," the groom stammered in surprise.

Max jumped on the horse and headed toward the spot where Virg had disappeared into the woods. He urged the gelding along the path that she had

taken through the trees but saw no sign of her or of
Black Lightning.

Max was almost to the meadow where they had
met when he heard a fierce snarl ahead of him. *Lionel!* Knowing Virg's penchant for trouble, Max
would find her with the beast.

He caught his first glimpse of the meadow
through the yellow and scarlet leaves of the trees.
A moment later, he slowed his horse abruptly at the
sight of Virg riding at full speed on Black Lightning
and twirling a rope loop over her head.

Now what the hell was she up to?

A few seconds later he emerged from the trees
and got his answer. She was chasing the lion and
still swinging the rope over her head. It was the
damndest thing he'd ever seen.

She had to have a death wish!

Max yelled at her.

If she heard him, she kept it to herself. The lion
and Virg disappeared among the trees on the opposite side of the meadow.

Terrified for her, Max galloped across the
meadow and down the path she had followed.

Twice the lane forked. He stopped and listened
impatiently, trying to determine which branch she
had taken. Max heard nothing, however, to guide
him. Fear was crushing him like a giant boulder.

He prayed that he had made the right choices.
Despite the raw, drizzly weather, his palms were
sweating.

After another ten minutes, which seemed like ten
centuries to him, he knew he should concede failure,
but he could not.

Then another meadow opened before him. And

Virg, astride Black Lightning, was there, riding in a circle around an old oak, wrapping the rope she had been twirling over her head earlier around the tree's trunk.

The hemp was pulled taut, and Max's gaze followed the line to its other end wrapped snugly around Lionel's neck. Max could not believe his eyes.

He prodded the gelding alongside Black Lightning. "Are you all right?"

"Of course I'm all right." Virg sounded as though capturing lions was a routine part of her day.

"Thank God," Max breathed, so relieved that he turned in the saddle. Leaning toward her, he circled her with his arm. He nudged her upper body closer to his and closed the gap between their mouths.

No gentle kiss was this, but hard and demanding, as his heart-pounding fear gave way to relief. Her mouth yielded willingly to his, and they were oblivious to all but their kiss.

Black Lightning danced sideways away from the gelding, and Max had either to release Virg or pull her off the stallion.

Reluctantly, he let her go, the sweet taste of her lips lingering on his own.

"I'm even better now," she confessed, her voice low and rich. The warmth of her smile fired an ache in his groin. "Why did you think I wouldn't be all right?"

"Despite what you apparently think, Virg, that is not a docile house kitty tied to the end of your rope. How the hell did you capture Lionel?"

"I lassoed him."

"What does that mean in English?" Max asked, exasperated.

"To throw the loop of rope over an animal's head to capture him."

"Someone should throw a lasso over you," Max grumbled. And he wanted to be the one to do it. Preferably before he had to leave for London to escort Lady Priscilla to that damned ball.

As Max and Virg rode back toward the castle, he shuddered to think what dangers Virg would bound headlong into while he was in London, unable to keep her under his watchful gaze.

Not that he had stopped her thus far from risking her lovely neck at every whim.

And not that she had needed his help either. For the first time in his life, he felt superfluous with a woman, and that made him angry. No, not angry. Furious.

"I told you I would handle the lion, Virg. Why did you not let me do so?"

She turned her face to him, clearly startled by his belligerent tone. "You seemed more interested in talking to the hunting party."

"I was with them only briefly. Could you not have allowed me those few minutes?"

"I was worried about Lionel."

"A few minutes would not have mattered." He glared at her. "Just once, Virg, I wish you would let me be the hero."

Chapter 22

The hostile look Max gave Virgie wrung her heart. She could not argue with him. He was right. She should have been a little more patient.

They rode the rest of the way to the castle in strained silence.

When they dismounted at the castle, the members of the hunting party were staggering down the steps. Apparently they had finally managed to imbibe enough liquid courage to get them outside.

"Going to kill that lion," Horton announced, his words slurred.

Given his inebriated condition, he was more likely to shoot himself. Or one of his companions.

The lion hunters halted at the bottom of the steps.

"Why are you stopping here?" Max asked.

"Waiting for the hounds and horses," Kingsbury said. "And the gun bearers."

"Oh, no, gentlemen," Max said. "No sportsman uses them to hunt lions."

"Why not?" Yarwood demanded belligerently.

"For one thing, a lion is faster than either hounds or horses, and the noise they make will alert the lion that you are coming. He will undoubtedly charge you, and you will not have time to retrieve your guns from your bearers."

The would-be lion hunters paled at Max's words.

"Surely, the hounds will corner the beast." Kingsbury sounded more hopeful than certain.

"No, he will tear the dogs to pieces and perhaps the horses and gun bearers too. I am sorry, gentlemen, but I am responsible for this estate. I cannot allow either the men or the animals of Penrose to be exposed to such a fate."

The men gulped in unison, their Adam's apples bobbing up and down like balls on a string.

Rotherman and Burland immediately backed away and sneaked up the stairs to the castle. After another minute or so of cogitation, the others followed.

Max sent Lionel's new keeper and several other men out with a cage on wheels, left over from the menagerie's better days, to collect Lionel.

An hour later, the keeper reported the lion was safely back in his own cage, and Max immediately passed the information along to Virg.

He did not see any of the shooting party again until dinnertime. He was on his way to the withdrawing room when Lord Rotherman called from behind him. "Wait, Chartwell, I must talk to you privately. It is of utmost importance."

When Rotherman reached him, Max's nostrils were assaulted by an overpowering odor that sent him reeling back a step. Rotherman must have dumped a whole damned bottle of musk over himself.

Max led him to the morning room because it was larger than the other sitting rooms and allowed him to sit farther away from the man and his overpowering scent.

"What is of utmost importance, my lord?" Max asked.

"Miss Blair is the daughter of Leonard Blair—*the* Leonard Blair—is she not?"

Max had a most unpleasant premonition of where this conversation was going. "Her father's name is Leonard, but I have no idea whether he is the man you call *the* Leonard Blair."

"The Leonard Blair is one of the richest men in America," Rotherman said.

"Why do you care about Miss Blair's father?" Max asked, although he knew damned well what the answer was. The earl had found his heiress.

"I intend to marry her."

The fool had no conception of how much Virg disliked him.

"I can see you are shocked, Chartwell."

"Yes, I am." How could Rotherman think Virg had the least interest in him?

He smirked. "I know what you are thinking, Chartwell. She is too far beneath me for me to consider marrying her."

It was all Max could do to keep from hitting the man. "Not at all, my lord. The opposite is true."

Rotherman frowned as his feeble wit tried to puzzle out what Max meant. Finally, he said angrily, "I believe you have insulted me."

Max stood up abruptly. "No, my lord, it is you who have insulted Miss Blair."

He wheeled and left the room. The fat idiot! Dammit all, Max could not leave the castle for London until the hunting party was gone.

He must protect Virg from these fools, but most important, he must save her from her stepmother. Virg could no doubt take care of herself, but Max feared that if Rowena learned of Rotherman's interest, she would strike a deal with him. Without Max there to intervene, she might well try to force Virg to marry him.

Virgie could not face another dinner in the shooting party's disgusting company, and she confided her plight to Isabel.

"I do not know the men, but Her Grace says they are stupid, boring braggarts. That is why we are eating in our apartment until they leave."

"Lucky you!" Virgie said fervently.

"The dowager and I would be delighted to have you eat with us tonight."

And Virgie did.

When she returned to her own room after the meal, she was still giving thanks for having escaped the company in the refectory.

She opened the door to her bedroom and jumped backward in shock. A few feet inside her room stood Rotherman, his thick lips pulled into a smile.

"What the devil are you doing in my room?" she demanded, more angry than afraid.

He moved into the doorway, nearly filling it with his girth.

She took a step backwards as waves of musk assaulted her nose.

"I have a wonderful surprise for you, you lucky girl."

Virgie doubted any surprise he had in mind for her could possibly be wonderful. "What is it? You want to play poker with me again?"

"No, I have decided to marry you."

"What did you say?" Virgie was certain she must have misheard him.

"I have decided to marry you."

Dear God, she hadn't misheard the egotistical fool. "And I have decided *not* to marry you."

"Oh, I see. You are one of those women who want pretty words, do you?"

"No, I only want you to leave me alone."

"But I will make you my countess." He made it sound as though he were giving her the British throne.

"I don't want to be *your* countess nor anyone else's."

He looked at her in clear disbelief. "Every woman wants to be a countess."

"Not this woman."

"Now, come, my sweetling."

"I am not *your* sweetling."

"I know you are not serious." He smirked at her. "I am up to all the tricks you nubile maidens play on your beaux. I'm no young fool."

No, an old one! The worst kind!

He stepped into the hall and tried to embrace her. "Don't you touch me!"

He ignored her warning. She grabbed his arm and flipped him, sprawling him out flat on the hall floor.

He looked up at her, puzzled. "What did you do to me?"

"When I tell a man not to touch me, I mean it."

Giggles floated down the hall. Virg looked toward the sound and discovered an audience of three young maids.

Hearing the laughter, Rotherman turned purple with rage. "You will pay for this. I am an earl."

"I'm terrified, your earlship," she scoffed. "The next time a woman tells you not to do something to her I advise you to listen."

She went into her room, slammed the door behind her, and turned the key in the lock.

Chapter 23

In the drawing room of the earl of Stonybrook's home in St. James Square, London, Max waited for Lady Priscilla to appear.

Originally, he was to have been in London the previous afternoon, but he had postponed his departure from Penrose until the shooting party had left.

Rotherman had been the first to go, departing abruptly two nights earlier without so much as a good-bye or thank you to the duke or his mother.

No one above stairs knew why he had left so rudely, so Max asked Jenkins and learned that Virg had become the heroine of everyone below stairs, especially the maids.

"The earl tried to make an improper advance to Miss Blair, and she laid him out flat on the hallway floor," Jenkins explained. "And her such a little thing too, and him so fat. The maids who saw the incident said they have never seen anything like it. An hour later, Rotherman was gone without a word to anyone."

Max had suspected Virg would handle Rotherman in her own unique way. Thank God the earl had gone to her first and not to her stepmother. Then it would have been a much more unpleasant situation.

Although Rotherman had been his primary concern, Max had stayed on at the castle until all of the party had gone, then caught the late night train from Ipswich and reached London in the early hours of this morning.

When he'd arrived at his London rooms, he'd found a note from Stonybrook awaiting him, inviting Max to dinner on the previous night to discuss the marriage settlement.

Although the earl had indicated earlier he would accept Max's last offer, Stonybrook had rejected it and listed his new—and outrageous—demands.

The earl had done this repeatedly during Max's protracted negotiations for his daughter's hand. But by now, Max had become heartily sick of it and intended to tell Stonybrook that when he saw him. In fact, Max had been so angry he'd been sorely tempted to go back to Penrose at once.

And to Virg.

Instead, when his temper had cooled, he'd sent the earl and his daughter a note explaining he had not gotten the invitation until after the dinner was over. He would, however, call at one o'clock that afternoon to discuss the settlement.

Max had been eating a late breakfast when a note, embossed with Stonybrook's coat of arms, arrived saying the earl had departed that morning for a hunting party in Scotland and would be gone from London for several days. His daughter, however, would be awaiting Max's arrival at one that afternoon.

Not for a moment had Max believed hunting had drawn the earl to Scotland, if indeed he had even gone there. The wily Stonybrook had hoped the delay would exert pressure on Max to capitulate to the earl's demands.

Max had arrived punctually at Stonybrook's front door as the church bells rang one o'clock. Now Max glanced irritably at his watch. That had been twenty-seven minutes ago.

Could it be that Lady Priscilla was making him wait in retaliation for his having delayed his London arrival?

Impossible. Not sweet, demure, biddable Priscilla.

The drawing room had been redecorated since Max's last visit, and he hoped Priscilla had had no hand in the abysmal result.

Paintings, both large and small, in elaborately carved and gilded frames covered the walls. Only the doors, windows, and the massive, carved marble chimneypiece that reached to the ceiling had been spared. The space above the doors, however, had not.

The paintings, most of them excruciatingly bad, had been placed with no regard for style, color, or content. Max decided the determining factor in hanging them had been how well the frames fit together so that no bit of wall was left uncovered.

The room was so overloaded with furniture—

sofas, chairs, tables—that Max had scarcely been able to navigate his way through the maze to the sofa where he now sat.

Porcelain vases, plates, cups, bowls, and soup tureens, in a variety of clashing colors and patterns, were displayed on every table and shelf.

Max feared he might suffocate in this Victorian excess if Priscilla did not arrive soon.

She finally appeared ten minutes later, and he stood to greet her. Despite how late she was, she glided as slowly as a glacier into the room.

"Max, we missed you last night. We delayed dinner for more than an hour waiting for you."

He could not mistake the edge to her voice. "As I explained in my apology, I did not receive the invitation until after the dinner was over."

Priscilla was a little taller than medium height and generously endowed in all the right places. Her complexion was pale, and so was the blue of her eyes. Her nose was the proper aristocratic length.

Max had thought her features perfect, but as he looked at her now, he realized for the first time how thin her lips were, especially her lower one—too thin to be truly sensual.

Or even all that inviting.

She wore a walking dress of pale pink foulard, and her blond hair was tucked neatly under a white lace hat topped with pink roses. Her gown had a voluminous pink underskirt. Its overskirt was caught up to the waist by large ribbons on each side. Wide flounces edged with pink ribbon trimmed the enormous bottom edges of both over and under skirts.

To Max's surprise, Priscilla also carried a dainty

pink parasol trimmed with white fringe.

"I was not aware we were going anywhere," he said.

"I hope I can persuade you to take me shopping." Priscilla looked up coquettishly at him and smiled. "Can I?"

He had learned long ago that whenever a woman wanted him to take her shopping it was to buy her something exorbitantly expensive. After her father's latest demands, Max was not feeling particularly generous.

"It depends on where you wish to shop. So long as a jeweler's is not your destination, I can be persuaded to go."

Color crept up her face, betraying that a jeweler was indeed her planned destination. But she recovered quickly. "No, no. I want to buy ah . . . ah . . . books."

This choice intrigued Max. He had never seen her with a book in her hand.

At the bookstore, he discovered that, if her selections today were any indication, her tastes ran to the Bible, improving stories of the kind taught to small children at Sunday schools, and embroidery.

No Isaac Newton treatises for Priscilla.

When they emerged from the store, the sun had disappeared behind one of the puffy white clouds floating across the sky.

Although neither sun nor rain threatened Priscilla and their carriage awaited them at the curb, she opened her fringed pink parasol the instant she stepped outside to protect herself during the half dozen steps it took her to reach the conveyance.

Or at least it would have been a half dozen for

anyone but Priscilla. She took such tiny, dainty steps that she required at least a dozen.

A damned snail moved faster.

At last they reached the carriage, and an exasperated Max helped her inside. He ordered the coachman to drive past the park on their return to St. James Square.

Priscilla chattered about her gown for the ball that night and all the distinguished guests who were expected to attend.

Since Max did not give a damn about either, he soon tuned her out. He was very good at this, having had considerable practice honing this skill with Daphne.

As they neared the park, traffic became heavier than he had ever seen it, and a huge crowd was gathered in the park itself.

"What can be going on?" Max asked.

"Oh, this must be the day of the balloon ascension."

Max had never had the opportunity to witness an ascension before, and he wanted very much to see this one. "Shall we stop and watch?"

Priscilla looked horrified. "No, please, I beg of you, no!" She clapped the palm of her hand over her heart. "The mere thought of watching such an unnatural occurrence gives me severe heart palpitations. I could not bear it."

Max swallowed his disappointment. "Well then, we shall not."

Virg would have been eager to witness such a thrilling sight. He suspected she would have begged him to take her—not only to see the balloon but to ride in it too.

* * *

That night, as Max waited once again in Stony-brook's overstuffed drawing room to escort Lady Priscilla to the ball, her voice drifted to him from the hall beyond the door. "I am ready, my lord."

Max looked up in surprise. He had expected her to come into the drawing room to greet him. Once he saw her, however, he realized why she had stayed in the hall.

The crinoline cage that she wore beneath the skirts of her white tulle and lace gown was too wide to permit her to pass through the door. Max only hoped the entrance to the duke of Portney's home would have sufficient breadth to accommodate her.

Otherwise, they would be out in the cold—literally.

He strode into the hall, where he had an unobstructed view of her finery. The boat neck of her gown was cut very low between its off-the-shoulder cap sleeves. He admired her décolletage and her trim waist.

The gown's underskirt consisted of row after horizontal row of tulle puffs with a long spray of silk dahlias extending down one side. A short puffed overskirt was trimmed with several rows of artificial zinnias in a kaleidoscope of bright colors. The combined effect of these elements and the crinoline cage was of a moving mountain abloom with fake flowers.

Her blond hair had been pulled up and twisted into a circular knot that was ringed with more artificial zinnias. As always, not so much as a wisp of her hair was out of place.

When Lady Priscilla was finally stuffed into the

carriage—a difficult task given all those horizontal steel bands in her crinoline cage—Max wondered whether he would be left out in the cold sooner than he'd feared. Her huge skirts left very little room for him in the carriage.

He finally managed to squeeze into the corner of the seat opposite her. As he did so, he noticed she was having a hard time catching her breath.

"What is it?" he asked in alarm.

"I believe my—er, an unmentionable of mine is laced a little too tight."

Did she think the word corset would shock Max? "Would you like me to loosen it for you?"

"How dare you!" she cried in outrage.

She sounded as though Max had just suggested they make love on the seat. If she had been Virg, she would have laughed and said yes.

Except Virg would not have been caught dead in a gown like Priscilla's. Virg had too much sense. And if being a lady meant wearing such a gown, he was glad she was not one.

The carriage sped along the London streets at a smart pace. Every time Priscilla moved, one or another of the horizontal steel bands in the crinoline banged and prodded Max's legs.

He felt as though he were riding with a hungry octopus, and he was tempted to climb up on the box with the coachman to escape the gouging tentacles.

Oblivious to the discomfort she was causing him, Priscilla talked on about the many fittings her gown had required.

Finally, as Max felt about to expire from boredom, she changed the subject. "You said nothing about our drawing room. Did you not notice it has been redone?"

"Yes." How could he help but notice such an abomination? That she asked, though, warned him she bore at least part of the responsibility for that ugly transformation, and he searched for something innocuous to say about it. "It is—ah, stylish." Which was true. He did not add that he despised the style.

"Papa gave me carte blanche to do what I wished, and I am very proud of the results. Perhaps after we are married, I will redo your country home for you."

Over his dead body.

The carriage slowed, and Max saw they were only a few doors from their destination.

Feeling bruised and battered, he asked, "Did you have to wear that da—" He started to say *damned*, then caught himself. "Darned crinoline cage tonight?"

Lady Priscilla stiffened in shock and indignation. "My lord, I will not permit a man to curse in front of me!"

He stared at her incredulously. She considered *darned* cursing?

What the hell was he supposed to substitute—*oh, fudge*?

Max swallowed his irritation and said politely, "I beg your pardon, my lady."

He had not realized how accustomed he had become to talking to Virg. With her, he never had to worry about an occasional *hell* or *damn* slipping out. Instead he could talk to her as he would one of his male friends.

As his equal.

That realization struck him with the force of a strong earthquake.

The carriage rolled to a stop, and Max did not wait for the door to be opened for him. He flung it wide himself and jumped out before the steel bands stabbed him yet again.

Getting Lady Priscilla out of the coach proved to be even more difficult than getting her into it had been. The effort required several minutes and the combined efforts of Max, the coachman, and three of the duke's footmen.

The great double doors of Portney House proved wide enough for Priscilla to enter. Max felt a pang of disappointment. He was rather hoping the entrance would be too narrow, and they would be forced to abort the evening.

In the ballroom, the orchestra played a waltz. Max, who loved to dance, turned to Priscilla only to discover her crinoline made dancing impossible unless they moved around the floor with their arms fully extended horizontally and only their fingertips touching.

Why would anyone wear such a damned ridiculous gown to a ball?

He led Priscilla to a seat only to discover she could not sit because the steel bands would pop up, revealing far too much beneath her skirts.

Worse, no one else could dance with her either. Max would be forced to stand attendance on her the entire night.

Her conversation consisted of a running commentary on various ladies and their gowns as they danced past.

Max fought a running battle to suppress his yawns. Would this interminable night never end?

After a while, he found himself wondering what Virg was doing tonight. What trouble was she getting into now?

". . . is that not so, my lord?"

Priscilla's question snapped Max's mind back to the ballroom. "Ah, yes," he said, although he had no idea to what he was acquiescing. He hoped he had not just agreed that Queen Victoria should abdicate.

Max had never tuned out Virg's conversation as he was doing with Priscilla's.

He would not have wanted to do so.

Hell, he would not have dared!

During a break in the music, Priscilla said, "I understand the American heiress, Miss Blair, is visiting Castle Penrose. I hear she hopes to trap the duke in marriage." Priscilla's voice took on a contemptuous edge. "Is she not the most shocking girl you have ever met?"

Not long ago Max would have agreed with her. Now, however, his anger flared, and he defended Virg, saying curtly, "Not at all. She is a lovely young lady."

Priscilla's eyes narrowed, and her mouth tightened into such a narrow line Max could barely see it. *Meet Lady Prissy.*

"Well, she thoroughly shocked London."

Max was not about to give Priscilla the satisfaction of inquiring what Virg had done that was so shocking. No doubt he would be subjected to a long, disapproving litany. Instead he shrugged carelessly. "London deserves to be shocked now and again."

Prissy looked as though he had just yanked her corset another inch or two tighter.

When at last the time came to go down to the midnight supper, the crinoline cage prevented Priscilla from choosing her food from the buffet. She gave Max such lengthy instructions on exactly what and how much to place on the plate he would bring her that he began to fear the food would be gone before he reached the table.

Then, when he brought her the plate, they discovered that the crinoline cage prevented her from sitting at a table to eat.

By now, Max was heartily tired of standing.

And of Lady Priscilla's company.

He could do nothing about the latter, but he recalled having seen a sitting room with a red plush sofa, two chairs, and several tables on the other side of the hall from the supper room.

He led Lady Priscilla across the hall, thinking she and her crinoline cage could occupy the sofa while he sat in one of the chairs.

Stepping inside, she trilled in shocked accents, "My lord, how improper!"

"What the he—er, devil are you talking about?"

She fanned herself. "We cannot be alone in this room together. It would be scandalous."

What the hell did she think Max was going to do? Force himself on her with half the polite world only a few feet away?

"The door is open and will remain so for all to see." Max's irritation and weariness crept into his voice. "The sofa is for you alone." He gestured toward the armchair farthest from the sofa. "Believe me, I do not intend to move from that chair."

"Still it would not—"

He cut her off. "Furthermore, this door is three feet away from where a hundred or so people are eating. If, at any time, you feel your virtue is in danger, you have only to scream. You will immediately have more rescuers than you could possibly need."

"Well," Prissy said dubiously, but she floated slowly into the room, taking her customary tiny steps.

At this rate, Max thought sourly, it would take her ten minutes to reach the low mahogany table in front of the sofa and another five to settle herself on the red plush cushions.

But an instant later, Priscilla proved him wrong. A baby brown mouse not much more than an inch long scurried across the Aubusson carpet in front of them.

Priscilla shrieked in terror and dropped her plate and its contents upside down on the rug.

She yanked up her skirts, crushed the steel bands of her crinoline together, and leaped on top of the low mahogany table in front of the sofa, giving Max an unparalleled view of her legs. They were not much more shapely than the logs burning in the fireplace.

She jumped from the table onto the sofa and then onto a second, higher mahogany table behind it.

Total elapsed time could not have been more than a half dozen seconds.

Never had Max seen Priscilla move so quickly.

Or heard her scream so loudly.

Guests rushed from the supper room to discover

what the caterwauling was about, and they gathered at the doorway.

Priscilla danced about on the tabletop as though by doing so she would keep the baby mouse, which had long since disappeared, at bay.

"What is it?" several voices demanded.

"A rat!" Priscilla gasped. "A huge rat! At least two feet long."

Max had not realized what a fertile imagination Prissy possessed.

An image of Virg in Lionel's den, rubbing the beast's ear, flashed into Max's mind. It was succeeded by a second image of her standing calmly in the corral, her back to a kicking, rearing Vesuvius, then a third of the footpad sailing through the air.

What a courageous woman—no, courageous human being—Virg was. She put most men to shame.

And here was Lady Priscilla cowering on top of a table in full-blown hysterics over a baby mouse not much bigger than Max's thumb.

It required several minutes for Max and their host to quiet Priscilla and coax her down from the table.

Max wanted to take her home at once, but now that she had made herself the center of attention she was in no hurry to leave the limelight.

A group of horrified women gathered around her to hear her account of her terrible experience.

"The rat was huge! And his fangs, you should have seen his fangs."

Max listened in disgust. Was this the perfect wife he wanted?

What a damned fool he had been!

Chapter 24

❧❧❧

"How silent you are tonight, my lord." Priscilla smiled coquettishly at Max.

He was in no humor to smile back. Not when he was again squashed into a corner of the carriage, traveling to Priscilla's home.

By now, both Max and his patience were exhausted.

In the distance, a muted bell sounded thrice. Was it only three a.m.? Beyond doubt, this night had been the longest of Max's life. He felt as though he had been trapped with Priscilla for at least seven years instead of seven hours.

After the mouse incident, she had loved basking in the attention of the other guests. Over and over, she had tearfully described to any and all who would listen her horrible ordeal with the "rat" that, during the course of her many retellings, had grown to three feet in length.

"A penny for your thoughts, my lord," Priscilla said with another coy smile. "From your expression, they must be most serious."

They were. To marry this woman sitting across from him, this woman he had thought would make him a perfect wife, would be the worst mistake of his life.

Before he left her tonight, he must tell her that he was breaking off negotiations with her father for her hand. Max offered silent thanks that Stonybrook had been so greedy in his demands. Otherwise, the marriage settlement would have been signed by now and the betrothal announced. Then Max, as a gentleman, could not have backed out.

He did not flatter himself that Priscilla was any more in love with him than he was with her. The blow he was about to deliver would not be to her heart but to her pride. He would do his best, however, to spare that as much as he could.

Still, he did not look forward to her reaction. Would she swoon? Or would she dissolve into hysterics and wake up everyone within earshot?

The coach stopped in front of her home. Max jumped out immediately, anxious to get the forthcoming scene over with as quickly as possible. He helped Priscilla down, earning a few more stabs from the bands of her crinoline.

Before Max could sound the knocker, a porter opened the door for them. Max escorted Priscilla inside, then dismissed the servant. The man vanished through a closed door off the entry.

"Why did you send him away?" Priscilla demanded in a scandalized tone.

"I have something I must say to you in private."

"Tonight? But I am so tired." She hid a yawn behind her hand, then left Max standing by the door and glided to the marble staircase. "Surely whatever it is can wait until tomorrow."

"Sorry, but it cannot. However, I promise I will keep you no more than a minute."

"Well, then, what is it?" Her voice was as impatient as her expression.

Max carefully hid his own annoyance behind a grave countenance and a regretful tone. "I will not meet your father's unreasonable demands for our marriage settlement, and I must withdraw my offer for your hand. I am very sorry."

Priscilla did not react as Max had feared she would. Instead she stared at him as though he were speaking Chinese or some other language she could not understand.

Then her pride kicked in, her back stiffened, and her expression became spiteful. "Good! I am much relieved."

"Thee and me," Max muttered to himself.

Priscilla turned and, without a backward glance at him, ascended the staircase. When she reached the floor above, he quietly let himself out the door. On the steps, he almost broke into a jig, but he restrained himself.

He climbed into his carriage and, with a relieved sigh, stretched his long legs out across the blessedly empty seat.

When he reached his rooms, he immediately sat down and penned a letter to Stonybrook, formally breaking off the marital negotiations.

Max finally crawled into bed well past four

o'clock, intending to sleep only two or three hours, then leave for Penrose.

And Virg.

But when Max awoke, he was astonished to see that the clock read five minutes past noon. He had slept the morning away.

He caught the midafternoon train for Ipswich. No other passengers occupied his first-class compartment, and he chose the wide, comfortable seat next to the window. He settled back against the soft beige leather and opened the *London Times* to catch up on the news of the day.

One story immediately attracted his attention. The balloon ascension scheduled for the park the previous day had been postponed, and another attempt was to have been made early that morning. Max wondered whether it had succeeded.

Darkness had settled on Ipswich long before Max arrived. As he left the train, rain was falling, and a cold, gusty wind forced the men and women on the station platform to hang on to their hats and umbrellas.

He had no desire to complete his journey on horseback in such wet, cold weather, and he took a room at an Ipswich inn for the night.

Max awoke as the first feeble gray light heralded the coming of the new day. He discovered he was too eager to see Virg—just how eager startled him—to go back to sleep.

He went to the window. The rain had stopped, although gray clouds still quilted the sky and wind rattled the tree branches.

Max dressed quickly, reclaimed his horse from

the stable where he had left it, and set off at a gallop.

By the time Castle Penrose came into Max's view in the distance, the cloud blanket had broken up enough that he could see large patches of blue sky.

He reached Penmoor, where the main street was more deserted than he could ever remember seeing it.

As he left the village behind, he saw the reason. In a fallow field ahead of him, a crowd large enough to include every one of Penmoor's residents was gathered around a huge balloon that looked as though it were wrapped in a Union Jack.

Curious, he rode toward the cylinder and dismounted at the edge of the spectators.

"What is happening?" he asked one of them, a thin man with a long handlebar mustache.

"Ain't ye heard? Balloon what left London yes'erday morning come down here. Now 'tis goin' up agin, tryin' to get back."

Perhaps Max would see a balloon ascension after all. He left his mount's reins dangling on the ground and pushed his way through the crowd toward the sphere, wishing that Virg were with him.

A dozen men acted as anchors, holding on to long ropes that kept the balloon from blowing away. A hemp net enclosed its red, white, and blue envelope. The net's ropes hung down below the bottom of the balloon, looping around a small hoop. Below that, the ropes were attached to a ridiculously fragile wicker basket that carried the balloon's passengers into the air.

Max could scarcely believe how flimsy it was. A

man had to be a blathering idiot to place his trust in that.

A gust of wind struck the balloon. The men, muscles straining, struggled to hang on to the ropes and keep the contraption on the ground. They succeeded but barely.

"Not gonna be able to keep it down much longer," one of the men clutching the ropes called.

A man standing beside the basket replied, "Very well. I'll get in."

His odd goggles told Max he must be the balloon's lunatic pilot. A bright scarlet cloak and feather-trimmed hat behind the aeronaut caught Max's attention.

Virg! His joy at seeing her vanished when he realized where she was.

Standing *inside* that wicker basket.

The pilot gestured theatrically toward her and announced in a loud, dramatic voice, "My brave friend and I will now ascend into the heavens."

Over Max's dead body!

He sprinted for the basket. One of the rope holders stepped into Max's path to stop him. Max shoved the man out of the way. He stumbled backward, dropping his rope.

"Damn it, Virg, get out of that basket," Max yelled.

"No."

Her chin tilted to a determined angle that told him he would be wasting his time to argue with her.

If the fool woman didn't have the sense to save herself, Max would have to do it for her.

Cursing under his breath, he caught Virg's waist in his hands, intending to lift her out of the basket.

"What do you think you're doing?" she demanded angrily.

"Getting you out of this damned balloon before it flies away with you."

"But I want it to fly away with me!" she cried. "Stop trying to rescue me!"

"Damned ingrate," Max muttered.

The pilot, who was climbing into the basket, pointed at Max and yelled, "Grab that crazy man!"

Which, in Max's opinion, was the pilot.

Two more men obediently dropped the tether ropes they held to go after Max.

A fierce gust of wind struck. The wicker basket rocked and tipped, dumping the pilot out on the ground. Max let go of Virg so he could grab the top of the wicker to right the basket.

Another savage gust hit them, ripping the tether ropes away from the remaining men struggling to hold the balloon on the ground.

The basket suddenly righted itself, catching Max in his midsection, lifting him off his feet and tumbling him headfirst inside.

He scrambled up as the balloon—and the wicker basket beneath it—began to ascend.

A roar went up from the assembled crowd.

Max, who believed in keeping his feet firmly planted on the ground, was incredulous and dismayed to discover that he and Virg were rising rapidly toward the sky with nothing beneath them but the bottom of that ridiculously flimsy basket.

They soared above the treetops and kept climbing.

This would be too much even for Virg. Any woman in such circumstances could be counted on to dissolve into hysterics. She was entitled to them. Hell, so was he.

Turning to reassure her, Max discovered her hanging far over the basket's edge, waving at the crowd beneath them.

Christ, she was going to fall out!

"What the hell do you think you are doing?" he roared as he grabbed her and pulled her back from the edge.

She straightened and turned to face him. The wind had blown her scarlet hat askew, and its once perky feather now stuck out sideways. She unpinned the hat and removed it.

Another gust hit them, freeing some of her hair from its restraints and blowing it about her face. Her lovely eyes sparkled like aquamarines, and her cheeks were pink from the cold.

"Oh, Max, isn't this the most wonderful adventure?"

So much for hysterics.

"If God had meant man to fly, He would have given us wings." Max had wanted to see a balloon ascend, but he sure as hell had not wanted to ride in it.

"God gave us intelligence instead so we can fashion our own wings."

A disgruntled Max refused to allow Virg to have the last word. He gestured toward the sphere above them. "I don't see any wings on this damned fool contraption."

"Don't worry," she counseled him. "It's perfectly safe. Aeronauts have been ascending in balloons for almost ninety years now. Two Frenchmen made the first ascent in 1783."

Damned French never did have any sense. "Are you trying to tell me none of these so-called aeronauts has been killed in the process?"

"Well, perhaps a few," she conceded.

"How do you define a few? A dozen? A hundred? Two hundred?"

Instead of answering him, she pointed toward the ground. "Look, the people down there are as tiny as miniature toys."

Max did not find that reassuring.

The people below shrank even more as the balloon rose higher into the gray sky. Finally the cheering spectators on the ground disappeared from sight altogether.

The balloon drifted southwestward on a course that he fervently hoped would take them over London. If they were lucky, they would end up at Hyde Park.

And then what? Max had not the foggiest notion how to bring the balloon back to earth.

An eerie silence settled over them. It seemed unreal and unnerving to Max that he could be soaring high in the sky without so much as a sound around him. Damn it, even birds could at least hear their wings flapping.

Virg sighed contentedly. "Isn't it peaceful and quiet up here?"

"I prefer my peace and quiet closer to the ground."

"Don't tell me you're afraid?"

"No!" he denied vehemently. *Well, perhaps mildly uneasy.* Still, as the shock of finding himself flying through the air wore off, he started to appreciate this bird's-eye view of the world beneath him.

How different it looked from up here. Even Castle Penrose seemed insignificant from this height.

"I love this." Virg closed her eyes, and her mouth parted in a beguiling smile.

How much Max had missed that smile—and Virg herself—during his brief stay in London.

He wrapped her in his arms, bent his head, and brushed his lips lightly, caressingly over her forehead. Her eyes opened dreamily, and she raised her mouth toward his. Their lips met and held in a kiss that began tenderly but soon grew hot and hungry. Her body seemed to melt against his.

She felt so good, so right in his arms that Max wanted to keep her there all day—and all night.

He might have tried to do so, but the balloon suddenly bumped hard several times and rocked wildly as though it had hit an invisible rough patch in the air.

"What happened?" For the first time since they were airborne, Virg sounded concerned.

Max tightened his grip around her with one arm and grabbed the top of the wicker basket with his free hand to anchor them.

He had no one to blame but himself for this dangerous predicament. Had he not tried to pull Virg from the basket, she would be with an aeronaut who knew how to operate the damned balloon.

If anything happened to Virg—the mere thought raised a stricture in his throat—it would be his fault. He swore to himself he would find a way to bring the balloon—and her—safely to earth.

He studied the ropes that held the wicker basket below the giant red, white, and blue balloon. They extended upward and became part of a hemp netting that encircled the top of the sphere. Not one of them looked as though it would be of any use in trying to steer or lower them to earth.

Suddenly the balloon soared upward with gut-wrenching speed. It was as if the wind had suddenly decided to blow vertically.

Instead of Hyde Park, Max thought glumly, they were going to land on the moon.

Virg clutched the arm that he had around her as though she thought he might let go of her. "What's happening."

Although the fear in her voice mirrored his own, he felt compelled to try to reassure and comfort her. "Winds frequently change speed and direction." Though it was not easy, he managed to keep his voice unperturbed. "Nothing to worry about." *Liar, liar!*

"But why are we suddenly going straight up like we've been shot out of a cannon?" Virg asked, still hanging on tight to him.

Better straight up than straight down! Max kept that thought to himself. "The wind will change again in a minute or two." Hell, if it did not, they would very soon be introducing themselves to the man in the moon.

In another minute, as though the wind had been listening to him, the balloon slowed its climb considerably, although it continued to drift upward as well as sideways. Virg released his arm, and the anxiety faded from her face.

As the sphere rose, the air around them grew colder. Much colder. When they exhaled, their breath hung before them like miniature clouds.

Virg started to shiver. Max gathered her into his

arms, hugging her as close to him as he could manage, so they could share their body heat.

It occurred to him how much more he wanted to share with her. But the odds on their living long enough to do so were becoming grimmer by the moment.

They floated into a cloud of damp gray, thicker than any fog he had ever seen.

The world beneath them vanished as though it had never existed. No light, nothing, penetrated the gloom. Max could scarcely see anything at all except Virg's apprehensive face. But at least she remained outwardly calm and quiet—something no other woman he knew would have been capable of doing.

He would not blame her if she started screaming at him for getting them into this perilous situation. She had every right to do so.

At long last, the balloon stopped climbing and drifted sideways, but they were still mired in dense, gray cold.

The wind strengthened and, blowing fiercely, switched direction. Max was too disoriented in the gray cocoon that encased them to be certain of what the new direction was.

After what seemed like an eternity to Max, the balloon finally emerged from the gray cloud.

Looking ahead, Max saw that the balloon was racing eastward. Already, to his shock, it was rapidly approaching the Suffolk coast and the North Sea beyond.

He swore silently. He had to figure out how to get this devil's device turned around and on the ground.

And quickly—before Virg and he were blown out to sea.

But he was baffled as to how he could accomplish that.

Chapter 25

❦❦

"**V**irg, do you have any idea how this balloon can be guided to earth?" Max inquired as casually as one would ask the time of day.

His calm astonished her. Although she was doing her best to conceal her fear, her heart was pounding harder than the surf below them.

"I asked the aeronaut that, and he said he uses one of those ropes." Virgie pointed to two ropes that dropped down through the neck of the balloon. "It opens a valve in the top of the balloon that releases gas and makes it sink."

"What does the other rope do? Turn the balloon?"

"Rips a panel from the balloon's skin, deflating it instantly."

"Wonderful. Do you happen to know which one is which?"

She gulped, knowing that if she made a mistake,

they could not possibly survive a precipitous dive into the sea from this altitude.

"From what he said, I'm ninety-nine percent certain it's that rope." She tried to touch the rope, but it dangled a few inches above her head.

Max, however, had no problem reaching it. "I hope you are right." As he pulled lightly, cautiously on the rope, her heart seemed to stop beating.

She heard only a slight hissing. The balloon dropped a little but was clearly not deflating.

Thank God, she had chosen the right rope! She offered up a silent prayer of thanks.

Max gave the hemp another tug, a little harder this time, and the balloon lost more altitude. "Is there any way to turn this contraption about?"

"Not that I know of."

"Then our only hope is to land on that island."

Virgie looked at the earth below and gulped at what she saw. They were already leaving land behind and racing eastward above the roaring, crashing breakers of the North Sea, which mercilessly pounded the English coast.

Ahead of them, as far as she could see, stretched the gray, wind-churned sea, unbroken except for an island that looked to be no more than a lonely speck on the water.

How could Max possibly hope to land on that dot? Yet she knew he was right. Unless the wind changed dramatically and blew them back over England, that island offered the sole spot for landing that they were likely to find.

Virgie clutched the top of the wicker basket. Now that they had left terra firma behind, panic suddenly gnawed at her as she examined the wild, angry sea that lay beneath her like a huge, yawning grave.

Max pulled the valve rope lower, and the balloon sank more rapidly. He frowned and appeared lost in thought that was clearly not pleasant.

"What is it?" Virgie cried in alarm.

"I am trying to gauge what rate of descent is required, given our altitude and distance, to land on the island."

To Virgie, it still looked no larger than a piece of flotsam. "It's so tiny."

"Yes," he agreed calmly. "Not much margin of error for an accidental aeronaut like myself, is there?"

"You'll make it."

A smile tugged at the corners of his mouth. "Are you certain about that, Virg?"

"Yes, I am." And, as she said it, she realized she was. She truly believed that Max could land the balloon. The terror that clawed at her subsided into dull fear.

She looked down at herself. Her full riding skirt would be a definite hindrance when they landed. She quickly unfastened its tapes and removed the garment, revealing denim pants and riding boots concealed beneath it. She wrapped the skirt into a bundle and stuffed it behind the supplies.

Max was so focused on bringing the balloon down that he did not even notice her changing costume.

As the sphere descended, the velocity of the west wind blowing it toward the island slowed precipitously.

For an instant, Virgie feared they would plunge

into the churning sea well short of the island, but Max immediately stopped pulling on the valve rope. The balloon leveled out.

Two minutes later, the wind picked up speed again, and he pulled lightly on the rope once more.

Virgie watched him admiringly as he manipulated the only means available to him to maintain the proper angle of forward speed and descent that would land the balloon on their target.

She was so independent that it had always been difficult for her to entrust her fate to someone else. Now, however, she found herself eagerly surrendering it into Max's capable hands.

"I estimate the island is approximately two miles wide from north to south and five or six miles, west to east," he said as they moved closer to it.

And what a pathetic patch of earth it was. Surveying the island, Virgie's heart sank at a considerably faster rate than the balloon.

Shingle beach along the dipping and curving coastline gave way to rounded hillocks—too small in her opinion to merit the name hills—sparsely covered with tufts of grass. The only trees she could see was a stand of scrubby evergreens, their trunks angled sharply to the leeward, in a small inland meadow. A few crumbling bluffs rose up behind the beach at the north end of the island.

If Virgie had a choice, it would be the last place she would pick as a likely spot for survival. But they had no alternative, and she kept her misgivings to herself.

Max continued to maneuver the balloon toward the island.

As they dropped lower, Virgie was again afraid

they would land in the water short of the island. Her heart seemed to leap into her throat and stayed there until the balloon finally crossed the island's shoreline. As it did, the wicker basket in which they rode was scarcely ten feet above the shingle beach, studded with pebbles and driftwood.

Max dropped the balloon slowly to earth, and the basket finally touched down among the rolling hillocks.

Before Virgie could congratulate Max on his success, a sudden, sharp gust of wind picked up both balloon and basket, carried them several more feet, then slammed the basket on its side against one of the hillocks with such force that Virgie would have been thrown out had Max not grabbed her.

More fierce gusts of wind hit them. Like a wounded bird, the balloon tried to rise into the air and fly again but could not manage to ascend more than twenty feet above the ground.

In the process, it jerked and dragged the wicker basket violently up and down the rounded hills. On the terrifying slide down, the open top of the basket became the bottom.

Virgie would have tumbled out had it not been for Max's powerful arm wrapped around her, gripping her tightly to his body, trying to protect her from the worst of the battering, while he managed somehow to keep them in the basket by gripping the wicker with his other hand.

No longer did Virgie scorn the terrain beneath her as mere hillocks. She was rapidly coming to think of them as mountains.

She looked at the neck of the balloon. In all of the tumbling about, the valve and rip-panel ropes had tangled together, and she could no longer tell which was which.

As the basket started up another hill, Max let go of his hold on the wicker edge and yanked both ropes as hard as he could.

The loud rush of escaping gas filled the air. Like a dying dragon, the rubberized taffeta skin of the rapidly deflating balloon fell limply to the ground, covering it like a red, white, and blue shroud.

At last the wicker basket stilled and came to rest on its side at the bottom of a gully.

Max had twisted so that he was beneath her. "Can you manage to crawl out first?"

Virgie did so, and Max followed her. Relieved of their weight, the wicker basket rose up an inch or two, then settled back on the ground.

She and Max scrambled to their feet.

"You did it, Max! You saved us!" Ecstatic that they were still alive, Virgie threw her arms around him and hugged him exuberantly.

"Ah, my reward." His mouth swooped down on hers, and he kissed her with such passion that for a few moments she forgot everything else but him and the fleeting thought that he was wrong.

This was *her* reward.

Chapter 26

Although Max and Virg survived their rough landing without injury, their meager stock of emergency supplies was less fortunate. The bundle had tumbled unnoticed from the basket, been lost during the wild ride up and down the hills.

"We'll have to retrace the basket's path and look for our supplies," Max said, turning to Virg.

For the first time, he realized that she was wearing pants. "Where did your skirt go?"

"With the supplies, I'm afraid."

They made their way slowly along the bruised tufts of grass that marked the bumpy route the basket had taken.

Several seagulls landed near the beach. A pair of white-breasted sanderlings followed them.

Virg gestured toward the birds. "I'm afraid they may have found our food. We'd better run, or we'll have nothing left."

When they reached the birds, they discovered the bundle had broken open, scattering the supplies.

Worse, the birds they had seen landing were only a small part of the gulls, sanderlings, and ringed plovers that were feasting on the emergency rations. By now, most of the food supplies had been eaten or ruined.

Max sorted through the pitiful remains. Only a package of jerky and two small bags, one of coffee and the other of salt, were salvageable. He wanted to curse in frustration.

"What happened to the water?" Virg asked. "And the matches? I'm most concerned about them."

So was Max.

They hurried over the next hill and found Virg's scarlet skirt and a blanket lying on the ground. They crossed another hill, where they found a second blanket and a small bucket containing soap.

Finally, on the other side of a third hill, they found the empty water container. It had broken open, spilling its precious contents into the wild grass and, in the process, soaking the matches.

The only eatable items that had been carefully packed and wrapped and that, therefore, had survived the tumble and the birds were four bottles of fine French wine.

Max's heart sank as he assessed their plight. They had no water and no matches with which to build a fire to protect them against the cold. He looked out at the icy gray surf.

Virg's survival, not merely his own, was at stake, and that was what bothered him the most. How the hell could he save her?

His jaw clenched in determination. By God, he would find a way.

He looked over at Virg, who was busily pushing aside the tufts of wild grass in the vicinity and looking beneath them. Did she have any inkling of what dire peril they were in?

She moved on to another tussock and peered under it.

"What are you looking for?" Max asked.

"Ah, here it is." She held up a hunting knife. "The aeronaut told me this was among the supplies. We're in good shape now."

Max decided against disabusing her of that notion. Did she think they could provide food for themselves by hand-to-paw combat with wild game? Assuming any game even inhabited this poor excuse for an island.

"You are taking our plight very well," he remarked.

"My father taught us to make the best of every situation."

"You were an excellent student. He would be proud of you." Max took Virgie's soft hand in his own and had to restrain himself from lifting it to his lips to kiss it. "Come with me."

He led her inland. "From the air, I noticed something that looked like ruins of some sort. I think this island was inhabited once. Someone had to have planted some of the vegetation here. It cannot have been native to the island."

They had not gone far when they came upon the remains of two small dwellings that had crumbled long ago. Only a little rubble remained where the walls had once been. They found a rusted tin tub, two iron cooking pots, some utensils, and a few chipped and broken dishes.

Virg knelt and began to examine the dishes. "I wonder who could have lived here."

A vague recollection stirred in Max's memory of something his grandfather had told him when he was a child.

"This must be Ives' Folly. Early last century, two Puritan families set out to start a colony on a remote island in the North Sea."

"And the man who came up with that asinine idea was named Ives?"

Max nodded. "Apparently Ives came from the West Indies. He thought they could plant trees, fruit, and vegetables, and raise pigs and rabbits, and generally turn this into another island paradise."

"Some people can only learn the hard way." Virg gathered up the cooking pots, the utensils, and the least damaged of the dishes—two bowls and three chipped plates—then got to her feet. Max took the heavy iron pots from her, and they headed back toward their collapsed balloon.

Max looked up at the sky, but all he could see was a thick quilt of low, gray clouds, angry and threatening, swirling overhead. Rain was in the offing.

"What happened to the colony?" Virg asked.

"Ives failed to consider this is the North Sea, not the Caribbean. The group nearly starved to death before they abandoned the island a few months later."

When they reached the balloon, Max said, "We must find a place to camp. I will explore the island some more. Perhaps I can find a cave and a water supply."

He hoped she would volunteer to come with him, but she did not. That both surprised and disappointed him. He set out alone, carrying the larger of the two cooking pots they had found.

When Max returned, he reported only partial success. He'd discovered a spring and filled the pot with water from it.

"The spring feeds into a small creek that runs into the ocean on the other side of the island," he told Virg.

"Did you find a cave?"

"Only one, and it is far too shallow to offer us much protection. I did find a place for us to camp, though. A row of cedars and pine that the Ives people must have planted protects the spot from the winds. I will take you there."

"First, we need to go down to the beach and gather driftwood for a fire," Virg said briskly.

What did she think she could use to light it? Max did not ask his question aloud. Knowing Virg, she would find a way, and he wanted to see what she intended to do. Silently, he fell into step beside her.

When they reached the beach, strewn with pebbles and driftwood, she pointed at a shrub, which grew here and there among the rock fragments. "What is that funny-looking plant?"

"Shrubby seablite. And the one over there with the dying white flower is sea campion."

As they began gathering wood, Max noticed Virg picking up a small agate with a pretty brown and beige pattern and dropping it into the pocket of her scarlet riding jacket.

A few minutes later, she discovered another agate, which also went into her pocket. Virg must collect agates.

By now, Max's arms were full of driftwood. "I've all I can carry. Let me show you the campsite I found."

"I have to pick up something that I left by the balloon first," Virg said. "I'll just be a minute."

As she started across the sand, she stooped to pick up another small stone. This one was not an agate but a black rock, dull and worn smooth, that Max could not identify. Still, it joined the agates in Virg's pocket.

She rejoined him a couple of minutes later, carrying a bundle wrapped in the scarlet skirt of her riding habit.

When they reached the site he had picked, her face brightened. "Oh, this is better than I expected we would find."

Virg arranged the wood for the fire.

"What will you use for tinder?" Max asked.

"Birch bark." She untied her skirt and revealed a large pile of paper-thin birch bark. "I gathered and shredded it while you were exploring the island."

She dumped some of it out next to the wood. Then she took her knife and struck it against the black stone she had picked up on the beach.

Sparks flew into the kindling, and she blew on them, igniting the shredded bark. Then, using a broken branch, she pushed it under the driftwood.

"What is that stone?" Max asked.

"Flint. If I had not found it, I would have used

one of the agates." She sounded as though she
started fires that way every day.

"How do you know all this?"

"My father insisted survival techniques be part of
my brothers' and my education."

Both her knowledge and her calm determination
to make the best of their situation greatly impressed
Max. What a remarkable woman.

His gaze settled on her lovely, inviting mouth,
and he could not resist kissing her, softly at first,
and then with growing passion.

He ended the kiss sooner than he wanted, fearing
if he did not stop now, he would not until . . .

She gazed at him with a dreamy light in her eyes.
"What was that for?"

Max smiled. "For being you."

Darkness came early at this time of year. It crept
over Virgie and Max as they ate.

In the light from the fire, she looked around the
camp they had fashioned for themselves. They had
water, food, a makeshift bed of cedar and pine
boughs, and even a colorful shelter of sorts, a lean-
to that Max had built and covered with material
from the balloon's red, white, and blue taffeta skin.

She smiled proudly at Max. "We accomplished
more than I would have thought possible in a few
hours, thanks to you."

He grinned. "See, Virg, I can be handy to have
around now and then."

Not merely handy—crucial! She held up a bit of
the sea kale shoots that Max had harvested. "This
is better than I thought it would be."

"It's often eaten as a vegetable. Tomorrow night, we will try wild cabbage."

Max had also caught plaice, which she'd roasted on sticks over the fire, and crabs, which she'd boiled in one of the cooking pots they'd found in the ruins.

"Thank you, Max, for such a good dinner."

"Thank *you*, Virg. You cooked it."

"But without you, I would have had nothing to cook."

Her father and brothers had taught her a great deal about wilderness survival, but Max knew far more about how to retrieve food from the sea and from its tide pools.

For her part, Virgie had fashioned two snares for whatever small game inhabited the island, but so far neither trap had captured anything.

When the darkness deepened, the temperature fell, and a raw wind blew in off the sea. Virgie could not suppress a shiver.

Max put his arm around her and drew her close to him. How comforting it was to nestle against his warmth. He held her like that for several minutes. She found it so pleasant and comforting that she did not want to move.

After awhile, her head was nodding.

Max said softly, "Time to get some sleep."

They crawled into the bed of boughs they had fashioned on the ground inside the lean-to. Max covered them both with the blankets they had salvaged from the emergency supplies.

Virgie lay her head down, the pleasant scent of cedar and pine filling her nostrils.

Max pulled her tightly against him so they could share their warmth, and Virgie loved having his hard, muscled body against hers and his arms around her.

Max lay awake on the aromatic boughs, listening to Virg's soft, deep breathing. She had fallen asleep within a minute of lying down.

A light rain pelted the lean-to. He was proud of this simple, crude structure. Virg had explained the concept to him, and he had built the frame and covered it with the balloon's tightly woven fabric, which had been rubberized and now protected them from the rain.

A frigid gust of wind off the sea shook the lean-to's fabric. Max was glad they had no thermometer. He did not want to know how cold it was.

Virg snuggled against him in her sleep. She was amazing.

Unique.

The most intriguing woman he had ever met.

Her courage was rare even in a male, and Max had never before met a woman who possessed it in such abundance. She was actually managing to enjoy being stranded on this godawful island.

And, dammit, Max was too. Her enthusiasm was infectious. For the first time since his grandfather had summoned him back to England to oversee Penrose, he felt as though he was truly living. Although he had been nervous at first, he had even enjoyed the challenge of landing the diabolical balloon on this sorry island.

Max listened enviously to Virg's deep, even breathing. He was as tired as she was, but he did not fool himself that he would get much rest tonight.

And it was all her fault.

In her sleep, she unconsciously kept trying to snuggle closer to him and his warmth. She squirmed and wiggled, trying to paste every last inch of herself against him as tight as wallpaper against a wall.

Thanks to her, he was no longer cold.

He was hot.

And hard.

He ached to bury himself in Virg's tantalizing body, but she slept on, totally unaware of the misery she was inflicting on him. She had innocently turned sleeping beside her into erotic torture.

Max had to do something. He could not spend another night in torment like this.

He was just a man, not a damned saint.

Chapter 27

Hearing the crunch of Max's footsteps approaching their camp the following evening, Virgie looked up from the rabbit she was roasting for their dinner. Her snares had finally yielded a meal. Most likely, the Ives party had imported the animal's ancestors to the island.

Max's lower face was already covered with thick, black stubble that made him look more than ever like a dangerous outlaw—or perhaps the secret agent he had once been. He carried a load of driftwood in his arms, and a bottle of French wine dangled from one of his hands.

Max dumped the wood beside the fire and held up the wine. "I thought we might as well drink this tonight. It should go well with the *lapin*."

"What will we drink it in?"

He pulled two large seashells from his coat pocket. "I found these on the beach." He looked at her as if he expected her to spurn drinking from them.

Instead she laughed. "What fun. I never drank wine from a seashell before."

Maybe the wine would make Max more cheerful. Virgie hoped so. He had been such a grump all day. When she'd asked what the matter was, he'd said he'd had very little sleep and was exhausted.

She'd exclaimed in surprise, "How could you not sleep like a baby? I certainly did."

"Yes, I know," Max had snapped, glaring at her as though his sleeplessness had been all her fault.

The rabbit turned out better than Virg expected. Max even complimented her on her cooking skill, which pleased her. He had been right about the wine going well with the food, and he seemed in better humor.

After they finished eating, Max refilled their seashells. Virgie sipped from hers while he watched her over the edge of his shell with such intensity that she finally asked, "Why are you looking at me like that?"

"Like what?"

He acted as though he had no idea what she was talking about, but she was certain he did. She thought about pursuing the subject, but the wine had mellowed her—and made her sleepy.

Night had stolen over them, ending their second gray, cloudy day on the island. Did the sun ever shine on Ives' Folly?

With the darkness came another drop in the temperature, and she was getting chilly. She thought of how warm and cozy she had been last night snuggled up against Max.

Virgie fought her need to yawn, then saw Max do so, and seized upon it. "Since you're so tired, why don't we turn in now?"

He gave her a look she could not decipher. "Excellent idea."

They settled into their bough bed, which was not as aromatic as it had been the previous night, and she pressed against Max again, seeking his warmth. Tonight, however, despite his professed exhaustion, he was terribly restless.

"What's the matter?" she finally demanded.

"I'm trying to get comfortable."

Well, he wasn't exactly making her comfortable with his squirming. He kept rubbing against her in a way that, even through her shirt, made her ache.

Then his hands moved slowly up and down her body, turning her bones to water.

"What are you doing?" Her voice was unsteady.

"Looking for a comfortable place to put my hands. Ah, I'll try this." Max settled his hands on her derriere, but instead of resting them, he caressed her there, intensifying her ache.

With the tip of his tongue, he outlined her lips lightly, teasingly. "My tongue is cold," he whispered huskily.

The instant she opened her mouth to challenge his claim, he slipped his tongue between her lips and explored her mouth with a tender thoroughness that thrilled her.

The chill she'd felt earlier vanished in a blaze of hunger so hot and fierce it frightened her. She pulled away from him and rolled over, presenting her back to him.

That proved to be a serious tactical error. Max

dropped his hands to her waist and casually unbuttoned her denim pants. He traced circles lightly with his fingers on her belly, sending sensations of desire and aching need shooting through her.

She pushed his hand away and immediately realized how much she wished she had not done so.

Before she guessed what he was about, he'd undone the top buttons of her shirt. Max slipped his hand beneath it and cupped her breast. His fingers toyed with her nipple in a way that made her moan with pleasure.

He returned his other hand to her belly and resumed drawing circles with his fingertips, rocking her with new and powerful sensations. This time, she could not have pushed that tantalizing hand away if her life depended on it.

Her breath came in quick gasps. He brought her to the edge of something wondrous, then suddenly stopped, and withdrew his hands.

"W-w-what?" she asked, dazed and wanting.

"Not without me, my sweet." His voice was dark and mesmerizing, full of mystery and promise. "Turn toward me."

She did, wanting to look into his eyes. When she could not even make out his face in the darkness, she groaned in frustration.

"What is it?" He gently caressed her cheeks with his fingertips.

"I want to see you."

"No more than I want to see you, my sweet."

Denied the sight of him, she resorted to her hands. She moved her fingers lightly over his face, touching his eyebrows, his nose, his cheeks and chin, with their rough growth of whiskers, and pictured his features in her mind.

Her hands slipped to his chest. She unbuttoned his shirt and ran her palms over his warm, hard chest and the surprisingly soft hair that curled there. He moaned.

Her inability to see made her other senses more acute. The surf sounded more pure and clear. So did the hiss and crackle of the fire's dying embers. She loved the different textures of Max's skin and hair beneath her fingertips, and she traced his muscles.

"You feel wonderful," she murmured.

"Not nearly as wonderful as you do." The husky warmth of his voice sent shivers of excitement tripping up her spine.

He pulled her hard against him, and his mouth covered hers in a deep, erotic kiss that unleashed a gripping sensation in her stomach that was almost painful.

He pulled her hips against him, and she felt the hard bulge of his erection. "I want you."

For a moment, Virgie did not move or speak. All the reasons why she should not give herself to this man flashed through her mind.

But what did these reasons matter? They might not escape this island alive.

And most important of all, she loved Max. Whether they died on this island or lived to tell about it, this might be her only chance to taste the mysterious union with the one man she had ever loved.

"I want you too." Virgie had meant her voice to come out strong and certain. Instead it had an embarrassing quaver.

If Max noticed, he did not comment. Instead he drew back and kissed her long and hard. Then he pushed away her clothes and caressed her everywhere.

Where his hands had been, his mouth followed, covering her with kisses, making her body quiver and throb with pleasure and need.

She felt like the sleeping princess Prince Charming had just awakened.

His hand moved to her secret place, rubbing it in a way that left her moaning and writhing beneath his touch.

When she thought she could bear his sweet torment no longer, he entered her, and she gulped at the size of him. Then she felt a stab of pain so sharp she cried out.

Max went absolutely still, bracing his weight on his powerful arms. He whispered sweet reassurances and endearments, his warm breath tickling her ear. Then he nibbled on her lobe.

Finally he began to move within her, slowly, carefully. Gradually her pain metamorphosed into pleasure, and she moaned. His pace increased, and this time she did fall over the edge into an ecstasy she had never known.

As her body convulsed around his, he followed her into that shattering oblivion with a hoarse cry.

Afterward he held her tightly against him. Even when his breathing relaxed into the deep rhythm of sleep, he continued to cradle her.

How she loved this man.

When Virgie opened her eyes the next morning, she was surprised that the sun, or what little she could see of it through thick gray clouds, was well above the horizon.

Max, his head propped on his elbow, lay beside her, watching her with an expression she could not read. She suddenly felt shy at facing him for the first time since making love with him—or any other man.

His sensuous smile warmed her in a way the sun could never have.

"Good morning, my sweet Virg."

Disappointment stabbed at her. She had hoped he would say *my love*.

"What a lazy bones you are," he teased. "And you claim to be the early riser."

"How long have you been awake?"

"Oh, for hours and hours."

She sincerely doubted that, but she noted, "You could have gotten up."

"What—and let you get cold? I could not be so cruel as to do that to you."

"Always thinking of others, aren't you?" she asked archly.

"Especially when the other is you."

"You're in much better humor today."

He grinned hugely. "After last night, what man would not be?"

Later they explored the island together, hand in hand, talking constantly except when they stopped to kiss.

That evening, as they were eating, Virgie told him about her parents and the great love they had shared. If only she could make him appreciate the importance of love in a marriage.

But he said, "That kind of love is so rare—the

exception that proves the rule. Mostly people fall into lust with each other and mistake it for love. Then they soon discover how quickly passion burns out."

"But true love does not burn out!" Virgie protested.

"How many people can tell the difference between lust, when they are in the throes of it, and love? If they make the mistake of marrying when their passion is hot, they are stuck with each other."

"And if they love each other, nothing makes them happier than to be—as you so felicitously phrase it—stuck with each other."

His skeptical expression irritated her. "Furthermore, if a couple has neither lust nor love for one another, which is what you advocate, they are still stuck with each other. And I mean really stuck like two hungry sharks trapped in a tank with no food."

He laughed. "What a way with words you have, Virg."

"It's true!" she exclaimed indignantly. "They don't have love to smooth the rough spots for them. Love is so important. It is the ice on which marriage skates smoothly."

"You are such a romantic, Virg."

"No, I know how wonderful and satisfying a marriage based on mutual love can be. I saw it firsthand with my parents."

"And such a marriage is as rare as a dodo bird."

"You are such a cynic, Max." What had made him that way? Had it been his own parents? "Didn't your parents love each other?"

Max thought for a while, then confessed, "Truthfully, I do not know. I hardly remember them at all.

They were killed when I was six, and I saw very little of them before that. They were much sought after in society and were often gone."

Virgie was truly shocked. "How could any parent ignore his or her child?"

He shrugged. "My grandfather paid more attention to me than my parents ever did."

How thankful that made Virg for her own parents.

Max rose and held out a hand to Virgie. "Come, that is enough talk. Time for bed." His sensual smile set her pulse rushing. "That is the one place where we are in complete accord."

A few nights later, after Max and Virg had made love and she had dropped into contented sleep, he lay staring up at the blackness and worrying whether they would ever get off this island. They had been here a week now, and not once in that time had they even seen a boat on the sea.

Time had not dragged, though. That was impossible with Virg beside him. They talked about any and everything—from cosmic theories to trivia. He told her things about himself that he had never dreamed of telling another human being. Indeed, he had never met anyone he could talk to as freely as he could talk to her.

She, in turn, entertained him with hilarious tales about her family and her and her brothers' childhood escapades. Her stories made him laugh and, paradoxically, made him want to cry. What would it have been like to grow up in a family like hers, bound so closely together by love?

For the Blairs, love was paramount.

For the Chartwells, duty was.

And that was the crux of the problem between Virg and him.

Now, she brought up the importance of love in marriage less and less. She had found arguing with him on that topic futile.

If she only knew. Max swallowed hard. The conflict between his heart and his honor was tearing him apart.

He desperately wanted Virg, but he knew how miserably unhappy she would be as an English lady. Max could not incarcerate her in the women's prison that was Victorian England. It would be like caging an iridescent hummingbird in a teacup.

But Max could not leave England either.

At least, not yet.

And perhaps never.

He had sworn to his dying grandfather that he would oversee both Es and Penrose until Max was convinced his cousin could properly administer the estate and had the strength to resist his mother's constant extravagant demands. Max had never in his life broken his oath. And he would not now.

His grandfather had been certain that Es could never meet either condition, but Max knew that his young cousin was well on his way to fulfilling the first.

Daphne, however, posed a more intractable problem. Until her son could stand up to her—and Max was not optimistic about that ever happening—he was trapped in England.

Try as he might, he could think of no way to untie this Gordian knot.

Chapter 28

Virgie might well have lost track of how long they had spent on the island had Max not insisted on scratching a mark for each day on the wall of the small cave, where the rain would not wash them away.

Each damp, gray day blended into the next with nothing to differentiate them.

But the nights—oh, the nights. Each one was precious. How she cherished the nights spent making love with Max and sleeping in his arms.

Now, standing in front of the marks in the cave, Virgie counted eight. And in that time, they had not seen a single boat. Would they ever be found?

She shivered and pulled her scarlet cloak more tightly around her. The days were growing colder and shorter, a sobering reminder of how quickly winter was approaching. If the temperature dropped much lower, she doubted they could survive.

When Virgie emerged from the cave, Max was a hundred or so yards down the beach, gathering driftwood deposited by the tide.

She looked in the opposite direction and saw a long piece of driftwood, bleached and gnarled. From its size, she surmised it must have once been a large tree branch. As she hurried to retrieve this generous length of wood, she caught a flash of something on the water.

Looking toward it, she saw the sails of what appeared to be a fishing boat skimming past the island.

She waved her arms and shouted, "Help, help!"

Then she realized her voice could not possibly be heard over the thunder of the surf.

With fingers awkward from the cold, she unbuttoned her scarlet cloak and waved it in the air, hoping the bright material would attract the attention of someone on the boat.

The fishing boat sailed steadily on a southeastern course away from the island.

Virgie wanted to cry in frustration and vexation.

She raced to the long piece of bleached driftwood and grabbed it. With frantic haste, she draped her scarlet cloak over one end of the wood, then gripped the other end with both hands and raised it high over her head.

The bright garment swirled, waved, and dipped in the wind.

Still the boat receded toward the horizon.

But Virgie refused to give up. She continued to wave the driftwood with the cloak on top of it.

Max shouted something at her, but she could not make out his words over the surf. He dropped the driftwood he'd been collecting and ran toward her.

Please God, Virgie prayed silently, make the people on the boat look this way.

Instead the boat moved away from the island until it looked no bigger than an oval toy under sail on the frigid, heaving sea.

Soon the boat would disappear from sight. And with it, their hope for rescue.

Desperation drove Virgie to wave her makeshift distress flag even more vigorously.

Max reached her and grabbed the driftwood. By now his ragged, fast-growing beard made him look like a California desperado.

"Let me have it," he said hoarsely. "I am taller, and I can hold it higher."

Virgie relinquished the bleached wood to Max.

He hoisted the long branch as far above his head as he could manage.

The boat was about to disappear over the horizon when it suddenly altered course and tacked toward the island.

"I am certain they see us," Max cried.

Virgie offered up another silent prayer, this time of thanks.

When the boat sailed within shouting distance, Max yelled, "Can you take us aboard? We are stranded on this uninhabited island."

"Aye, providin' us can get in close 'nuff," a rough voice from the boat replied.

The vessel tacked closer but was still fifteen or twenty yards from shore when the rough voice called again. "Water's gettin' too shallow. Here's as far as us can come. Can you wade out to us?"

Max looked anxiously at Virgie. "I am certain I can, but what about you?"

The question miffed her. "Don't worry, my lord. I'm no helpless female."

His gray eyes lit with amusement.

"You, Virg, are the least helpless person, male or female, I have ever met. And that's a fact."

"Why, thank you," she stammered in surprise.

"What concerns me is that you are much shorter and lighter than I am. The waves will hit you higher, and it will be harder for you to retain your footing against the outgoing tide."

Max was right, and his anxiety for her generated a glow of warmth that made her forget for a moment how cold she was.

He grabbed her cloak from the end of the driftwood and tossed away the makeshift pole. He wrapped the cloak around his neck.

"I hope I am tall enough to keep it dry," he explained, reaching for her hand and enveloping it in his own. "Come, we will head for the boat. No matter what happens, hang on to me. Do not let go."

Side by side, hand in hand, they splashed into the sea toward the fishing boat. The foaming gray water swirled about the ankles of their riding boots.

Although the surf hit them hard, the first few yards were easy enough. Then a breaker, higher and more fierce than its predecessors, slammed into them.

The force of the wave nearly knocked Virgie off her feet. She clung to Max's hand as though he were her lifeline—which he was. Even then, she would have been flattened against the sand, but he quickly pulled her against him, using his body to anchor hers so she remained upright.

Still, the icy seawater drenched her to the shoulders, and a strong chill shook her.

Max wrapped both his arms around her. He held her so tightly she could feel his muscles straining and his heart beating hard and fast.

Virgie struggled to retain her footing against the power of the tide, but its insidious force sucked her legs from beneath her.

Clutching her to him, Max half pulled, half dragged her through the angry, churning sea toward the boat.

A few yards from their goal, another large breaker crashed over them with such fury that Max staggered too. For a heart-stopping minute, Virgie feared the stormy tide would suck them both under the water and out to sea.

Somehow Max managed to retain his footing, but barely.

He lifted her off her feet and shoved her toward a burly fisherman hanging over the side of the boat. The man's outstretched arms caught her beneath the shoulders.

Then, like an invisible stalker, the treacherous tide ripped her from the fisherman's arms. Each grabbed for the other's hands. Their fingers met and gripped.

Another wave crashed over her, leaving her choking for air. This time, however, the fisherman managed to maintain his hold on her and lift her over the railing into the boat.

He set Virgie, coughing and gasping, on the deck.

She looked out to where Max was. Another wild wave broke over the boat and him. He vanished beneath the frigid gray water.

Endless seconds ticked by, each one an eternity for her, and he did not reappear. Horror paralyzed her.

In that terrible moment, she felt as though her heart had been sucked out to sea.

One of the crew on the other side of the boat yelled and tossed a rope out into the cold, bubbling cauldron that was the sea.

"He caught it," the man yelled, and he began pulling the hemp in.

Praying that Max could hang on in the violent, frigid water, Virgie clung to the railing with fingers that felt like shards of ice, fighting to make her way on the rolling, pitching deck toward the man with the rope.

A second man joined him, and together they strained to draw the rope in.

Virgie reached them as they dragged Max over the side and into the vessel. He lay gasping on the deck.

She would have fallen on her knees to help him, but one of the fishermen grabbed her and held her back.

"Ma'am, ye must get out o' them wet clothes afore you freeze." He tried to turn her toward the cabin, but she would not move.

"Max! Are you all right?"

He tried to push himself to his knees but failed.

He tried again and succeeded. Thoroughly soaked and exhausted, he struggled beneath the weight of her scarlet cloak, which hung around his neck like a wet anchor.

His shirt was so wet that it was semitransparent and plastered against his shoulders and chest in a way that uncoiled a lovely warmth in Virgie despite her chattering teeth.

His dripping hair curled about his face in unruly black swirls, and rivulets ran into his ragged black beard. Virgie itched to push his hair back with her fingers and wipe the water from his face.

She jerked out of the fisherman's grasp and dropped to her knees beside Max on the deck just as a blast of bone-freezing wind struck them. She began to shiver and could not stop.

Max pulled her into his arms, but he was as cold as she was. A fisherman appeared with blankets that he wrapped around them. Then he took them below to change out of their wet garments.

Twenty minutes later, Virgie, now dry and dressed in ill-fitting clothes borrowed from the fishermen, went into the galley and found Max there, drinking from a steaming mug of hot tea.

When he saw her, he got up and poured a mug of tea for her. They sat together, sipping their tea in silence, while she searched for words that would properly express what she wanted to tell him.

Finally, she set the mug down and turned to him.

"I have so much to thank you for, Max. Without you, I would not have survived on that island, or even landed on it. Without you, I would never have made it to this boat." She reached up and stroked his bearded face gently with her hand. "You saved my life several times over, and I am so grateful to you. You are truly my hero."

He looked startled, then he grinned so widely that his mouth seemed to extend to his ears. "At last, Virg!"

He put down his mug, pulled her into his arms,

and held her so tightly she could scarcely breathe. She felt his heart beating strong and steady against her breast.

When he finally loosened his hold on her, he said, "We make a great team in dire circumstances, Virg."

And what about in life? Instead of asking that question aloud, though, she hid her sadness behind a smile. If only her hero loved her as she loved him.

Chapter 29

The fishing boat put into port that night at Aldeburgh.

After thanking their rescuers profusely, Virgie and Max hurried along the dock.

"I know a very good inn nearby where we can spend the night," Max said.

He led her to the King George, which looked like a large country house. When they stepped inside, the inn proved to be as elegant as its name—all mahogany paneling, tapestry-upholstered furniture, and crystal chandeliers.

Virgie glanced down at the fishermen's clothes, ragged and smelly, that she and Max wore, then up at his face and its untrimmed growth of black beard that obscured his lower face.

She must look even worse, her hair a wild tangle from the salt water. The ragged pants she wore were so big that she'd had to tie the drawstring waist just below her armpits and roll up the legs almost to the knees so she would not trip on them. The jacket was so large that it hung to her knees.

She had not bothered to push up the sleeves, which hung inches below her fingers, because they kept her hands warm.

"They may not rent to us," she said dubiously. "We are dirty and stink of fish."

"Yes, they will," Max assured her. "I will see to that."

When they presented themselves to the clerk at the registration desk, however, he was clearly appalled by their appearance and odor.

Not only did he look down his nose at them but Virgie thought he was about to pinch it closed with his fingers. She was certain he would turn them away, but she had reckoned without Max.

"Give us the very best room you have, the one in the corner that looks over both the ocean and the town." In manner and voice, Max was the unmistakable scion of eight centuries of British aristocracy.

The clerk's nose snapped up, and he looked uncertain. "We have other rooms—"

"Only the room I requested will do."

The clerk's gaze swept over them contemptuously. "But that room is very, very expensive."

"I know what it costs. I have stayed in it many times."

The clerk was clearly still skeptical. "Well, sir—"

Max cut him off. "I am not sir, I am Lord Chartwell."

It was the first time Virgie had heard Max invoke his title, but when she saw the way the haughty clerk paled, she understood why Max did so.

"Also tell Josiah Bailey I wish to see him in my room in ten minutes."

"Y-y-yes, m'lord," the clerk stammered. "Will you be so kind as to sign the register?"

Virgie watched as Max wrote Lord and Lady Chartwell, and the clerk handed him the key.

Then Max took Virgie's arm and led her toward the stairs.

"Who is Josiah Bailey?" she whispered.

"The inn's owner."

As they walked along the upstairs hall to their room, Virgie said, only half teasing, "I was much surprised to learn we are married."

"It was necessary to register that way to protect your reputation."

His reply hit Virgie like a bucket of icy water. She had expected a more romantic response than that. Deep in her heart of hearts, she had hoped he would say, "We soon will be."

But, of course, that was impossible. Max, always the realist, clearly knew that.

And he was right. But it still made her want to cry.

"Here is our room." Max stopped before a door at the end of the corridor and inserted the key in the door lock.

Virgie stepped inside and examined the spacious corner room, which had been tastefully, indeed opulently, furnished.

A large four-poster bed boasted a feather mattress so thick that it required a three-step bedstair to climb into it. The head of the bed was placed against one of the interior walls so that its occupants could enjoy the views through the windows on both exterior walls.

A table and two chairs had been placed beneath the windows that looked out on the lights of the town. On the adjacent wall, the windows revealed only darkness, broken by an occasional pinpoint of light across the sea.

"Why did you insist on this room?" she asked.

"Two reasons. First, I am determined to make love to you in a proper bed."

His hot, intimate smile ignited a smoldering fire deep within her. She looked longingly at the big, *comfortable* bed and sighed. "That would be wonderful."

"Second, this room has a bath."

Max pointed to a closed door that she'd assumed was a closet.

"Go ahead, Virg. My business with Bailey will take a little time."

While Virgie was washing her hair and bathing, she heard voices speaking too low to be intelligible. Bailey must have arrived.

After drying herself and her hair, she could not face putting on clothes that were not as clean as she was. So she ignored her borrowed garb and, instead, wrapped a towel around her.

She opened the bathroom door a crack and asked, "Are you alone?"

"Yes, come on out."

She took a few steps into the bedroom and stopped. Even though the towel was large and covered her quite adequately, she felt shy at Max's lazy perusal of her and clutched it together nervously.

With an enigmatic smile, he crossed the room to

her, kissed the tip of her nose, slipped the towel from her hand, and opened it. He stepped back and studied her leisurely, starting with her bare feet and moving up her legs to her thighs, her hips, her waist. Then his intense gaze stopped at her high, firm breasts.

Virgie felt her face burn with embarrassment, and she knew her cheeks must be blazing a bright red. Even though she had made love with Max, he had not actually seen her naked before.

He raised his gaze to hers. "You have no reason to be embarrassed, Virg." His voice was as soft as the downy feathers of a baby wren. "You are too lovely to be anything but proud. Even more lovely than I had dreamed, sweetheart."

Her startled, skeptical eyes saw the appreciation—and something else she could not identify—in his gaze.

"I speak the truth, Virg. Do not doubt it."

He made her feel more beautiful than she'd ever felt in her life.

"I long to cover your delectable body with kisses, but I must bathe and shave first. I hope you will still recognize me when I emerge." He drew the towel around her again, fastened it at the neck, and lifted her hand to hold it.

Then he bent his head and kissed her, keeping a space between their bodies. Only his lips touched hers. The kiss was long and sweet, a promise for later.

He headed into the bath. "You will find a robe in the closet. Also I ordered dinner for us. We will eat when I get out."

He stopped and turned to look at her with a

wicked grin. "I cannot vouch for the rest of the meal, but I promise dessert will be wonderful." His gleaming eyes left no doubt as to what dessert would be.

She pulled the robe of blue flannel from the closet and wrapped herself in it, then sat down at the dressing table to attack her wet, snarled hair with a brush and comb that had appeared while she was bathing.

By the time Virgie managed to dispose of the tangles, a manservant arrived with a heavy tray of covered dishes. He set two places at the table that overlooked the town and unloaded the contents of the tray.

A minute after the servant left, Max emerged from the bathroom. He'd shaved and wrapped a towel around his waist, leaving his powerful chest bare.

Her breath caught, and she could not take her eyes from him. She longed to go to him and run her hands slowly over his muscled shoulders and through the curling black hair on his chest.

At last, he said quizzically, "Virg?"

Her gaze snapped up to his face. She was not certain how long she had been staring at him, and she felt like an idiot.

Amusement softened his gray eyes and the hard planes of his face. "Thank you," he said softly.

They sat at the table with Max still wrapped in the towel. He lifted the cover from one of the dishes, revealing poached salmon garnished with prawns.

He picked up one of the prawns and dangled it in front of her. "A morsel for you, my sweet."

Their gazes locked, and she could not tear hers away as she ate the tidbit from his fingers. With his gaze still fixed on her face, he lifted another prawn to her lips, and she ate that too.

Passion smoldered in his eyes, igniting her own. Suddenly her hunger was not for food.

She cast a longing glance at the big, *comfortable* bed, then looked back at him. "Please, can we have dessert first?"

He laughed, clearly delighted. "Indeed we can, and we will, sweetheart."

His endearment thrilled her.

Max replaced the cover on the platter of salmon, rose, and helped Virgie to her feet.

Then he gathered her in his arms. Virgie caressed his naked back, delighting in the smooth warmth of his skin and the muscles rippling beneath her hands.

Max kissed her lightly, brushing his mouth across hers like a gentle breeze. Her lips opened slightly, giving sound to a contented sigh.

He took advantage of that to deepen their kiss, filling her with delight while making her ache for more.

He opened her robe as he dipped his lips, delivering a string of nibbling kisses down her neck and the slope of her breast, until his mouth closed over its rosy tip and gently suckled. She gasped in pleasure.

Max pushed the robe from her shoulders, and she let it fall to the floor. He swept her up into his arms and carried her to the bed, laying her on it as gently as if she were a priceless piece of crystal.

His gaze roamed her body admiringly. "So lovely," he murmured.

Once again, he made her feel beautiful and treasured.

He untied the towel around his waist and let it drop beside the bed. She raised her head slightly from the pillow to examine his lower torso that she knew so well by touch but had never seen entirely naked before.

Max grinned at her. "Do I pass muster?"

Oh, yes, he did.

Instead of telling him, though, she teased, "I'll let you know after we've made love."

"Ah, a most intriguing challenge."

And one he clearly accepted, for he explored her body with aching slowness. He teased and tormented every last inch of her, using his mouth, his tongue, and his hands to bring her to the edge of ecstasy and then drawing back time after time.

"No more. Please, no more," she finally gasped.

"Does that mean I passed muster?"

"You won the grand championship!" she gasped. "Now, have mercy and love me!"

And he did, until they both soared in unison to the edge of paradise.

Afterward they lay still joined together, and she marveled at how his outlaw face had relaxed. He looked almost boyish.

Virgie swallowed hard. She had given her body, her heart, and her soul to this man. She wanted to tell him how much she loved him, how much she longed to spend the rest of her life as his wife, but she could not bring herself to do so.

Virgie could not bear the pain of having him remind her that love had no place in marriage.

Chapter 30

When Max and Virg arrived at Castle Penrose, Jenkins stared at them as though he were seeing two ghosts.

"We feared you were dead after that balloon vanished without a trace."

"We are harder to dispose of than you think, Jenkins," Max said with a smile.

"I am much relieved, my lord. Miss Lake has been terribly worried about you, Miss Blair. Perhaps you could set her mind at ease. I believe she is in the drawing room."

Max silently noted that Jenkins said nothing about Rowena. The witch was probably delighted her stepdaughter might be dead. "Go ahead, Virg."

She nodded and headed for the drawing room.

"Where will I find the duke, Jenkins?" Max asked. "Or is Lady Albert with him?"

"No, her ladyship took to her bed three days ago and has not left it since."

"What illness felled her?"

Jenkins, at his most wooden-faced, said, "The duke's announcement of his betrothal to Isabel Lake."

"Does Lady Albert not approve of the match?" As if Max needed to ask.

"No, my lord, and she assured them that you would put a quick end to it."

"Did she now? You had better tell the duke that I must see him in the library as soon as possible."

Instead of finding Belle in the drawing room, Virgie discovered Rowena. She was talking to a stunningly beautiful blond woman with the type of tall, well-endowed figure that Virgie had always envied.

Neither woman noticed Virgie immediately, and she stared with admiration at the lovely stranger. From her modish lavender gown to her carefully coifed hair, she was perfectly turned out.

Virgie cringed at how bad she must look in the ill-fitting brown linsey-woolsey gown and gray cape that Max had purchased for her from one of the maids at the King George Inn. Although Virgie had pulled her hair back and twisted it into a knot, she could feel unruly tendrils that had escaped and were curling around her face.

Never had Virgie felt so small and insignificant and unattractive as she did with this woman, whom she silently dubbed Miss Perfection.

Virgie turned to sneak quietly away, but she had

taken only three steps toward the door when Rowena screeched, "Missy, is that you?"

Cursing her bad luck, Virgie reluctantly turned.

The beauty spared her only a quick cursory glance. Her expression betrayed that she found nothing of interest about Virgie.

Her stepmother looked her up and down critically. "So you have survived after all." Rowena sounded as though that disappointed her enormously.

She turned to the beauty beside her. "Virginia, let me present you to the earl of Stonybrook's daughter, Lady Priscilla."

Oops, not Miss. Lady Perfection.

Rowena smirked at Virgie. "Lady Priscilla is betrothed to Lord Chartwell."

"What?" Virgie croaked in shock.

"Lady Priscilla, this is my stepdaughter," Rowena said.

The blond swiveled her head and examined Virgie as critically as her stepmother had. "Is my darling Max safe?"

Virgie nodded, too stricken to speak.

Rowena smiled, her eyes glittering with pure malice. "Won't Lady Priscilla and Chartwell make a handsome couple? I believe we shall stay for their wedding, which is imminent."

"I hope you will." Although polite, Lady Priscilla's answer was devoid of enthusiasm.

Virgie's heart seemed to implode and disintegrate into a million broken shards. She was plunged into the center of a vortex where the world seemed to be whirling around her.

I will not faint, she told herself sternly, gritting

her teeth, clutching the top of a chair back for support, and willing herself to remain conscious and on her feet.

Slowly the dizziness cleared, and she heard Lady Priscilla say, "You must excuse me. I cannot wait to see my dearest Max."

"And I must pay poor Daphne a visit." Rowena followed Lady Perfection from the room.

Still dazed with shock, Virgie sank down into the chair she had been using for support.

Memories of Max and their lovemaking haunted her.

Memories of the ecstasy he had brought her.

Memories of his warming her with the heat of his body.

Memories of his mouth, his hands, even his eyes caressing her as though she were the most beautiful creature alive.

Not once had he so much as hinted that he was already betrothed. But neither had he said he loved Virgie, only that he wanted her.

Her father and brothers had warned her often enough that men, unlike women, did not confuse lust and love.

What an incredible idiot she was. She had known better than to fall in love with Max, but she had not been able to stop herself. Then she'd deluded herself into thinking that Max cared deeply for her too.

But it did not matter whether he did or didn't. In either case, he would not marry her. He had been emphatic that he would never marry a woman he loved, only a woman who would make him the proper blue-blooded wife.

Which Lady Perfection clearly would.

And Virgie would not.

She rose and hurried quietly down the hall to the backstairs to avoid any chance of seeing Max with his fiancée. Gathering up her skirts, she started up the stairs two at a time.

At the top, she dashed down the hall to her bedchamber, where she rushed inside, threw herself across the big bed, and buried her head in the pillows to muffle the torrent of tears that she could no longer suppress.

Damn Max!

Damn the lying scoundrel.

Damn him for smashing her heart to smithereens. Virgie would have nothing to do with him again.

Not ever.

Chapter 31

M ax crossed the threshold of the library and stopped abruptly. Es and Isabel sat together on one of the sofas, holding hands and talking. Although Max was only a few feet from them, they were so engrossed in each other that they did not even notice him.

He smiled at the way Isabel regarded Es adoringly. Virg was right—as usual. Isabel truly loved his cousin.

Isabel was urging the duke to reinstitute the tradition of a harvest dinner for all his tenants and dependents and to hold an additional one at Christmas, too.

Good for her. Max smiled approvingly to himself. She would make Penrose a fine chatelaine.

"An excellent idea, Isabel."

Max's voice startled her and Es, and they hastily jumped up.

"Max! Max! You are safe!" his cousin cried, clearly overjoyed.

"My lord, is Vir—Miss Blair safe, too?" Isabel asked in a voice wobbly with fear.

He nodded, and her eyes shone with happiness and relief.

"I am so happy!" Es exclaimed, a wide smile on his face.

He started toward Max, then stopped abruptly, his smile fading into a frown and apprehension creasing his face.

Puzzled by his cousin's sudden change in mood and demeanor, Max asked, "What the devil's the matter, Es?"

The duke squared his shoulders, and his expression became so markedly like their paternal grandfather's at his most stubborn that Max wanted to smile.

"Belle has done me the honor of accepting my offer of marriage, and we are betrothed," he said with stiff formality so unlike him. "We will be married as soon as the bans are published."

Daphne burst through the door, clutching a pink silk wrapper around her.

"Chartwell, I just heard you returned. Thank God, you are here." For once, she was clearly delighted to see Max. "I warned my son you will forbid him to throw himself away on that . . . that . . . creature."

Daphne glared at Isabel, who flinched as though she'd been struck physically.

Max winced in sympathy with Isabel.

"Mother, you will not insult my future duchess," Es ordered, sounding just like their grandfather at his most forbidding. "I will not tolerate it."

Daphne gaped at him in shock, then turned to Max. "Tell him he cannot marry her."

"I *will* marry Belle." Es faced Max, staring him straight in the eyes. "Neither you nor anyone else can stop me."

"Nor do I want to stop you, Es. I am well pleased with your choice of a bride. I think you two will suit admirably." Max smiled at them both. "Your marriage has my blessing and best wishes."

"No!" Daphne cried. "You cannot allow my son to wed such an inferior, penniless creature. Why, she is nothing but a paid companion."

"Actually, Daphne, as the granddaughter of both a duke and an earl, Isabel's breeding is far better than yours," Max said sharply.

Daphne looked at him with murderous fury, then turned and ran from the room.

Es gathered Isabel in his arms and comforted her.

Max glanced after Daphne. She had stopped outside the door and turned to look back at her son. When she saw him embracing his betrothed, her face crumbled. Clearly, she had expected Es to follow her. She vanished through the first open door she passed, slamming it shut behind her.

Silently Max applauded his cousin. At last, Es had cut himself free from his mother's apron strings.

"Darling Max, here you are."

Recognizing the carefully modulated voice behind him, Max froze in surprise and dismay, nearly uttering a groan aloud.

What the hell was Lady Priscilla doing here?

Then her father said, "You cannot imagine how

terrified my daughter has been for your well-being, Lord Chartwell."

Well, hell! His relief at having extricated himself from negotiations for Priscilla's hand had apparently been premature. Reluctantly, he faced father and daughter, knowing full well that what was about to transpire would be extremely unpleasant.

Stonybrook nodded almost imperceptibly to Priscilla.

In response to her father's signal, she minced toward Max with those tiny steps that exasperated him. "Darling, I feared you were dead. I cannot tell you how relieved I am."

She leaned from the waist toward him and planted a brief kiss, cool and prim, on his cheek. So different was her chaste, emotionless peck from Virg's passionate, fiery kisses that Max nearly recoiled.

Priscilla hastily straightened and stepped back, saying, "I have wonderful news for you, my darling Max."

Her wooden smile and stilted delivery warned her darling Max that she was embarking on a well-rehearsed speech he would not find wonderful at all.

Before she could continue, however, her father interrupted, gesturing toward Es and Isabel. "If this pair would leave us now." The earl's tone left no doubt he believed them of no importance. "What we have to say requires privacy."

"My lord," Max feigned shock, "surely you are not so rude as to try to oust the duke of Penrose from his own library!"

Stonybrook stammered, "No . . . of course not. Sorry, Your Grace, I did not recognize you."

"Come, we will find our privacy elsewhere and leave the duke and his betrothed in peace," Max said.

He deliberately chose a small sitting room. Musty and rarely used, it was overcrowded with Daphne's Victorian excesses, which included everything from ornate furnishings to displays of mismatched china that made up in quantity what they lacked in quality.

Priscilla should love the room.

She did not disappoint Max. "What a pretty room."

Max nodded toward a sofa upholstered in a bilious lime green. "Please be seated."

Priscilla took one corner of the sofa. Her father chose a matching armchair, clearly intending for Max to join her on the sofa.

Instead Max pulled one of the narrow chairs upholstered with frayed tapestry from several feet away, turned the chair toward the visitors, and sat there.

Max's choice of seat clearly displeased both Priscilla and her father. Stonybrook almost imperceptibly nodded again at his daughter, cueing her to restart her performance.

She leaned toward Max. "My darling, as I was saying, I have the most wonderful news."

He winced, knowing full well he was not *her* darling. He dreaded what was certain to come next. He would never marry Priscilla now, but the original error had been his in assessing her, and he did not want to hurt her. He absently picked up an apple of red glass from the table beside his chair and rubbed it.

Pausing for dramatic effect, Priscilla looked up coyly through her lashes at him. "I have managed to persuade Papa to accept your last offer for a marriage settlement."

"And I tell you, Chartwell, she had considerable difficulty bringing me around."

Right, and the earth was square! "Tell me then, how did she succeed?"

"Well, ah, ah . . ." The earl floundered about for an answer and finally managed weakly, "Her happiness is more important to me than anything else."

It was all Max could do to keep from laughing out loud. Stonybrook had never considered anyone but himself in his life—or anything but his own gain.

The earl's statement apparently sounded so false even to his own ears that he quickly added, "Still, my daughter is far too fine a woman for me to give her in marriage to a man who does not recognize her value and appreciate it."

One last try for a better settlement. Max seized this small opening Stonybrook had unwittingly given him. "You are absolutely right, my lord, and you should not for a moment consider doing so."

The earl blinked in surprise. "Ah, so you are now willing to meet my requests. Good."

Max tightened his grip around the glass apple to keep from throwing it at Stonybrook. This was going to be even more difficult and awkward than Max had feared.

"No, I meant that I esteem your daughter so much that, like you, her happiness is my paramount concern." Max told himself that lies as egregious as those Stonybrook had just uttered deserved a lie in reply. "You have forced me to the reluctant conclusion that you are right when you say she deserves a richer and more appreciative husband than me."

Before father and daughter could recover from their shock, Max stood and bowed to Lady Priscilla. "It is my dearest hope, lovely Lady Priscilla, that you will find a husband truly deserving of you and live happily ever after with him."

When Max reached the door, he turned. "I know the duke and his betrothed would not mind having you stay for dinner and spend the night. I hope you will do so. I wish that I could stay too, but I must return immediately to my own estate."

Which, of course, was another lie. Max fervently wished for them to leave immediately. Knowing how contrary Stonybrook was, Max had gambled that he could most quickly speed their departure by inviting them to stay.

Leaving the sitting room, he shut the door behind him.

"My lord, there you are," Jenkins called from farther down the hall. "The dowager duchess wishes to see you immediately."

Max groaned, fearing his aunt intended to champion Lady Priscilla's cause.

He found the dowager alone in her apartment, sitting in her favorite chair and looking out the window at the park, where more leaves now lay on the ground than remained on the trees.

When she saw him, she held out her gnarled hands, and her eyes filled with tears.

He had never seen her cry before. He gripped her hands tightly in his own. "What is it, Aunt? Is the rheumatism paining you badly?"

"When no trace of that balloon was found, we thought you had been killed. I cannot tell you how relieved I am to see you again."

Before he could speak, she went on hastily, as though embarrassed by her unprecedented show of emotion. "As you no doubt know by now, your betrothed is here. Why did you not tell me you were negotiating with Stonybrook for his daughter's hand?"

"*Were* is the operative word."

"Oh? The earl and his daughter say you *are* betrothed to her."

Damn them. He hoped they left the castle before Virg ran into them. "They no longer say that. I just made certain of it."

His aunt gave him a sharp, piercing look.

"I withdrew my offer while I was in London, and I thought I made it clear I would not make another, but they chose to think otherwise."

Max girded himself for his aunt to do her best to change his mind.

"Good." She gave a quick, approving nod of her head. "You were a fool, Max, to even think of marrying her. You deserve better. She would have made you miserable."

"So I belatedly concluded."

"If only you had told me what you were doing, I would have warned you. Speaking of betrothals, have you heard about the duke's?" She watched him carefully, clearly to gauge his reaction.

"Yes. What is your opinion of Es's choice, Aunt Elizabeth?" Max wanted to hear what his aunt had to say, so he would know what tack to take with her. "Isabel is your companion. You know her better than I do."

"She will make Esmond an excellent wife and duchess. I do not know why I did not think of her for him before."

His aunt's determined tone told Max she expected him to dispute her assessment.

Instead he said, "I am delighted with the match and with the way Es is standing up to Daphne. He reminded me so much of Grandfather today. I believe this duke will make the Chartwells proud."

"You may be right. Who would have thought it?"

"Virg did. She was also the first to recognize that Es and Isabel would make a good match, and she worked to bring it about."

His aunt gave him a searching look. "Yes, she did. You were right. She is an intelligent woman, spirited too, and generous." Aunt Elizabeth hid a yawn behind her crippled hand.

How exhausted she looked, as though she had not slept in days. "You need a nap," Max told her.

A soft knock sounded on the door, and Isabel came into the room. She stopped when she saw Max. "Oh, I am sorry, Your Grace. I did not realize you had company." She turned to leave.

"No, stay," Aunt Elizabeth said, then yawned again. "You are right, Max. I require a nap."

Max kissed her forehead and left. He went down to the estate office.

Grigsby looked up from the open ledger on the desk before him, dropped his pen, and jumped to his feet.

"My lord, we are so thankful you are safe."

"So am I. What has arisen in my absence that I must handle?"

"Several things have arisen, but the duke has taken care of them. I am certain you will agree with me that his decisions were all good ones. I am very impressed with how skillfully His Grace took over managing the estate when you disappeared."

Max took the chair across the desk from Grigsby. "Sit down and tell me about them."

Nearly an hour later, Max left Grigsby, intending to find Virg.

But he failed. Finally he asked Jenkins if he knew where she was.

"I believe in her room, packing."

"Why would she be doing that?" Max demanded, much shocked.

"Mrs. Blair has decided that she and Miss Blair will leave the castle as soon as they finish packing. The duke's decision to marry Miss Lake, rather than Miss Blair, infuriated Mrs. Blair."

"Ask Miss Blair to join me in the library at once."

Jenkins nodded.

But when the butler came downstairs several minutes later, he was alone. "I am sorry, my lord, but Miss Blair said she is too busy to meet with you."

Her stepmother must have insisted Virg continue packing. Knowing Virg, though, she would soon find a way to meet with him. Confident of that, Max went into the library to wait for her.

But he waited for more than an hour, and Virg did not appear. Finally, he went up the backstairs, intending to go to her room himself.

When he turned the corner by Virg's room, he saw her starting down the main staircase in her green riding habit. He hurried after her, calling to her to wait for him.

She stopped on the second step from the top and gave him a look so hot with anger and contempt that it would have instantly fried the largest fish they had caught on Ives' Folly.

"I have nothing to say to you, my lord, now or ever."

With that, she descended the steps, leaving him at the top of the staircase, staring after her. What the devil was the matter now? He had done nothing to merit her poisonous response.

He sighed wearily. The day had started out so well. He thought of waking up in the big bed at the inn with Virg nestled beside him, of the smile she had given him when she opened her eyes, and of their good morning kiss, at once tender and passionate.

He sighed again. The day had been all downhill since then. What the hell else could go wrong?

Someone banged the knocker three times with such force that Jenkins and two footmen scurried into the hall to answer the summons. The butler reached the door first and opened it to one of the handsomest young men Max could ever remember seeing.

Virg was crossing the hall, and the newcomer held out his arms to her. "Hello, love."

"Scott!" She ran into his embrace.

They hugged each other so fervently that a wave of intense jealousy hit Max. It was all he could do to keep from running down the stairs, grabbing the pair, and yanking them apart.

Max's question of what else could go wrong had just been answered.

The damned day was going from bad to hellish.

Chapter 32

~~~~~~~~

From the stairs, Max watched Virg pull the handsome newcomer into the small sitting room adjacent to the hall and shut the door behind them.

That was too much for Max. He hurried down the stairs, intent on putting an end to whatever was going on between them in the sitting room.

As Max reached the bottom of the staircase, the most distinguished man he had ever seen strode through the open door into the castle, bringing Max to an abrupt stop. Even Jenkins was clearly impressed.

Now what?

The stranger's face, with its broad jaw, combined with his tall, muscular body, looked too youthful for his full, thick head of white hair. He crossed toward Max with the purposeful stride of a man who knew precisely where he was going and what he wanted.

Max had met kings whose countenance and bearing were not nearly so commanding as this man's.

"Who are you?" he asked Max.

"Lord Maximilian Chartwell."

Hope flared in his eyes. "Is Virg safe?"

"Yes, she is in that sitting room. Who are you?"

"Her father, Leonard Blair." He extended his hand to Max. "You sent me a cable a few weeks ago."

"And you did not answer it." That had so disappointed Max he was not certain he wanted to shake Blair's hand.

"You're wrong. I'm answering it now in person. I sailed for England immediately after receiving the cables."

"Cables? I only sent one."

"Virg sent the other. They arrived together."

"You call your daughter Virg?" Max asked in surprise.

"Yes. Everyone in our family has done so since she was a little girl. She'd be furious if we called her anything else. She loves the nickname."

The door to the sitting room burst open, and Virg flew into the hall and her father's arms. "Oh, Daddy, I'm so happy you've come. I can't tell you how much I've missed you."

Father and daughter hugged as though neither one ever wanted to let the other go.

The man she'd called Scott appeared in the doorway of the sitting room, smiling broadly.

Max eyed him suspiciously. What had gone on between Scott and Virg while they were alone that made him smile like that? Was he a serious suitor for her hand that Leonard Blair had brought with him?

Max strode over to him and asked bluntly, "Who are you?"

"Virg's brother Scott. And you are?"

Max's relief was so great that it was a few seconds before he answered, "Chartwell."

"Ah, the author of the other cable to my father. I have never seen him so angry as when he received those messages. Too bad he couldn't have gotten his hands on Rowena at that moment."

"You do not like your stepmother?"

"No," Scott answered with the same frank honesty that Virg displayed. "She has done everything she can to try to alienate our father from his children, especially from Virg."

"Why Virg?"

"Jealousy. My father and Virg are extremely close, and Rowena can't stand that."

Virg and her father were no longer hugging, but he still had his arm protectively around her.

Then Blair nodded to his son, released his daughter, and the two men went toward the door.

Mrs. Blair's shrill voice rang out from the hall at the top of the stairs. "Virginia, get up here at once."

Leonard Blair winced.

"Your wife always orders your daughter around like that—as though she were a scullery maid," Max told Blair in an undertone.

"I told you to help my maid pack my clothes." Rowena bent over the balustrade and looked down at Virg. "Why are you still standing there, missy? Are you deaf, you stupid girl?"

Chapter 33

"**E**ven if she was deaf, she could still hear you, madam—as can everyone else in Suffolk," Virgie's father told his wife.

Virgie had never heard him speak with such icy contempt before. He returned to her side and again put his arm protectively around her.

"My daughter is not one of your servants, and you will not order her about as though she is. Nor is my daughter stupid. I am the one who is stupid for having married you."

Rowena's several chins dropped on her ample chest, and she froze. For a full minute, her listeners were granted blessed relief from her ear-grating voice.

Then she managed in the softest voice Virgie had heard her use in weeks, "Leonard, dearest, I am overjoyed to see you. What a . . . a wonderful surprise."

She clearly considered it nothing of the kind. Virgie stole a sideways glance at her father. From his expression, he was no more fooled by Rowena than Virgie was.

"Leonard dearest, I am so glad you have come. I am at my wit's end with Virginia."

"Why? Because she refused to marry the duke, whose mother you bribed?" His words were like chips of ice.

"I . . . I did nothing of the sort." Rowena pumped up the anger in her voice higher with each word. "Who told you that ghastly lie? I know—it was your daughter, wasn't it?"

Rowena glared at Virgie with such hatred and malevolence that her father tightened his arm around her.

"How can you lie to your father like that, Virginia?"

"You are the liar, Mrs. Blair," Max said coldly.

She seemed to notice him for the first time. "How dare you accuse me of such a thing, you evil man."

"Because it is the truth. And who are you, the devil's own handmaiden, to be calling anyone else evil?"

Rowena sputtered in fury.

"Furthermore, Mrs. Blair," Max continued calmly, "I am the one who sent your husband a cable telling him about the bribe, so you may rail at me for informing him."

Had Max done that? He'd said nothing to Virgie about cabling her father.

Max turned to her father. "Your poor daughter's calm forbearance in the face of all your wife put her through was remarkable. Miss Blair is a true lady. You should be very proud of her."

Why was Max praising her to her father? Was he easing his conscience for making love with her when he was betrothed to another woman?

Easing his conscience for breaking Virgie's heart?

"Rowena, come down here."

Only once before had Virgie heard her father speak in that tone—and that had been to a ranch hand who had been caught stealing cattle from him. "I want to talk to you privately."

She hastily backed away from the stairs. "I . . . I must finish packing."

"I said come down here."

She came.

He turned to his daughter. "I see by your costume you were about to go riding. Why don't you take Scott with you and show him the countryside?"

"Yes, Virg," Scott said, "I'd like that."

Out of the corner of her eye, she saw Max start to say something. Before he could speak, she said hastily, "I would love to do that—just the two of us, Scott."

She brushed past Max without so much as a glance at him, took her brother's arm, and swept out of the castle.

As they walked down the worn stone steps, Scott said, "Dad clearly wants us to take our time. I think he intends to have Rowena gone from the castle— and your life, all our lives—before we return from the ride."

"That would be so wonderful. I pray you are right." She hesitated, then asked, "Was Max telling the truth when he said he cabled Dad about Rowena bribing the duke's mother?"

"Yes. In fact, your cable and his were sent the same day and arrived together."

Had that been the reason he had gone to Ipswich that day?

"His cable was quite lengthy and spelled out the situation—and Rowena's reprehensible behavior— in much greater detail than yours did. I think his was what convinced Dad to sail immediately for England."

Her thoughts of Max threatened to soften until she reminded herself that his cabling her father was meant to save his cousin, not her.

Quiet returned to the castle. Following a session with her husband, Rowena Blair departed in a hurry without a word to anyone and without her baggage.

After the door shut behind her, Max chanced to see her husband's face. Rarely had Max seen a man look so happy.

Max pulled out his pocket watch for at least the hundredth time while he paced the floor of the small sitting room off the castle's entrance. Why had Virg and her brother not returned? They had been gone nearly three hours, and it would soon be dark.

Perhaps they had had an accident? Should he launch a search party?

At last he heard the great iron strapped door open and saw Virg and her brother come in. Max hurried into the hall.

"Virg, I must talk to you," he said quietly.

She did not stop walking, nor did she even turn

her head to look at him. "I told you before I have nothing to say to you ever."

"I, however, have a great deal to say to you." He took her arm firmly, pulled her into the sitting room, and shut the door almost in the face of her startled brother.

"Now, would you be so kind as to tell me what the hell is the matter? Why are you acting as though I have the plague?"

"Not the plague—a fiancée." She yanked her arm from his grasp with a look so cold that the North Sea in January seemed hot by comparison. "I was not aware of your and Lady Priscilla's forthcoming nuptials."

So that was it. "Neither was I."

"I see. You somehow forgot your betrothal to her?"

The way Virg was glaring at him, Max hoped she did not have that derringer on her. She reminded him of an infuriated porcupine about to fire its stinging quills. Given the choice, though, Max would rather take his chances with a porcupine.

At least the animal would not emasculate him.

"Only a rotten sonofabitch makes love to one woman while he's betrothed to another!" Virg cried.

"Who told you I was betrothed to Lady Priscilla? Your lying stepmother?"

"Lady Priscilla herself, among others."

"She told you that?" How damned confident Prissy must have been that after her father dropped his demands, Max would marry her. "Well, she told you wrong."

"Are you calling your betrothed a liar?"

"Listen to me, Virg. I am not, never have been,

and never will be betrothed to Lady Priscilla."

"I don't believe you. I want to hear the truth."

He sighed. "The truth is I did negotiate with her father for her hand, but he kept increasing his demands and nothing was settled. When I went to London to escort her to a ball, I discovered I no longer had any desire to marry her, and I broke off the negotiations."

"Why did you no longer want to marry her?"

"Two reasons. I belatedly realized she would not make me the kind of wife I wanted. Second, I found another *lady* who was exactly the wife I did want."

"And who is that unfortunate *lady*?"

This was not going at all the way Max had planned. He jettisoned any thought of a romantic, flowery proposal to Virg and said bluntly, "You are."

She looked at him so blankly that he had to fight to keep from smiling.

"What . . . what are you talking about, my lord?"

He seized upon the only way he dared to caress her—with his eyes. "I am asking you to marry me."

Virg's expression turned to outrage, and she flung open the door. "I would never, never, ever marry you. Don't insult me by asking me again."

She ran into the hall.

Max was not quite certain what reaction he had expected to his proposal, but it certainly had not been this one.

For a moment, he was too stunned to move. When he recovered, he headed for the door, reaching it in time to see Virg running up the stairs, taking them at a most unladylike two steps at a time.

Cursing under his breath, Max went after her.

In the hall, two figures moved out of the shadows into his path. It was Virg's father and brother.

"Do not try to stop me," he warned them fiercely. "This is between your daughter and me, no one else."

As he strode past them, her father muttered something, but Max was certain he had misheard the man.

Surely Leonard Blair had not said, "Go for it."

Chapter 34

Virgie ran into her bedchamber, slammed the door behind her, and threw herself on the bed.

"Open the door, damn it," Max called, pounding on the door.

"Won't! Go away!" She held her breath. Would he discover she hadn't thought to turn the key in the lock?

Her question was answered seconds later when he burst into the room.

"Get out of here!" she ordered.

Instead he headed for the bed, looking for all the world like an avenging devil. Virgie rolled across the bed and jumped off on the other side.

"I told you to leave."

"Not until you answer me two questions." He glared at her across the width of the bed. "What kind of rotten woman makes love to a man she has no intention of marrying?"

That so surprised Virgie she could not think of a retort.

"And here is the second: Why will you 'never, never, ever marry' me?"

This one she could answer. "I told you the reason the day we met. I said then and I say it again now—I will never marry except for love."

His unreadable expression both frightened and thrilled her. Then his eyes narrowed speculatively.

"I think you do love me, Virg. Now dammit, be honest with me. And with yourself."

Virgie would not deny the truth. "Yes, I love you, but I would never marry a man who doesn't love me in return, and you don't."

A hint of a smile played at the corners of his mouth. "Ah, now we are getting somewhere. How do you know I do not love you, Virg?"

"Because you said you would never marry a woman you loved. Therefore, since you proposed to me, you clearly can't love me."

Her answer seemed to fascinate him. "Was, perchance, logic one of the subjects you studied at college, Virg?"

"Yes. Why?"

"Because that sounds exactly like what professors teach in beginning logic. Your logic, however, has a fatal flaw."

She drew herself up, torn between indignation and hope. "And what is that flaw?"

"When I told you that, I did not know what love was." He was making his way cautiously around the bed to her. "But people can learn and change, even useless English lords like myself."

"What are you telling me?" She tried to rein in her hope and failed.

"You taught me what love is, Virg." He reached her and took her cold hands in his warm ones. "Now that I know, I would not marry for any other reason."

Virgie's heart pounded like an Indian war drum, and she could not seem to catch her breath. It was as though she'd been laced into that too tight corset that Rowena had always wanted her to wear.

"Nor would I marry any other woman than you." His hands tightened around hers as though to emphasize his words. "You are the love of my life."

How Virgie had ached to hear such words from him. She had been certain she never would. Now that she had, she was so overwhelmed by happiness she could not even speak.

Max looked at her a trifle warily. "Now, my beautiful prickly porcupine, will you let me kiss you?"

She threw her arms exuberantly around his neck, and their mouths joined in a long, passionate, soul-shaking kiss.

At last he raised his head a fraction. "Can I take that as your acceptance of my marriage proposal?"

Oh, how she wanted to tell him yes, but cold reality reared its ugly head and sneered at her. Much as she loved Max, much as she wanted to marry him, she knew that she could not bear to live her life trapped in the narrow, stultifying strictures prescribed for a Victorian lady.

Even more important, she did not want her daughters, should she have them, to be raised in such an atmosphere. She could not do that to them.

As she told him how she felt, she could not prevent tears from running down her cheeks.

He gently wiped them away with his thumbs. "You have nothing to cry about, darling."

"Wh-a-a-t," she stammered.

His smile softened his harsh face that she loved so much.

"I know your heart is set on living in that beautiful valley of yours. I love you too much to deny you that pleasure. We will live there."

Hope rose within her like the dawning of a warm sunny day. "You would do that for me?"

He nodded. "An adventurous woman of your spirit and courage deserves a properly splendid setting."

"Why, I think you have just complimented me."

"I know I have."

She could hardly believe that he had just agreed to leave England to live where she wanted to live. "But what about your responsibility for overseeing Penrose and the duke?"

"You were right yet again, Virg. What Es needed was to be trained and freed from his mama's apron strings. Now he has done so, and he is also proving himself to be an excellent administrator of the estate. Our grandfather would be proud."

"And astonished."

Max chuckled. "That too. Seriously, I have no qualms whatsoever about leaving Penrose in Es's hands, especially not with Isabel to help him and Daphne gone from the estate."

"Where is Daphne going?"

"Es has decided to send her to London to live. She insulted Isabel once too often."

"What about your own estate?"

He shrugged carelessly. "Perhaps I will sell it. Unlike this castle, it has not belonged to my family for eight centuries. I bought it only a few years ago."

His mouth settled over hers in a long, deep, erotic kiss that made her long to use the bed beside them.

"So you will give up England and your own estate for love of me?"

"For that and . . ."

She eyed him suspiciously. "And what?"

His eyes were alight with laughter. "My hankering to live among *real* mountains."

Epilogue

~⌒⌒⌒⌒⌒⌒⌒⌒⌒~

Max looked up at the monumental gray granite cliffs rising thousands of feet against blue sky. Once again, Virg had been right. The Sierra Nevada truly were real mountains.

This was Max's third May in Eden Valley. To his right, a narrow waterfall cascaded down a vertical wall with a muted roar. To his left, a riot of white blossoms decorated a grove of Pacific dogwood.

Contrary to what he'd once thought, Virg had not exaggerated the valley's loveliness. He turned his attention to the two most gorgeous things in this spectacular valley: his wife and his eighteen-month-old daughter, Jenny, who were playing tag together.

His gaze moved slowly, lovingly over Virg's beautiful face and petite body. It lingered on her derriere, displayed to perfection in her denim pants.

370

Jenny looked back at her mother, trying to elude her.

The toddler failed to see her father sitting on the ground against the trunk of a ponderosa pine. She tripped over him and fell into his lap.

Jenny was a miniature of her mother, with the same eyes, button nose, and rippling laugh. She even wore a much smaller edition of her denim pants. Max lifted his daughter onto her feet, and she rewarded him with a loud, smacking kiss.

Virg strode over to them, a teasing smile in her eyes. "Careful there. I might get jealous."

Max reached for his wife, pulled her down on his lap, and kissed her long and thoroughly.

"That should cure your jealousy."

"It did." Virg made no attempt to get up from his lap. "I'm so happy about Belle and Esmond's new son."

They had received two letters from England that morning. One had been from Es, telling them of the birth of a second son, named Maximilian in honor of Max.

"Maybe our next child will be a boy," Virg said.

"I would be delighted with another daughter. I wouldn't trade Jenny for a hundred sons." Max turned and kissed his daughter, still standing beside him, lightly on the tip of her little nose, and she giggled.

The second letter was from Grigsby. He wrote that the duke's administration of his estate was being heralded in British publications as a model to be emulated.

"You must be very proud of Esmond." Virg gave

Max a smile that left him yearning to take her to bed that very instant.

"Play tag ag'n, Mama," Jenny begged.

Virg jumped up. "You were an excellent teacher, Max. You're not a bad cowboy, either."

No, he wasn't, Max thought, except for roping. It irritated him that he could not seem to get the hang of that skill.

Watching Virg play with their daughter, his thoughts mellowed. After all, he had managed to lasso the only woman he had ever loved as his wife.

Much as Max hated to end their outing, they had to go home to greet Virg's father, who was coming for a visit in this valley he had given them on their wedding day. How much happier a man Blair was now that he was divorced from Rowena.

Max scrambled to his feet. "Time to go home, Lady Chartwell." Knowing how much his egalitarian wife hated titles, he occasionally used hers to tease her.

"*Mrs.* Chartwell," she retorted and blew him a kiss.

That was his Virg.

Never a lady.

And if he was very lucky, their daughter would grow up to be just like her.

Coming in September from
Avon Romance
Two historical love stories you'll never forget . . .

Much Ado About Love
by Malia Martin

What if the greatest male writer the world has
ever known was really . . . a woman? And what
if the man who uncovered her secret was the
only one who could set her heart free?

Always and Forever
by Blackboard bestselling author
Beverly Jenkins

Grace Atwood was desperate for a man . . .
to lead a wagon train full of brides out west.
Jackson Blake took one look at Grace and
decided to help her . . . and to keep her by his
side—always and forever.

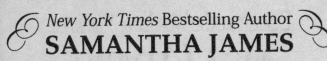